SHADOWS FROM THE PAST

DAY OF THE DEAD

Maria Broadhurst

DAY OF THE DEAD

Keeping the memories of loved ones alive.

CHAPTER ONE

I believe that dreams are like champagne. The smaller the bubbles the better the champagne, but my dreams have possibly been just a cava wish with no sparkle. I have always been a big believer that you should find your dreams, live your dreams and be them, but I feel that I have not been following my dreams and that I have been trying to live the life my husband wants, being the person that he wants me to be, not the person I want to be.

My name is Saskia and I am thirty-two years old. I acknowledge that I have problems in my life and believe that all of my dreams, hopes and wishes are crashing in around me. My little world of pretense has been one big misconception. It is time for me to get a grip of the situation and to move on, so that I can find the dreams and wishes that I crave.

I have eventually come to this decision after residing in a psychiatric rehabilitation unit for the last three months. I have had a lot of time to think about things and I have had chance to talk to my psychiatric counselors regarding matters too.

I was firstly diagnosed with dysthymia. If you have never heard of this, it is a form of depression. I would suffer a state of unease, anxiety, misery, irritable mood and other symptoms, such as eating and sleeping disturbances, fatigue and poor self-esteem.

Dysthymia often co-occurs with other mental disorders and occasionally there would be periods of slight euphoria, so I would then experience intense feelings of well-being and happiness, sometimes exaggerated in pathological states of mania.

My husband, Daniel, thought it best that I be admitted, as he was finding it difficult to cope with my mental health issues. I was aware that I was in a very dark place and I was trying to cope and deal with things in my own way. I thought I was doing fine, but according to the professionals, I wasn't coping at all.

My difficult situation and my moods revolve around my recurring dream and nightmare, which I shall explain shortly. I can be fine and happy when the pleasant dream comes to me, but I always fear that when the lights go out and I am alone in the dark, that my nightmare may come to haunt me instead.

My pleasant dream includes the most gorgeous man that I have ever seen. His beautiful blue eyes enchant me and I'm sure that I know him from somewhere. I have thought long and hard about where I could know him from, or how I could know him, but I never find the answer. In my dreams, we dance together and roll between the sheets making passionate love to each other. I never want the strong feeling of love to ever leave me. He brings a certain feeling to my life, which I have never felt with Daniel, my husband. That feeling is true love.

My nightmare is a different story and I want to stop having it. I dream that I am a passenger in a car with the same man. We are travelling fast and he loses control of the car on a narrow cliff-edge road. The sun is shining strongly and brightly, like I have never seen before, almost like it is an angel calling me and drawing me near. As the car leaves the road I feel my body leave the car seat, and I feel like I am falling in mid-air. This is when I sharply wake up screaming and sweating. It is so terrifying that my body tenses up and I am powerless to move, as though I have frozen. I later feel that I have lost control of my life and I can sit and cry for hours. It's the feeling of heartache and having lost something special, somebody special.

I have had the same repeating dream and nightmare for as long as I can remember. They have travelled with me throughout my life but at this point they were getting more frequent. The nightmare played on my mind, making me go insane. I was anxious when it wasn't there, I dwelled on when it may come, and I was terrified when it arrived.

Daniel informed the doctor at the psychiatric unit, "I can't cope with her restlessness, distraction, sleeplessness, extreme irritability and her provocative behavior. She wakes up screaming and then cries for hours. There is nothing that I can do with her and I am afraid that I could end up having a breakdown myself, trying to cope with the situation."

I just sat there and rocked in the chair, looking out of the window onto the beautifully maintained gardens of the unit, whilst Daniel spoke. It wasn't a rocking chair, just a stool, but I liked to rock backwards and forwards, and it helped me to think. I agree I was restless, distracted, extremely irritable and hardly slept, but I didn't think that I was provocative. I don't have a provoking bone in my body, unlike him, who was forever galling me. I didn't want the nightmares any more than he wanted me to have them, but they wouldn't go away.

I always thought that Daniel would be there for me and I needed him in my life, at this point, to support me. I have nobody else, but all he wanted to do was abandon me at a time when I felt that I needed his help.

The doctor sympathized with him, "Don't worry, Daniel, we will assess her, and we can look after her until she is well again."

Daniel looked relieved and spoke gently to me, "It will be like a holiday, darling. It is what you need. It is what we both need. You can't go on with these nightmare situations."

I didn't answer him or say goodbye. I carried on rocking, looking out of the window, until he left the room and building. After he drove off, two nurses in white coats escorted me to a cream room with only a bed in it. I threw myself on it, kicking and screaming to relieve my frustration. I felt like the walls were closing in to suffocate me, but the administered drug injection made me feel drowsy and happy.

I was brought up by my Grandma Alice and Grandfather Jack who have unfortunately now passed away. My mother fell pregnant at the age of 15, and later ran off with an artist from Paris leaving me to be brought up by my grandparents. I still receive the occasional card on birthdays or at Christmas … when she remembers. My grandparents always described her as a troubled soul. I believe she must have never loved or cared about me to have left. I came to the same conclusion about Daniel, when he left me at the psychiatric rehabilitation unit.

I must admit that I have actually enjoyed my time at the rehabilitation clinic. I have been to counseling sessions where they have trained, accredited counselors that provide a confidential, safe and professional service. I can speak openly and in confidence about my dreams, my feelings, and about the ups and downs that I have felt in the past and I am now feeling in day to day life.

I don't suffer any high or low mood swings whilst I am here at the clinic.

This could be because my psychiatrist has prescribed some medication called mood stabilizers. They make me feel normal, or as normal as I think normal feels, and they help me think straight and rationally. I don't keep getting upset like I used to, because everything seems to make sense in my mind. The more I talk with my counselors, the more everything starts to come together and seem logical. I have been encouraged to forge both the skills and the confidence required for a fulfilling and meaningful life and I have been taking part in an intensive recovery program.

The recurring dream and the nightmare seem to have now left me with the aid of a tablet before I go to bed. I can turn off the light at night and know that I can sleep peacefully. I still think about the dreams with the gorgeous man with the ocean blue eyes and wish he would return, but I am happy to be living without the nightmare.

My husband, Daniel, hasn't visited me whilst I have been on my intensive recovery program. My counselor suggested that it would be a good idea for him to give me some space. Catherine, my good friend, visits. She is the mother to my husband's child and I will come to her later.

Whilst at the clinic I have learnt to cope with my depression by trying to find my true self. I had previously based my worthiness on the approval of Daniel. I wanted to please him and thought I needed him in my life in order to survive, which I have now come to understand was not right. I know that I have lost myself and need to find out who I am, and what I am about.

Julia, one of the patients, has helped me along my journey here. Julia is 45 years old, petite, very attractive with a smooth complexion. She dresses elegantly and has short mousy hair that she brushes straight every day. She decided to befriend me when I arrived, and often sits next to me during mealtimes and various programs. She has some interesting conversational topics and a really unusual way of looking at life. She has been a good friend to me and we have talked a lot. She advised me a little while ago, "Even if Daniel is in your life, you don't have to abandon yourself."

I appreciated her point. I knew that I wanted Daniel in my life because I had nobody else and needed somebody there for me. After my grandparents died, he was the only family that I had left.

It is a bright sunny day and I am sitting on a bench in the garden of the psychiatric rehabilitation home looking out over the beautiful green lawns. I have reached the dizzy heights of being allowed out of the unit, into the grounds alone, a privilege to only a few here. I understand that this rule is to do with health and safety, but I am clueless as to what harm can be done with only grass and a surrounding high wall. Some health and safety fanatic must have thought of something though. Madness gone crazy; that's what this place is all about.

I am really happy today. I have just had my final session with my health psychiatric counselor and have been told that I am now well enough to go home. I could leave tomorrow, but apparently, my husband, Daniel, can't collect me for a couple of days. He has used the appalling excuse of being too busy with work. I think that I would rather be here than with him anyway. It also gives me time to say a proper goodbye to some of the friends I have made.

I am distracted from my thoughts as I hear Julia call me, "Saskia!" She also has permission to come outside, and she joins me on the bench.

"I heard that you may be leaving soon, and I have got you a little present."

She kisses me on my cheek as she hands me a small blue velvet box. I open the box revealing a dark blue velvet lining and an intriguing small crystal cherub shooting an arrow. It is lustrous and has a delicate soothing influence on me. The cherub is perfect, with a light glow that enhances the detail.

"Thank you, Julia, it is really beautiful." I have never seen anything so enchanting.

Julia watches me and smiles, "It had the same effect on me when I first saw it, and later it helped me find true love. When you meet someone special, you will know."

"When I meet someone special?" I ask, "I am already with somebody; I am with Daniel."

She frowns, "But, do you love him? I mean really love him?"

I shake my head. I don't love him, but I am brave enough to admit it now.

She shrugs her shoulders, "When the cherub shoots its arrow, you'll know that you have found the one, and fall in love forever. You can then pass it on to someone else who needs the cherub's help."

I nod and place it back in its box. It's a nice thought but I am unsure if I believe her.

She looks at me for a moment, "Saskia, a number of years ago I had a lovely home, a professional job, and I was with a young man named

Robert, who I lived my life for. I felt that he was my food and my water; I couldn't live without him. Robert didn't feel the same about me."

"What did you do?" I ask concerned.

"Well, being with him became my primary goal, overriding everything else in my life, because it gave me comfort and satisfaction seeing him and being with him. I tried to control his life for him."

Nervously, she carries on, "When you think that you may love somebody, your body releases mood altering chemicals that affect your brain. They tamper with your common sense and judgement. The more I told myself that I needed him, the more I believed it, but I had to eventually let him go. Robert didn't feel the same about me as I thought I did about him"

I look up at the sky, "I don't feel that I love Daniel or want to be with him anymore."

She looks concerned. "If you do have any doubts, let him go. I once read that if you thought that you loved a person and it wasn't working out, you should separate. If you come back together, you are supposed to be together, and if you don't then it was never meant to be. I set Robert free and we went our own separate ways."

"It must have been terrible for you. I take it that Robert didn't come back?"

She smiles pleasantly, "Robert married his one true love and has two beautiful daughters with her."

"What about you? Do you still have feelings for him?" I have to ask.

"We have kept in touch with each other as friends. I don't love him and know that I never did. It was just those crazy chemicals in my mind. Robert was just a passing fancy and he was not my true love. Chang is my one and only true love."

I am puzzled, "Well, how do you know that he is the one?"

She laughs, "When your cherub shoots his arrow, you will feel love like you have never felt before. You will know that you have found your soulmate. Love is a two-way road and when Chang and I met, we just knew."

"How did you meet Chang?" I am interested.

"After Robert, I wanted to do something for me. I found out about tai chi classes. It is the perfect workout for your mind, body and soul, and it releases any anxiety that you feel. Chang became my personal instructor, then later my husband. He is my true love, my heart." She crosses her chest. "He passed away two years ago. I wanted to end my life and be with him. I tried and was unsuccessful, which is how I ended up here." She wipes her tears away from her eyes with her cardigan.

I knew that she had tried to commit suicide but didn't know the reasoning behind it. Poor Julia, I give her a big cuddle, wanting to support her, and she absorbs my affection.

"Are you ok?" I ask concerned, looking to see if a nurse or doctor is anywhere around.

She nods, "I am fine now, and don't worry. This place has really helped me come to terms with my life and Chang's death. I still miss him, but that's normal. I have met lots of wonderful people, like you, who have also helped me whilst I have been here. I don't really get down anymore and I am looking forward to eventually leaving this place. I am looking forward to moving on with my life. Chang and I travelled the world together. There are certain places I would like to re-visit that were special to us both. We will meet again one day, in another life."

I am unable to sleep at night. I keep getting in and out of bed and walking the floor. I am thinking about what Julia said about true love. I don't love Daniel, I have never loved him. I have never felt about Daniel, like Julia felt about Chang.

I have tried to convince myself that my marriage to Daniel was the real deal, real love, that I had found the man of my dreams, but I know deep down in my soul that I haven't. I just haven't been strong enough to admit it and walk away, until now. I have been scared of being on my own. I have been holding on to him for all the wrong reasons.

Perhaps my body has been releasing mood-altering chemicals that have had some influence on my brain and tampered with my common sense and judgement. This in turn could have been causing my recurring nightmare. I think about the pleasant dreams frequently. I think about the gorgeous man that I feel a sincere love for, but then I question why he also appeared in my nightmare, and this tarnishes the thought of him.

Romance has always been simple and carefree when it has been acted out in my imagination. It has been acted out in my head over and over again, making the best romantic movies look amateur. It has been so easy to fantasize about the most amazing romance, but I have never experienced it in reality. I open the blue box Julia has given to me and speak to my cherub, "I hope that one day you shoot your arrow and find me true love. I hope that you find the man of my dreams, without any nightmares attached."

When I married Daniel, I married him for better, for worse, in sickness and in health, but not for love. I am looking for somebody, something, in my life, but Daniel is not that somebody or something. I need to find 'what' or 'who' is missing. Until I achieve this, I am going to feel like a lost soul in a lost world.

I mentioned my friend Catherine to you earlier. She is the mother to Daniel's son, Joshua. Daniel met Catherine on his stag night, just before his marriage to me, and Joshua is the outcome of their one-night stand.

A year after the wedding, Daniel's announcement that he had slept with another woman and was now a father had washed over me like an unexpected wave in the sea. I did not know what had happened until it was too late, and I was then gasping for breath trying to recover and work out where the wave had come from. That was four years ago.

During my time in rehabilitation, I have worked out where that wave came from. There was no love in our relationship and Daniel was looking for something else, somebody else, as I wasn't the one. He stayed with me because he knew that I needed him. It was thoughtful and kind of him, but we should have been honest. The fact is that we didn't love each other and were not meant to be together.

His son is the spitting image of Daniel in the face but has his mother, Catherine's, bright red, raven hair. I worked really hard to build a good relationship with Catherine. I did this for the sake of Daniel and Joshua. I think that we both found the situation really difficult in the beginning, but we get on great now.

Catherine is a very open person, and I like her honesty.

She once told me, "Daniel certainly wasn't what I was after, and I wasn't what Daniel was looking for."

Through what she has told me, it transpires they were just two lost and needy souls who came together for one encounter, which has been regretted by both parties. Don't get me wrong, they both love their son, and don't regret him. Let's just say that emotions and drink have a lot to answer for.

Catherine explained a long time ago what happened that led to her sleeping with Daniel.

She had just separated from her boyfriend Scott when she slept with

Daniel. She was on the rebound and it is one of her biggest regrets. She never thought that she would get back together with Scott, but when they did, she realized that she was pregnant and that it may not be Scott's baby.

Although they were in love, Scott couldn't find room in his heart to forgive her and bring up somebody else's child. He was happy to act as Joshua's father until the paternity test proved that Daniel was the father. He could have lived with the unknown and been in hope, but he couldn't live with knowing the truth.

She once told me, "We parted company and went our own separate ways. I wish that he had just kept in touch with me, or at least let me know where he is. There isn't a single day that I don't think about him. He was and is the only man that I've ever loved."

I never got to meet Scott, but I would have liked to. He must have been really special for her to admit that he was the only man she could and would ever love.

I believed that Catherine was still in love with her ex-boyfriend and didn't hold any feelings for Daniel. He was just a mistake that she had to pay the price of heartache for. Due to Joshua, we ended up spending a lot of time together, and that's how we have become great friends, in fact I look upon them as family.

Daniel wanted us to have children, but I secretly kept taking my contraception pill. He had idealized that our children would have his curly golden blond hair, his big dark brown puppy eyes and my olive-colored skin. A boy and a girl would have been perfect, in that order. Despite actually wanting children, he wasn't the father I wanted for my kids. I am sure that we could have brought beautiful children into the world, but I knew deep down that I did not love him, and I didn't want to make the same mistake as Catherine, having a child with someone I didn't love.

I was relieved when Daniel eventually informed me, "I no longer want to try for a baby with you, because it doesn't feel right." By this point, our relationship had deteriorated further.

Often, he would go out and not return until two o'clock in the morning. He was then unwilling to offer any explanation of where he had been, although it was easy for me to guess, I could smell the scent of other women on him.

Things in the bedroom had been rushed between us, unsatisfactory and occasionally even painful. The night before I went to rehab, I had been waiting for him to come home into the early hours. I was scared of going to bed alone, in case the nightmare smothered me. I was probably at my worst point of mental illness and I was curled up on the floor crying. It was a regular occurrence at this point in my life to get myself into this state, due to the darkness of my depression.

He arrived home drunk slamming the door behind him. I knew that he was in a bad mood with me, although I didn't know why.

He stared down at me and slurred his words, "Why don't you want to be with me? I am sick of your behavior and your nightmares, waking up screaming and shouting. You are mentally unstable."

He grabbed my hair, pulled me up, unzipped his trousers, and threw me on the sofa. He thrust himself inside of me. I closed my eyes and counted. I just kept telling myself that it would be over soon.

Afterwards he was sorrowful and nearly crying, "Look what you have made me do. It isn't nice when you know your wife doesn't want to make proper love to you and lies about wanting children with you. I know that you were taking contraception, so it didn't happen."

I felt used, dirty, bruised, hurt and sick. I crawled to the downstairs toilet and vomited at what had just happened to me. He had never treated me with such disrespect before. I didn't question him on what had happened, because I did partially blame myself for being deceitful by taking the pill to prevent pregnancy, and I questioned if I deserved his treatment. I should have been honest with him.

Towards the end of my rehabilitation program, I realized how badly I was treated that night. Of course, there are always two sides to every story. Daniel possibly had his own reasons for his actions. His behavior may have been his way of dealing and coping with my problems and our loveless marriage, but I can make no excuse for what happened that night. I was poorly, and he should not have treated me the way he did. Perhaps he really was close to a breakdown.

Whilst in rehabilitation, the reality has hit me that our marriage needs ending, for both our sakes. It may sound strange, but I am actually relieved to have come to this decision. I no longer need Daniel or ever want him. I just want happiness in my life. The time away from him has helped me think. I feel that there is still something missing in my life, but I don't know what. I just need to decide where I want to go now, and what I want to do with the rest of my life.

The day has eventually come for me to leave rehabilitation. As I finish packing my bags to leave for home, Julia knocks on the door of my room, "I've come to say goodbye." She looks sad. I am sorry to leave her, but in a way, I am also looking forward to what the future may have planned for me. She grabs hold of me, giving me the tightest cuddle I have ever had, and offers some words of wisdom, "I believe that everything that happens in life, be it good or bad, happens for a reason. Sometimes people come into our lives and we know that they will affect our life in some profound way, almost to serve some sort of purpose. Some of these people help us, other people hinder us, and some help us to figure out who we are and what we want to become."

I smile at her, "You've helped me figure out what I want, Julia. You have been a bigger help than what you probably know, and I am really grateful to you."

She smiles at my acknowledgement of her help, "The people that we meet along the path of life help to create who we are. I have met lots of people who I have never really understood but something has attracted me to them. I wish that I had never got involved with some people, because they have disappointed me or hurt me in some way. It's nice to meet somebody like you. I have always felt an instant connection with you, Saskia, like I know you. Perhaps our paths have crossed at some point before, but we don't remember."

I hold the cherub crystal she gave me proudly in my hand and reply, "You have been a great help to me, Julia, and I have really appreciated your advice whilst I have been here. This is the right place for thinking, and your words have given me a lot of thought. Your words and memories will stay with me forever, and I will certainly remember you if our paths ever cross again."

She smiles and nods, "Well, you take those words and memories with you wherever your travels may take you, and let's hope our paths cross again at some point in the future, hopefully somewhere away from here."

We both laugh, and I know that she is happy for me to be leaving and getting on with my life.

Daniel collects me from the clinic and as we drive off, I wave goodbye to Julia and the other friends I have made. I experience an empty hole in my heart leaving them behind. They have been a large part of my life recently.

Daniel is playing the dutiful husband as he drives me home. He says things like, "Nice to see you," and, "I have missed you." I don't think the words mean anything to either of us. He is trying to be nice and probably still thinks that I need his attention.

I previously clung to Daniel because I'd nobody else. It is time for me to move forward and find the path I lost somewhere along the way. I need to find myself and my dreams. My future no longer includes Daniel.

Like one of my counselors said, "It is easy to take a wrong turning in life, as long as we eventually get back on the right track." I am going to follow my natural instincts and see where my road to destiny takes me.

CHAPTER TWO

A day after I return home, I hear my mobile bleep in the kitchen drawer advising me of a text message. I didn't take it away with me as mobile phones weren't permitted at the rehabilitation unit. To be honest, I had forgotten all about even having a mobile. I am surprised that the battery hasn't run flat during my time away. I open the text enthusiastically, wondering who is sending me a message…

> Daniel. Can't stop thinking about our mind-blowing sex sessions. They were erotic. You are a real gentleman booking us into a 5-star hotel and I can't wait to roll between the silk sheets with you again. I know that Saskia is probably home now, and you may be a little busy with her issues, but give me a call when you are available. Sarah xx

I stand looking at the text in disbelief. Sarah, whom I thought was my friend, was supposed to be texting my husband, but has texted me by mistake. I wonder if she has done it deliberately. She was our bridesmaid, and before I went to rehab she had spent hours sat around my kitchen table, drinking coffee and asking how things were in my marriage. Perhaps this was the reason behind her enquiring. I can't believe that she has been bonking my husband in a 5-star hotel, whilst I was in rehabilitation recovering from depression.

My body slides down the oak kitchen cupboard doors of our country cottage, and I find myself sat on the cold slate floor with my head in my hands, repeatedly crying whilst my lip quivers, "The bitch, the bastard, the bitch, the bastard." I mean, what else is there to say at a time like this. I am lost for any other words. I would never have guessed they would do this to me.

I feel like my world has come to an end and I cry continuously for two hours, but then I instantaneously just stop. My mind goes back to rehabilitation and things start to make sense. I am not upset about the fact that Daniel and Sarah have cheated on me. I am upset because the bastard had never taken me to a 5-star hotel, not even on our honeymoon.

Looking back, our wedding day had been an event that any bride would have envied. With the help of numerous wedding planners, I wanted perfection. Over a year had been spent planning in detail every little aspect of our big day, from the napkins, to my wedding dress, to the venue. The honeymoon was the only imperfection. Daniel wouldn't fly, he was scared of flying and even though I tried to persuade him that it would be lovely to go to Mexico, he refused point blank. His exact words were, "It's not my destiny."

We didn't get a honeymoon, not even a night in a 5-star hotel. We married in the village medieval church, the reception was held in a marquee in the grounds of an old castle ruin, and we celebrated with friends and family, toasting our future together with champagne.

As the day progressed plenty of glasses had been spilled. Being superstitious, I believed this meant that great fortune lay ahead, but then a bottle was smashed. I instantly recalled that if this happens at a wedding the celebration is premature - it was a bad omen. Daniel and Sarah tried to convince me that it was just a myth and not to worry myself about it, but being superstitious, it did concern me. I knew that I was going with the flow and this marriage was not what I really wanted. I had gone through all of this to try to paint the perfect picture, one that didn't actually exist. In hindsight, we should have poured the champagne down a plughole.

Anyway, the fact that Sarah, who broke the bottle at our wedding, is now having an affair with my husband and is bonking in a 5-star hotel (this is really bothering me) has convinced me that I need to leave Daniel as soon as possible, and stop prolonging this unwanted relationship. This is the final nail in our coffin. After making umpteen excuses for him, I don't love him and never did, and he doesn't love me. I don't wait for Daniel to return home from work. Instead, I go to bed early and sleep the best that I have for over a year. I sleep for close to twenty hours; I must have needed the rest. I awaken feeling energetic, but my eyes are still a little red from crying yesterday. I look in the bathroom mirror and the dark circles that I used to have under my eyes are certainly fainter.

I can hear Daniel clattering about downstairs making breakfast and the alluring smell of bacon and eggs is drifting upstairs, encouraging me to join him. The rehabilitation unit used to encourage a healthy appetite and my appetite's certainly grown. In fact, some of my jeans are a little tight now, to the point that I will have to go shopping for some new ones.

I've decided to sit at the end of our long oak country table, placed in the kitchen, whilst Daniel cooks on the Aga. It is quite cold today, even though the sun is sporadically shining through the small sash window. It leaves a comforting warm glow on my skin. Daniel looks me up and down and I feel the need to fasten my dressing gown belt tighter. He places my bacon and eggs in front of me, along with a mug of black coffee, and he looks confused.

"When I came upstairs last night you were asleep in the spare room. Is there a particular reason for that? You haven't slept with me since your return."

I want to say, 'I'm not sure who's been in our bed,' and, 'I don't love you,' and go off on a rant, but instead decide to keep things pleasant.

"I just needed a good night sleep. The doctors said that I must get plenty of rest and you sometimes snore and it keeps me awake."

He frowns, "I certainly do not snore. I just want our relationship to get back to how it was. I want us to have a physical relationship again, Saskia, we have to work at this."

I look down and gulp my coffee. I don't want to be here listening to this bullshit. I just want the floor to open up and swallow me.

"Saskia, are you listening to me? We need to talk about our relationship." He speaks with authority in his voice.

I pick up the brown sauce and tomato ketchup and absolutely smother my food. I know that this will completely annoy him and will make him change the topic of conversation. I see the disgusted frown upon his face as he snatches the bottles from me.

"Have you picked this disgusting habit up from the rehabilitation place?"

He is staring at me and shouting like a teacher does at a naughty school child. I am finding it quite amusing watching his reaction.

"I just like brown sauce and love, love, love tomato ketchup. Is that a problem?"

Of course, I don't like the taste when I put it in my mouth and can't even taste the bacon or eggs. It's disgusting but I keep taking mouthfuls of black coffee to swill it down. I just want him to go to work, out of my way, and leave me on my own, so I can put it in the bin.

He turns to me, "I have arranged for Sarah to visit today and keep you company. I need to work a little later today."

I can't believe the nerve. He has arranged for Sarah, his 5-star slut to visit and keep me company. The cheeky bastard! I push my plate away because I can't pretend to like it anymore. I need to get on the right side of him though, to prevent Sarah, 5-star slut, coming around. I don't think I could face her too today.

"Daniel, you are right when you say we need to talk about our relationship. I was planning on cooking us a special meal this evening and we can then discuss the future over a lovely bottle of Chianti. What do you think?" I flutter my eyelashes at him.

He nods and agrees, "Ok, that will be wonderful. I shall collect some shopping on my way home."

"No," I interrupt, "I will go shopping today for the food, and I don't want Sarah to visit."

He shakes his head, "You can't go alone. Sarah will help you."

I sigh, "You need to give me my independence. I am completely capable of going shopping on my own. In fact, I have decided to go into Manchester today and treat myself, and Sarah is not coming with me."

He picks up his brief case and puts on his heavy brown wool coat and scarf without replying. I get the feeling that he isn't happy because he is muttering to himself as he walks out of the door. I recently learnt that 99% of people talk to themselves, and surprisingly 98% of people admit to doing it. I would bet my bottom dollar that Daniel would be in the 1% that wouldn't admit to doing it, just like he won't admit to snoring.

When I was in the rehabilitation unit, a lady used to visit as a day patient once a week. Her family would drop her off and she would sit in the lounge and mutter words into space all day long. I don't think that she used to know she was doing it, or where she even was. I don't even think she knew what she was saying. She was always going on about dolls and water. None of what she said made sense.

Julia used to say, "She is a lost soul but will find herself one day."

Perhaps Daniel will one day see what he's like and find himself too. Perhaps he should have been the one admitted to the psychiatric rehabilitation unit.

I am enjoying myself shopping in Manchester. It's quite a long time ago since I was here last. I have felt the need to wear my favorite Prada sunglasses, not for style but to disguise my slightly red eyes that are living proof that I was crying yesterday. They probably don't look as bad as I think, but I am certainly conscious of them. People are looking at me strangely for wearing my sunglasses in October whilst the sky is grey and the rain has started pouring, but I think that they would look more strangely at my eyes if I removed my glasses. Besides, I feel that I can hide behind the tinted lenses and this gives me some comfort and a little confidence.

It's a shame that such an enjoyable day will have to come to an end and I will then have to go home and face Daniel. I haven't decided what I need to say to him, but I do know that we need to face up to the truth. We need to be honest with each other; we should have been a long time ago. I also understand that when we have discussed going our separate ways, I will have to find somewhere else to live.

Suddenly, I find myself on the floor in the middle of St Ann's Square in a deep puddle, with bleeding knees and shoppers surrounding me. Whilst deep in thought I have got my heel stuck in a gap between two flags and gone head over heels, to pardon the pun. I blame Daniel. If I hadn't been thinking about our situation, I wouldn't have made a complete idiot of myself in front of all these people.

A few shoppers rush to help me and I thank them, but then in the corner of my eye I see it, something invitingly shining and grabbing my attention. It's a new penny. Being superstitious I must get to it, because if you find a penny on the floor, pick it up and give it to a friend, it will bring you good luck. I desperately need good luck, so I find myself back on my feet racing and limping the few yards to the penny, whilst bystanders watch me in disbelief, but it doesn't matter because I've got it. I'm holding it in my hand and I am going to have good luck, once I have given it to a friend, of course.

A lady looks out of a shop window at me and I find myself staring back, not at the lady but at the window of opportunity that has come my way. I know at this point that I want to be taken away, rescued from my situation. I have wanted this for such a long time, probably before the rehabilitation unit, even before marriage to Daniel, definitely before I found myself standing looking through the travel agents window with the big letters 'MEXICO' jumping out at me. It's the answer that I have been looking for. It's somewhere that I have always wanted to go. I can tell Daniel that it's over between us and go on holiday to think about what I want to do next.

The lady inside is waving at me so I wave back and decide to go in. I tentatively step inside and I get the feeling that she knows me by the way she is smiling at me. When I study her face, I think that I used to go to school with her.

"Martha?" I ask, wondering if my guess is correct. She has changed quite significantly if it is her. I remembered her as being short and dumpy, not long legged and gorgeous. Having had said that, I haven't seen her for years.

Martha smiles at me and nods, "It's Saskia, isn't it?"

"Yes, that's right."

"I thought so. You haven't changed one bit. In fact, I was just telling my colleagues that I remembered you being really superstitious at school. I can't believe you are still the same. I couldn't think of anybody else who would go to the efforts you have just gone to, with bleeding knees, to pick a penny up off the floor. Do you really need luck so much?"

I hand her the penny, "Well, looks like I really do need some luck, so please can I give this to you as you were a friend at school."

Martha laughs, "Of course you can if you intend booking a holiday."

"And that I intend to do." I smile as I hand her the penny.

Her colleague gives me some cotton wool and cream to clean up my knee whilst Martha looks on her computer. She seems surprised that I am travelling alone and that I am happy to go for as long as possible. She doesn't know that I have nothing to hurry back for.

"I just want to get away, Martha. I saw a holiday to Mexico being advertised in the window. It's somewhere that I have always wanted to go and there's no better time than the present."

"There are quite a few holidays to Mexico. When would you like to go?"

I hadn't even thought about that, but I suppose as soon as possible, after I have talked with Daniel this evening, that is.

"When is the next flight?"

"I have a flight tomorrow afternoon, but that may be a little soon for you? And there are only premium class seats available which are quite expensive." She looks up for a reaction as she tilts the computer screen in my direction showing me the information she has displayed.

I think seriously about this and the price for the all of a moment and quickly reply, "Absolutely perfect, let's get it booked."

I don't mind the price because if Daniel can afford luxury with his tart and stay in 5-star hotels that cost a fortune, then I can certainly afford luxury with my air travel.

Martha looks up at me, "You have a choice of hotels…."

Before she even finishes her sentence, I find myself interrupting, "It's got to be a 5-star hotel, the best you would recommend and don't worry about cost." I really do need to get over this and perhaps staying in one will help me. Let's call it a late honeymoon or separation treat that's just for me.

"This sounds like a special occasion, with no cost spared." She says.

"It is." I remark, "It's the starting point of the rest of my life."

Martha looks at me curiously, but I don't go into detail. I know what I mean and that's all that matters.

Martha and her two colleagues are really helpful and offer some useful advice about Cancun. I decide to upgrade everything, I just can't resist. They arrange private transfers for me and I upgrade from a standard room to a suite. I also request Champagne, flowers and chocolates to be in my room upon arrival. I've decided that I should treat myself - there's nobody else to treat me and I have been through a lot.

I decide that I will need some new clothes for my holiday and I am spoilt for choice with all of the boutiques, department stores and shops in Manchester. I buy some beautiful bikinis and sarongs. I treat myself to a pair of very expensive designer shoes that I have wanted for so long. I am feeling a little guilty, but I really can't resist the other three pairs, especially since there's a sale on. I also purchase some summer dresses in the sales and a couple of evening dresses. My wardrobe is complete. Daniel will get a well-deserved shock when our joint savings account statement arrives. He did say that the money was there for a rainy day, and today it is definitely raining. It's pouring!

It is said that time passes quickly when you are having fun. That's certainly been the case today but it's getting late and the fun will soon have to stop. Daniel will be heading home from work shortly and we need to talk. I've just remembered that I'm supposed to be cooking for us this evening. Looking at my watch, I'm worried that I'm not going to have time to cook now, and more to the point, I haven't bought any food. I suppose that I could suggest that we dine out, but I don't really want us to be discussing our situation in a public restaurant. I now know what I want to say to him, but I could have done with some more time to recite it in my mind. I've been busy having a good time shopping and I'd put him to the back of my mind. It's the best place for him, but time has caught up with me, and I will need to deal with this situation sooner rather than later.

As I walk through the buzzing city of Manchester, I suffer from a nail-biting tension attack. I only notice because I am holding about fifteen bags in my right hand and the weight of them is making it really difficult for me to keep my hand up to my mouth. Julia used to shout at me for biting my nails, and, to be honest, she had helped me to stop. In fact, until today, my nails were looking healthy and long. I am going to have to buy a nail file now. I can't go on holiday with nails looking like this.

I stop in my tracks and take a deep breath. I am getting myself all worked up worrying about the conversation I am going to have with Daniel this evening. My counselor at rehabilitation once advised me, "Don't get worked up or upset about things. There is always a solution to a problem." When I think about it, she is right.

Tonight will be the last night that we spend together. I want our break up to be amicable and civil, and the least I can do is make us a delicious meal to eat, whilst we discuss everything through. In hindsight, I shouldn't have offered to cook for Daniel as I can't really cook. I can make beans on toast, or put chicken nuggets and frozen chips in the oven, and I know how to turn the oven on, but that's as far as it goes. I want tonight to be special though, and I want the food to be absolutely perfect, like on those television commercials. I know that I can't cook, but I know somebody who can, and it will make my job much easier. More to the point, I can just stick it all in the oven without much prep. Here I come, Marks and Spark's food hall.

The food is purchased, and I now have time for a coffee. It is relatively quiet inside Selfridges' café bar and there are only a few tables occupied. I sit at table eighteen. I always try to sit at this table when I visit here. I truly believe that eighteen is my lucky number. The number has popped up repeatedly over the years in really important events of my life. I was born on the 18th, the first house that I bought was number eighteen and I passed my driving test when I was eighteen on the 18th of the month. It's strange how a number can have such an importance.

A couple sit at the black granite table opposite me whispering sweet nothings to each other and giggling whilst sharing a half-bottle of champagne. They are clearly in love. They remind me of how my Grandfather Jack and Grandma Alice used to be…like soulmates. I hope that the cherub I was given one day shoots its arrow and finds my soulmate.

An elderly lady approaches me.

"Excuse me? I hope that you don't mind me asking you, but are you Jack and Alice's granddaughter?"

She is in her eighties and would be a similar age to my grandparents if they had still been living. She is petite, with grey hair that she has in a net bun at the side of her head. She wears a long grey coat down to her ankles and a hand-knitted scarf wrapped tightly around her neck.

She carries on, "Please accept my apologies if you aren't, but it's been a long time and you look similar. Having said that though, my mind isn't what it used to be."

I have to smile. "Yes, I'm Saskia. I am sorry, but I don't recognize you. Did you know my grandparents? I recall that they had lots of friends."

"I'm Joyce. I was a friend of Alice's. I knew her from the dancing classes at the village hall. Please may I join you?" she quietly yet politely asks. "It's nice to have some company."

Grandma used to go dancing every Tuesday afternoon without fail. She used to say that it made her feel alive. It feels strange that I had just been thinking about my grandparents when this lady came along claiming to know them. It feels right that she should join me.

"May I order you a tea or coffee? You look like you need a nice hot drink to warm you up."

She has rosy red cheeks and her hands look cold and are trembling. The waiter approaches to take her order.

"How considerate of you, that would be lovely. I would appreciate a pot of English tea and I always have a toasted teacake when I come here. They are the best in town." She winks at the waiter being mischievous.

I can't help but chuckle. She sounds just like my grandma. Whenever we would go out to a café, Grandma always requested a pot of English tea and a toasted teacake. Joyce unbuttons her coat placing it over the chair and unwraps her very long scarf from around her neck, before sitting herself down.

She sighs, "It's now been over ten years since your Grandma Alice moved on. I choose the words 'moved on' rather than died, because she told me that she was going somewhere very special. At my age you know that the end of your life is fast approaching, but your grandma gave me hope."

"She gave you hope?" I query.

"Yes, I can remember her words exactly. She said that the beat of her heart would disappear from Earth but it would still ring loudly, that death was part of life and was nothing to fear, it was just another stage of life, like going from day to night. Your grandma believed that death was a transition from one life to another and that she would come back to Earth to celebrate her life in spirit and soul. She said that she would be living, dreaming, loving, smiling and would always be with the ones that she loved in some disguise."

I recall something similar, "Grandma used to tell me that there are many beliefs about what happens after we die, but the eternity of life is a fact and we are a part of it."

I am unsure why Joyce has come to sit with me and to immediately start talking about my grandma's death. Perhaps it's her age, but I feel a warm glow in my heart thinking and talking about my grandparents. They are always in my mind and I still love them both lots. It's a love that is irreplaceable and they're deeply missed.

"My grandparents really loved each other" I say, "It was a magical relationship. They meant the world to each other and nothing or nobody was ever going to come between them. Grandma always said that soulmates are very special people that you will never forget. She knew that there was only ever one man for her, and there would only ever be one man for her; my grandfather. Their relationship was special and unforgettable."

Joyce nods in agreement. "I only met your grandfather a few times, but your grandma always spoke very highly of him, and when they were together…" she pauses for a moment recalling them, "you could see that they loved each other dearly. Just the way that they looked at each other gave it away."

Joyce was a good listener. "When my grandad passed away, Grandma started to deteriorate. She gave up on life and longed to join the man that she had always loved. She longed for her soulmate. Before she moved on, she slowly whispered her last sentences gasping for breath between words. She told me that as one door closes, another one will open, and stated that she would meet my grandfather again, and they would be together again, happy to be living their life as one. I feel tears fill my eyes, "Those were her last words to me."

Joyce pulls her chair close to me and touches my shoulder. "Oh love." She gives me a sympathetic smile. "Your grandparents would not wish for you to be upset. They would want you to have happy memories about them."

I feel comfortable in Joyce's company and it's nice to speak with somebody who knew my grandparents. "I do have many happy memories, but my last thoughts are unbearably sad."

She queries, "Why sad?"

"I held my grandma's hand as she lay in her death bed. Trying to hold back my tears, I did not want her to know that I was upset. I wanted to be her rock and strength because she had been my inspiration during my childhood. I stayed with her until the end you know, the final chapter of her book, that's how she would have described it."

"You were with her until the end of her life. She would have appreciated that."

"Life had just passed her by. I remember glancing around studying the generations of photographs that surrounded her bedroom. We had discussed each picture during the years and each had a story portraying different stages of her life, from birth to death, all memories of her past."

I run my fingers through my hair and sigh. "She has remained in my thoughts since, and I have carried her forward in my mind and life. I just hope that I can keep hold of my grandparents' memories forever and hope that they never fade."

I glance across the table and Joyce looks a little preoccupied. "Are you ok?" I ask.

She replies quietly, "Sorry, you have just given me something to think about. I have many photographs from when I was younger, looking carefree and beautiful. I have aged so much since then and feel that my youth has been stolen from me. Time has slowly crept up, and I will soon be in the situation where there will only be photographs left for people to remember me by too. They will tell my unique story of my time on Earth and help my family remember me, even when their memories are jaded in years to come."

I observe Joyce looking thoughtful, "I hope that I haven't upset you, Joyce, talking about my grandparents moving on."

She sincerely smiles, "Not at all love, you have helped me and given me inspiration. I was just thinking that it's been a long time since I've had my picture taken and I would love a nice up-to-date family portrait taken by a professional photographer. It will tell the story of my existence with the people that I love the most and will capture the essence of my spirit." She smiles, "It would be lovely to have a family portrait on my wall that I can enjoy now, knowing that I can leave it behind when I am no longer with them. My family will have the portrait to remember me exactly as I was, and I feel that it will leave my imprint on Earth."

I agree, "What a lovely thing to do. I wish that I had done that with my grandparents when they were with me. I am sure that your family will love the idea."

Joyce nods, "Do you ever wonder if your grandma's theory was right and if she will meet your grandfather in another life?"

I suppose that it is an interesting question. "Following Grandma's funeral, I gave her words a considerable amount of thought. She often spoke in riddles that used to confuse me." I pause, "She once claimed that life was like the song, ten green bottles. She said that when one green bottle falls there will still be nine green bottles standing on the wall. I asked her to explain what happens when the last green bottle falls and there are no green bottles left. She answered that you should always recycle your bottles, so they can come back again." Joyce smiles and I carry on, "As I've got older I have come to understand Grandma's belief. She believed that people we have known through past lives will reoccur from lifetime to lifetime, and she would meet us all again in one of our next lives."

Joyce raises her brows, "It's a lovely thought. If you think about it, as one person leaves the world, someone is born into it. In fact, she used to compare life with her daffodils that always died each year, but always returned the following spring."

I remembered how Grandma loved her daffodils and it brings a happy memory to me. "I used to help my grandma in the garden. It was only a small garden, but she took pride and contentment in having it pristine. Daffodils always appeared amongst the rockery in the spring, I used to think that they appeared from nowhere, like magic." I smile remembering the situation. "She would smile at them and sigh with relief that they had arrived again, another year. They were the bright rays of sunshine in her life. When Grandma moved on, I planted daffodils near her graveside. I believe that wherever she may be there will always be some sunshine with her. They return to visit year after year, just like they had when she was with us."

Joyce has now finished her tea and teacake and stands to put on her coat and scarf.

"I have really enjoyed our conversation today. I have concluded that time is always ticking, and the clock will never stop, just like life goes on today and always. As we reach the last chapter or paragraph of our life, a new book is started for a new life. We just need to enjoy our time on Earth and not worry about the end. That's what I am going to do. I am going to live life to the full."

There is a moment of silence whilst Joyce concentrates on wrapping her long scarf round and round her neck.

"Do you come in here often?" she asks, "It would be nice to see you again."

I sip the last froth from my cappuccino which leaves me with a moustache and I see Joyce smile.

"I come in here occasionally, but I am going to Mexico tomorrow, so it may be a while before I'm here again."

"Mexico?" She raises her brows, "well that should be an adventure for you. Take lots of photographs and remember that your life is like a book. As you turn a page you can start a new paragraph or chapter with questions and new findings along the way. You are still young and there is still a lot for you to learn. I'm off now to arrange that family portrait we discussed. It's been lovely talking with you my dear."

As she leaves I am still trying to work out the rather unusual conversation I have just had with the lady who claimed to have known my grandparents. I am sure that I have never seen her before and I can't remember Grandma mentioning a Joyce. Still, I suppose stranger things can happen.

As I wait for the bill, I stare out of the window at a big wheel that is decorated with twinkling, bright lights. The cosmopolitan square of Manchester city is buzzing with wandering crowds meeting up, shopping, and bar hopping. It's obvious that the weather is not deterring the people below from enjoying themselves even though the rain is pouring down. It is slashing against the floor to ceiling windows that form the building and it has started to thunder and lighten.

I feel that I am now ready to close this chapter of my life and move on with the next. I have to be honest with Daniel. Our relationship is over, and I want to move on. I can't wait to go to Mexico, even if it's only to get away from this terrible wet weather.

I arrive home a little later than intended, but fortunately Daniel hasn't arrived home from work. I quickly put the food in the oven. None of it will take longer than an hour to cook. I have bought mainly from the luxurious range, so I have high expectations that it will look just like it does on the M&S television advert. I just hope that it tastes as good as it looks. We shall be eating crepes filled with butternut squash to start, followed by beef bourguignon, and melt-in-the-middle chocolate pudding for dessert. I'm starving and can't wait to eat this delicious looking food. In fact, I think I've put on a few pounds just thinking about it.

I place all of my designer shopping bags in two suitcases and slide them under the bed before Daniel arrives home. This is my little secret for now, and nothing that he needs to know about yet. I've bought so much that I hardly have to pack anything from my wardrobe or drawers. It's probably been the fastest holiday packing that I have ever done. It will be great to go on holiday with a new suitcase of clothes. I have a new wardrobe for a new chapter of my life.

I have a lovely hot shower and dry my bobbed dark hair before applying my makeup. I put on my emerald blue flared jumpsuit. The silk finish fabric is soft to the touch and the hems are finished with pretty white cross-stitching. I question why I am making such an effort. I think that part of it is pride. Daniel cheated on me and I want to look my best when I tell him that I know, and that we are over.

I hear a key turn in the door and know that Daniel is home. I put on my wedges and walk down the stairs to greet him. He has brought home a large bouquet of flowers, probably to ease his guilty conscience. The thought annoys me, and I wish that he would just turn around and walk out of the door.

He holds out the flowers and leans to kiss me on my cheek, "You smell very nice. Are you wearing the perfume that I gave to you at Christmas?"

I don't know why he is trying to creep around me after everything that he has done, and as for that perfume; I hated the smell of it but never really had the bottle to tell him, pardon the pun. I tried to wear it to please him, but it's a strong scent, which gave me a headache. I very occasionally used it as air freshener around the home, until I couldn't stand the smell any longer.

"Sorry, I lost that somewhere. I can't think where."

I know really, it ended up in the bin. I smelt the same scent on him when he returned home late one evening, after being out with one of his conquests.

I see a pitiful frown flash across his face and he follows me into the kitchen where I am pouring two large gin and tonics. I raise my glass, "To the future."

He doesn't join me but watches me knock it back and pour another. "I can't have a drink with you tonight because I have to go back out later."

That explains the flowers I think to myself, before sarcastically asking, "Are you off out to meet your slut in a 5-star hotel?

He looks shocked as his mouth opens in amazement. I don't think that I have ever talked so bluntly to him. I think the drink is giving me Dutch courage. I didn't know I had it within me.

After a long silence he answers. "I haven't a clue what you are talking about and I don't think that you should be drinking alcohol. It's obviously having some reaction with your medication."

I place the glass to one side and hand him my phone showing him the text that I received from Sarah. My comment probably was out of order, but I just couldn't help myself.

"I'm sorry, that was really horrible of me. I am happy that you have met somebody and hope you will be very happy together."

He looks annoyed, "Sarah was just something that happened. It wasn't love and I have no intention of leaving you to be with her."

I roll my eyes, "It's your life Daniel and you can do whatever you please. We have had some good times and we have had some bad times, but I think the time has come to say goodbye."

He puts his head in his hands and quietly asks, "What do you mean? Goodbye? Is this because of Sarah?"

I shake my head, "No, it's because of us and by the way; I am leaving you tomorrow."

"Why are you leaving me tomorrow? We need to talk about this."

This isn't really going how I planned. I can see this ending in an unpleasant, hurtful argument and I'm possible being the main instigator. We have been together for years and gone through thick and thin. I am sure that we can be amicable with each other and bring this to a pleasant ending.

I take a deep breath, "Tonight is our last night together and I have cooked us a really nice goodbye meal so we can discuss our separation. I fully understand if you have other plans, as long as you appreciate that I have plans to go tomorrow, and this may be our last chance."

He moves slowly out of the kitchen towards his mobile phone which is on the hall table. He looks slightly baffled, but then turns and makes eye contact, "I just need to make a private phone call and you'll have me for the evening. Please will you pour us both a large glass of Chianti and also serve dinner? I won't be going out now."

He closes the door firmly behind him, but I hear him on the phone making pathetic excuses to some woman. It was me who used to be on the receiving end of his excuses.

Daniel returns to the kitchen looking a little ruffled. He looks flustered and has removed his tie and undone the top two buttons of his shirt. His curly blonde hair looks sweaty and is sticking to his forehead. He sits at the table opposite me and runs his finger from side to side through the flame of the candle that I have placed in the middle of the table.

"Is there somebody else?" he asks.

I nearly choke on my butternut squash crepe and have to take a sip of my wine to get over the shock of his question. He is actually being serious.

"I cannot believe your nerve. I have always been faithful to you. It was you who fathered a child with somebody else and had affairs whilst you were with me. You couldn't even resist whilst I was in rehabilitation."

I carry on eating and after a short silence he picks up his cutlery and decides to join me.

He looks down in shame, "I am sorry, I shouldn't have done what I did."

I decide not to make any comment and keep looking down at my food whilst he talks.

"I owe you an explanation."

I look up, "No you don't, Daniel, I already know."

"What do you know?" he frowns.

"We have made compromises with each other and we aren't meant to be. A close friend called Julia told me that you should never compromise what you are looking for. We have both made compromises with each other and the truth is that we aren't right for each other. No matter how hard we work at this relationship, it will never be right, because we aren't right for each other. We may care for each other in some guise, but we don't love each other."

Daniel looks doubtful at me, but says nothing, so I carry on speaking.

"I have been doing a lot of thinking whilst we have been apart. I want the kind of relationship that my grandma and grandfather shared. I want the kind of love that will last forever, that will take the world by storm. I want sweet nothings whispered into my ear, excitement, passion and romance."

He rolls his eyes annoyed with me, "Not everything can be perfect. I am sure that we can work at things."

I shake my head, "There hasn't been any special magic between us for as long as I can remember. I was once willing to work at our relationship and live in hope that it comes, but I now know that's an impossible task. It's time to move on from each other. We just need to admit it."

I stand to clear the plates and start to serve the beef bourguignon. There is an uncomfortable silence between us until I return to the table. I try to pour myself another glass of wine but notice that he has finished the bottle whilst I've been away from the table. I can't understand why he can't sip and savor it, rather than gulp it. He gets a further bottle from the wine rack and fills our glasses whilst he speaks.

"Our relationship has been stuck in a rut for a while, but I am sure that we could get through the pain of this affair and end up stronger, if you give me another chance."

"I am really sorry, Daniel, but there is no love between us. I have thought long and hard about our relationship, but it's over. I need to make the break that is needed for both of us."

He sounds annoyed, "What's that supposed to mean?"

I shrug my shoulders, "My time at the rehabilitation unit has made me look at my life from a different perspective. I don't really know what I want anymore, but I do know that I can't be with you. There is lust between us, Dan, but there isn't love, and we both need to move on and stop holding each other back from getting on with our lives. I feel that there is something missing in my life, and I need to find myself, in order to find out what it is that's missing. It's a journey that I need to take alone."

He nods in agreement, "I've been selfish and haven't respected you. I am really sorry, but I want you to know that I didn't mean to hurt you. I regret my actions and really wish that we could have been the perfect dream couple, just like you wanted."

I smile, "We will both find our dreams one day."

He glares at me, "What if we are saying goodbye to our dreams? What if we do actually love each other?"

I recall what Julia said to me, "If we are meant to be, we will go our separate ways but will one day come back together. If we don't reunite, we were never meant to be. If we were to stay together, we may never find that special person that everybody is destined to find, and we may end up sad for the rest of our lives."

He smiles across the table, "Interesting theory, wherever did you get that from?"

I stand to clear the plates. "Rehab actually. I was really sad when I was there. I am fearful of being sad again."

He nods, "You seem to have all of the answers, so what next?"

I feel a pang of guilt, "Well I have a confession to make."

He raises his eyebrows.

"I have arranged to travel to Mexico, on a journey to discover myself, and I have raided our savings account to go. You did say the money was there for a rainy day."

I am expecting him to be annoyed but he half smiles.

"Well, it's somewhere that you have always wanted to go. I just hope the weather is better there than here, and it's not raining."

The atmosphere between us lightens and I serve melt-in-the-middle chocolate pudding and we share the scrapings left in the Ben and Jerry ice cream tub.

Daniel admits, "I wish that we had discussed our true feelings before we were married. It would have saved us both a lot of wasted time and heartache."

"I don't think that I knew my true feelings then."

He nods, "Yes, I know what you mean. I hope that you don't regret me though. I know that I have done some really stupid things, that I honestly do regret, but I did care for you."

"I know." I smile at his honesty. "I don't regret you or anything in my life. I think that everything that happens in life happens for a reason."

He agrees, "I am pleased that you say that and don't hate me."

I am happy that we have both come to the same conclusion and are happy to move on and go our own separate ways.

He smiles at me. "We probably could have ended up good mates, but for spoiling everything and getting together as a couple."

"Yes, we possibly could have." I actually agree with that thought.

As the glasses clink, I know that another chapter has finished. Tonight, we told each other the truth about our feelings. We were probably closer than I think we ever had been. I am really pleased that our separation has been civilized. I was worried that the evening may have ended up in an argument, but we have both come to terms with the fact that our relationship had been just a passing fancy and wasn't meant to be.

I can't remember going to bed, but I have woken up feeling worse for wear. I drag myself out of bed remembering that I have a flight to catch.

I desperately need some strong coffee and painkillers. My head is banging but there's definitely no loud music playing, it just feels like it. I eventually make my way downstairs into the kitchen and find a note from Daniel, who has left for work.

Sas,

No doubt you will be feeling sorry for yourself this morning, when you're suffering the morning after the night before feeling. The dreaded hangover! Hope you have a great trip despite this.

Here are MY words of wisdom for you on your travels. I appreciate that you may have a collection from the friends you made at re-hab.

1. Have enough money not to worry about having enough money.

2. Keep wherever you live presentable for any unexpected guests.

3. Do one hundred consecutive sit-ups a day to keep your flat stomach.

4. Finally, find your dreams, live them and be them. It's the only way you will ever find happiness.

Sorry that we weren't meant to be.

Dreams and wishes,

Dan x

Looking around I feel like I am somewhere that I no longer belong. The house doesn't feel like my home any longer, it doesn't have that homely feeling that it used to have. I wander around the house and say my goodbyes to each room. I am happy that I have made my decision to leave. It feels right that I am going.

I look at my watch. The taxi that I ordered last night will be collecting me to take me to the airport in half an hour. I have a quick shower and throw on my tracksuit. I want to wear something comfortable for my journey. I struggle to carry my heavy suitcase downstairs. My head is still banging, and I am now suffering from nausea.

It was really stupid to drink so much last night, especially when I knew that I had such a long journey ahead of me today. There is only one answer for this and it isn't painkillers. It's something that I haven't tried before, but I am willing to give anything a go if it might make me feel better. I believe the term is known as 'hair of the dog'. Apparently if you are hungover and take a glass of the same wine previously drunk, it will soothe your nerves and lessen the effects of being hungover. I pour myself a glass of red wine and drink it quickly. I am already starting to feel better. I wonder why I have never tried this before.

It's only 10am but it's been an emotionally-draining morning. I remember that I haven't let Catherine know that I am going away for a while. I phone her mobile, but it is just ringing out, so I leave her a message telling her that I will call her when I arrive in Mexico. It would have been nice to say goodbye to her and Joshua before I left, but not to worry, I will see them when I return. I just hope that she isn't annoyed with me. I usually talk to her about everything.

Whilst I am deep in thought remembering memories good and bad shared in the house, my mobile starts to ring. I think for one second that it's Catherine calling me back, but I am disappointed to see Sarah's name flash up on the screen.

Even though I didn't love Daniel, I feel betrayed by Sarah. She was supposed to be a friend and even though I probably expected an affair from Daniel, I would never have expected her to deceive me. Friends are supposed to look out for each other, not stab each other in the back. I won't hold a grudge against her, and I can't turn back the clock and stop it from happening, but she isn't really somebody that I want to remain friends with. She is the last person in the world that I would want to speak to now. I have nothing nice to say to her, so I reject her call and send her a text. In fact, I just reply to the one she sent me by accident a few days ago.

> Traitor Sarah, with an air of tranquility I would just like to say that you are wickedness, poison, dog poop, sarcasm and just simply a mean bitch on the loose. I feel totally betrayed by you, and I just hope that your fling with Daniel was worth our friendship. I am off to Mexico now, to stay in a luxury hotel, so Adios, bye. I won't bother sending you a postcard! Saskia.

I hear the taxi beep outside, so I check my new designer handbag to make sure that my tickets, passport and phrase book are all enclosed. I close the front door behind me and post my keys through the letterbox. I feel a sigh of relief pass through my body. It is like a heavy weight has been taken off my shoulders. My sweet dream for now is to achieve peacefulness in my mind. For some reason, I feel Mexico is going to help me reach this. I have a really good vibe and I've just seen two magpies for joy!

CHAPTER THREE

What is it with air travel?

I am sure that it brings out the worst in people, making them irritable and irrational. It's almost as if people's lives depend on how quickly they can get on the plane, pushing to get in line to the boarding gate.

Perhaps it's just that they are bored of wandering around the airport, worrying about delays, worrying about missing their flight, and wanting to have a seat and rest. You can guarantee that once they are seated though, they will be complaining about the plane, the food, their head phones, the air conditioning, it's too hot, it's too cold, or anything else that they believe they have a viable complaint for.

You would hope that people would think themselves fortunate to be going on holiday, without complaining and spoiling it for themselves and others. I am sure that most of these people are reasonable human beings, and I just can't understand why they act like this. I think that there should just be a rule to throw rude people out of the plane with an attached parachute. I am sure that the air hosts would welcome this suggestion.

My seat row number is announced, and I drift breezily to the front of the queue, whilst I receive frowns and moans from other travelers. Luckily, I don't have to suffer the sore ribs from being elbowed, or the swollen toes from being stood on. I have priority check in and a priority boarding pass, because I have booked Premium class tickets. I would have travelled first class, at Daniel's expense, if the option had been available, but unfortunately it wasn't on offer.

Fortunately, I had extra luggage allowance and I certainly needed it after my shopping spree. I am sat in a stylish, wide leather seat with a really comfortable head support and I have my very own widescreen seatback television with a great choice of sixteen movies that I can watch throughout the journey. I won't be doing any complaining.

I politely greet the strangers seated close by with whom I will probably interact with on the flight. The gentleman on the row opposite is drowning his flight nerves one mini bottle of gin at a time, the lady behind me is complaining about a child crying and kicking the back of her seat. She speaks sternly to her husband and everybody hears, "Screaming, unruly children should not be allowed in this section. We paid extra to fly Premium, so we did not have to tolerate things like this. I am going to speak to an air hostess about this if it carries on, because it isn't good enough." I hear the mother of the child apologize and I feel sorry for her.

The gentleman in front is moaning to the air hostess that he hasn't been given a pillow or blanket despite asking twice. I don't know why he can't get off his backside and get them himself, because they are only in the overhead compartment.

One of the air hostesses offers me a glass of Champagne before take-off and I politely accept. A lady sits in the seat next to me after loading her large black bag in the overhead compartment. Perhaps she hasn't brought a suitcase looking at the size of the bag. She seems pleasant enough and says, "Hello." I return the greeting and she also accepts a complimentary drink.

The lady is dressed completely in black and is Gothic in her style. She has long shiny black hair and a skull stud through her nose. It's hard to put an age on her but I would say that she could be anywhere between 40 and 50. She has a rather unusual smell about her. It's almost a mixture of perfume and mustiness but still smells quite pleasant, quite sweet actually. I recognize the scent and I am trying to work out from where.

I keep discreetly sniffing to try to work out exactly what the smell is. She opens her handbag which is placed on her knee and the smell gets even stronger. I can't help but wonder if it's cannabis, but she couldn't have got through customs with drugs in her handbag. I suppose that it could be incense.

She starts rummaging through everything that's inside her bag and there appears to be quite a lot. She pulls out a small bottle of perfume and hands it to me.

"Your nose was twitching in my direction. A lot of people ask me what perfume I am wearing when I wear my white musk. I guess that you must like it, so please try some."

"Thanks," I say to be polite, and feel compelled to put a little on my wrist.

She smiles, "I don't buy designer perfumes. I like to make my own perfumes that are unique to me and my personality. I always use natural ingredients, and a lot of people comment when I wear them, probably due to them being very different. One of the officers coming through security said to her colleague that she could smell dope on me. She checked all of my bags and then said I was fine to go. I was extremely offended, and I plan to complain when I return from Mexico."

Despite her gothic appearance she seems sweet and innocent. I just hope that she doesn't start complaining to the air hostesses. Looking around, I think that they are busy enough with pre-flight procedures and a few difficult customers.

I am still feeling terribly hungover and, to be honest, it's only 'hair of the dog' that has kept me going. I am hoping that I shall be able to have a sleep on this long flight and hopefully wake up feeling refreshed (without a hangover) when I arrive in Mexico.

The pilot makes an announcement to prepare for take-off and I feel myself being drawn tightly into the seat with the powerful force, as we hit the runway, and start to take off into the sky. I stare out of the window for a long period, watching the views below become smaller and smaller, until they disappear. All that I can see is white fluffy clouds.

I quietly say to myself, "Goodbye, rainy Manchester."
Hopefully, I shall soon have some sunshine in my life.

The lady at the side of me has now closed her eyes and is wearing earphones. I think that she is listening to classical music. I can vaguely hear it and it sounds quite relaxing. I remove my complimentary noise reduction headsets from my luxury pampering pack and place them over my ears to stop any noise. I am feeling really tired. My eyes close and I feel myself drifting, drifting asleep.

I am unsure how long I have slept, but I awaken suddenly with the sense of falling, in a state of distress and screaming and shouting at the top of my voice, "Please don't leave me." I am surrounded by close up faces staring at me with concern. I have a damp towel placed on my forehead and I find out that the man who was knocking back miniature bottles of gin is actually a doctor. (Apparently, the pilot put out a request asking if there was a doctor on board). The tipsy doctor is holding my wrist and taking my pulse rate. God knows if he is getting it right after the amount of alcohol I saw him consuming earlier. I wish I had an ejection button that would shoot me out of the plane, but I think that even this is too much to ask from premium class, so I face the embarrassment.

Trying hard not to draw any more attention to myself, I apologize, "I am so sorry to trouble you all, I was just having a bad dream."

The gothic lady touches my hand in a kind, caring manner. "Sweetheart, you experienced a nightmare, but it is ok because you are back in this life now."

I think that it is quite an unusual thing to say, but I suppose that she is quite an unusual person.

The faces start to slowly disappear from before my eyes, whilst the doctor asks me personal questions for reassurance that I am actually ok. The air hostess brings me a lukewarm cup of stewed tea and I sit back in my seat. Yes, tea still tastes terrible and stewed in Premium class. I check and there's definitely no teabag left in the cup. There are still a few hours left before we land at Cancun International Airport. Despite my nightmare, my hangover has fortunately now disappeared.

I have decided to look out of the window, so that I don't have to make eye contact with anybody. I feel sorry for the people who have booked Premium class seating and have had to suffer my freak show. It is pretty obvious that 70% of the cabin have decided that I must be some sort of mad, crazy woman. Well, I suppose that they are right, and I am now just something else for the travelers to complain about for the rest of their holidays.

It isn't that long ago that I came out of the psychiatric rehabilitation clinic believing that my nightmares and dreams had left me for good. I can't believe that they have returned, and I am mortified. I thought this holiday could be a new start in every way, leaving my past behind me, and that included the dreams and the nightmares.

The Goth touches me on the shoulder, "My name is Hania, which means Spirit Warrior."

I smile, "That is a nice name, and meaning." At least one person is being nice to me and not giving me frowns. "My name is Saskia," I introduce myself.

"I know," she remarks, I heard the Doctor speaking with you.

I smile, "Yes, Of course you did."

"Have you experienced the same nightmare before?" She seems interested.

She stares into my eyes and I feel hypnotized by her amazing crystal blue eyes.

"Unfortunately, the nightmare has haunted me all of my life." I look down disappointed.

"I could help if you like, but only if you would like me to."

"How could you help?" I ask interested. "Nobody else has been able to help, so how can you?"

She stares into my eyes like she is studying me, "I have many special gifts, one of which is to interpret dreams and nightmares, and I would like to help you understand what is happening."

I believe her. "What do I need to do?"

"Please tell me about your dream. Tell me everything that happens. We have plenty of time to discuss it."

I feel comfortable discussing my situation with her. I recall my dream in detail, "I am a passenger in a car that is travelling rather fast and I can feel danger ahead. The sensation of this extreme danger is causing emotional chaos in my stomach and I am feeling physically sick. I can see a narrow road ahead that is winding around a high cliff edge and the sun is shining strongly and brightly, like I have never seen before, almost like it is an angel calling me and drawing me near."

"Where are you?" she asks.

I think hard about this before answering. "It looks familiar, but I honestly haven't a clue. The calm turquoise sea that I see below is shimmering like a large crystal and there are large birds swooping down and hovering above the car. The only safety that I feel is from the man who is sat next to me in the driving seat."

"Who is this man?" she enquires.

I think for a moment. "I feel that I know him very well, but on reflection, I don't think that I do. He has the most beautiful ocean blue eyes though, that enchant me."

I smile for a second thinking about his beauty, but then my happiness turns to sadness.

"He then starts to scare me because his beautiful eyes are reflecting fear and horror. For some reason I feel that death is upon us, and he is trying to protect me and hide his fears. I grasp tightly hold of his hand because

I don't want him to leave me. I think that he could be my soulmate and if we are to die, then I want us to do it together."

I look at Hania, and her eyes are wide with horror.

"Sorry, this is crazy isn't it? I should stop here."

She touches my hand, "No, Saskia, this is important. Please carry on."

I shrug my shoulders, "I feel that we should never be apart and that we are meant to be together." I pause again recalling the end of the dream. "I then feel my body leave the car seat and I feel like I am falling in mid-air and this is when I wake up."

Hania nods, "That explains why you woke up screaming a little while ago."

I look at her and she appears deep in thought. "So, what is your interpretation, Hania?"

"I have special psychic powers that allow me to interpret your dream and see your life. I am going to tell you something, but I worry that you won't believe me or will not accept what I am telling you."

"It would be nice to know your interpretation. Even if I wasn't to believe you, I would still like to be told."

Hania takes a deep breath, "I believe that you have experienced the survival of your soul after death. It is the phase of the soul that is in the background of your physical world, and this is why you are experiencing this repeated nightmare. Your dreams and nightmares are telling you that there is some unfinished business in your life."

I open my mouth, but no words come out. I am shocked.

Hania observes my reaction, "I believe that you have died in a previous life, and that your soul from your previous life is still here with you now in this life."

I am still unable to speak. I want to ask questions, but when I open my mouth, I am unable to talk, nothing comes out.

"The mystery of life and death has always existed, Saskia, and I am sure that you have previously asked yourself many questions to try to understand your finite presence on this earth."

I had asked myself many questions in the past. How did I get here? Why does life end? Is there life after death? Is death a transition from one life to another? Perhaps the reason I asked these questions is linked with my issues.

Hania carries on talking, "Your past life traumas hold the key to your recurring nightmares and any anxiety attacks. There are a number of people who claim to have experienced their past life."

"Is there really?" I quiz, still trying to take in what she has just told me.

"Yes, for some, details of a past life have filtered in through their dreams whilst they sleep. Others report having had experienced some form of déjà vu and some just seem to know that they have been here before."

"What can I do about my nightmares, Hania? I am really worried." I feel myself shaking.

She holds my hand, "Tell me, and be honest, why are you going to Mexico?"

"I have come to find myself. I have felt lost for a long time, like there is something missing in my life. I have always wanted to go to Mexico and destiny has brought me on this trip."

Hania nods in agreement. "Destiny is bringing you to Mexico, destiny is a powerful source. Your trip will help you to resolve past life issues and put matters to rest that have been subconsciously troubling you. Evidence of your past life is in your everyday life, and your past life is still very present. When the two paths eventually cross, it shall have a great significance for you."

I feel a cold chill overtake my body and I have started to shiver. I nervously stand and take a blanket from the overhead cabinet and cover my body. It isn't having the affect that I hoped for. I am still feeling really cold, ice cold in fact.

I have often imagined what it would be like to read the story of my life before it happened. I would know how to make the most out of the opportunities that life gives to me. I would know how to avoid negative influences that could distract me from achieving my true life purpose and which path to take in order to have the happiest, most fulfilling life available to me. I am quiet now though, because I could never have imagined, or even come up with the scenario that I have died in a previous life, but my soul has survived, and is now in the background of my present life. Not even in my wildest imagination. I wonder how Hania has come to this conclusion, just because I have experienced a nightmare. She is either as crazy as me, or really does have special powers.

"Saskia, I am going to predict your future, but I don't want you to be scared, as you will finally get a resolution to your issues."

"You can tell my future too?" I enquire. "I am unsure if I want to know."

"Sorry, I have to warn you. I wouldn't be doing my job if I didn't."

"Ok," I reply reluctantly, "If there is something that I need to be warned about, then I should know."

"There is no easy way to tell you this," she stammers, "Your past life soul is being called for 'Dia de los Muertos'"

I have no idea what she means by Dia de los Muertos, but before I have a chance to ask the question, she tells me the answer, "Day of the Dead."

Hania looks up and then holds her hands together as though she is praying.

I feel my blood flow coldly through my veins. I am shivering again. How the hell is she doing this, but more to the point why is she doing this to me? I need to know, I demand to know, "What is this Day of the Dead?"

Hania opens her eyes and offers explanation. "It isn't like it sounds."

"Am I going to die whilst on holiday?" I am terrified and confused.

"I believe that you have died in a previous life, and that your soul from your previous life is still here with you now in this life. It is your past life being called for 'Day of the Dead' and you will be taken along to assist."

"What shall happen?" I am confused.

She explains, "Dia de los Muertos, Day of the Dead, is a yearly tradition celebrated in Mexico where families celebrate the idea that death is a transition from one life to another. Departed souls return to visit on the 1st and 2nd of November. The first day is set aside to commemorate deceased infants and children, the second day to commemorate deceased adults. For each deceased relative a candle is lit, and incense is burnt. The light and the aroma help guide returning souls."

"Is that why I am on my way to Mexico? Is my past life being guided here, and I am along for the journey?" I ask intrigued.

"Communication exists between the living and the dead, Saskia. Your soul from your previous life is being called for Dia de los Muertos and this is why you are on your way to Mexico. Your soul from your past life is in the background of your present life. There are issues that need resolving, and this is something that you and your past have to do together before you can move on. Your nightmares will then leave you."

I watch Hania closely and hope that she will give me further explanation, but she has now closed her eyes tightly and is fidgeting with her necklace. I observe the necklace for some time because it is rather unusual. It is a string of 40 beads and a cord of 40 knots. She is running her fingers over the beads and quietly chanting to herself.

I listen to her, "I call the spirits of all that have passed and those yet to come." She is rocking her head from side to side in the chair, "I call on the Moon, Earth, stars, Sun, water, air and fire. Priest and princess come bless this woman now."

When she opens her eyes, she tells me, "Baldur the god of light will protect you now. You have nothing at all to worry about."

I feel uncomfortable in her company. "Sorry, Hania, but I need to go to the ladies."

I need some space, and that is the only place to escape to on a plane. She is either telling me the truth or she is more insane than me. I will just have to see what happens when I arrive in Mexico, and then come to my own conclusion.

I escape to the urine stinking bathroom to wash down my face and body with cold soapy water. I change out of my sweaty tracksuit into my red Ralph Lauren summer dress. I hope that things can only get better.

When I return to my seat, Hania passes me her business card and a leaflet. The business card confirms that she is a spirit warrior. The leaflet says that she is a world-leading natural clairvoyant, psychic and medium. It claims that she will provide detailed information regarding your future and your past and will guide you through your life providing closure on your past. There are comments and references provided from leading and famous people all over the world who have confided in her and confirmed that she has tuned into their past, present and future, and used spirit guides to provide readings and advice that has been accurate.

"Saskia, should you need any help or advice, please don't hesitate to contact me, this is what I am here for. I am in Mexico for the next six weeks to help others like you. I have also written details of my hotel on the back of the card. Please look after this card, because I have a feeling that you may require my help in the very near future."

I place her business card safely in my purse, just in case I need her help, but I am going to try to put her to the back of my mind and get on with my holiday.

I am relieved to land safely, and before we vacate the plane, Hania informs me, "Magic is all around us. It is about knowing how to tap into the magical energy that surrounds you, so that you get what your heart desires. Mexico will be a journey to discover yourself, and hopefully your past soul will eventually rest. Just remember that even when you are really down, there's something always out there to smile about."

"I hope so," I comment. I just wish that I had something to smile about now.

I look up to the heavens and plead, "Please God, look after me, Amen."

CHAPTER FOUR

I've eventually arrived in Cancun. It's been advertised in the booklet Martha gave to me as the biggest party resort in the Caribbean. There are superb curving beaches of dazzling white sand and the sea is a perfect turquoise in color. As I am driven to my hotel, in the luxury Mercedes that I ordered, I pass old colonial haciendas and lavish hotels.

There appears to be a non-stop bright and breezy party atmosphere in the bars and restaurants that I pass. The high temperature is sending my heart racing. This modern, glittering resort excites me, making me feel like I am actually living a dream. I have a feeling that this place will help me to move on and decide what I want for my future.

My hotel does not disappoint at all and it is certainly a head turner. I stare in amazement at its white washed elegance, standing tall and proud, eighteen floors high. It is surrounded by soft blonde sands, palm trees, tropical gardens and sapphire clear waters. It is in a breathtaking location, yet it is still conveniently located for the designer shopping malls and nightlife. I think I am going to have lots of fun. I am so excited that I feel like jumping up and down. I hope that the inside of the hotel is just as good.

Air conditioning and a marble lobby greet me as the porter opens the door upon my arrival. I admire the vast sumptuous reception with numerous elegant sofas, granite tables, gleaming silver chandeliers and warmly-lit silver contemporary décor. The scent of the tropical flowers that are scattered throughout the reception make me sneeze. Some older guests are enjoying a civilized afternoon treat consisting of sandwiches, cream cakes and pots of tea and coffee. Not what I expected of Mexico, but I suppose anything goes on holiday.

I detect a party atmosphere through the open double glass doors at the far end of the lobby, where I can hear the hotels entertainment program in full swing. Loud music, pool games and laughter fill the air. It makes me just want to put on my bikini, dive into the pool and join in all the fun.

There are also two serene swimming pools overlooking the ocean, each with whirlpool baths and swim up bars. They must serve every drink possible looking at the selection of bottles on display. The vast sun terraces are decked with wicker tables, umbrellas and chairs where people are relaxing after an al fresco lunch. Palms and flowering shrubs lead to the whitewashed beach where there are numerous motorized sports, and children taking part in beach games such as volleyball. This place has heaven written all over it. I couldn't have wished for a better tropical escape.

Whilst taking all of this in, I am approached by a waiter dressed in black trousers and a palm tree patterned shirt.

"Excuse me madam. Please may I serve you a refreshing cocktail whilst you are awaiting allocation of your room?"

"That would be perfect, thank you." I answer, clocking his name badge, Alonso.

Alonso serves me with a tall glass, decorated with two small paper umbrellas. The cocktail is a mixture of tropical fruit juices with crushed ice to keep it chilled. As I suck through my straw I feel instantly relaxed.

"This drink is definitely refreshing," I comment, "It's just what I needed after my long journey from England."

"Where in England do you live, Madam, if you don't mind me asking?"

"No, I don't mind you asking at all. I live near Manchester."

"Wow, I love Manchester. It is a great city, but when I visited, it just never stopped raining. In fact, when I returned to Mexico where the skies are always blue, I joked with friends that I had flown over a rainbow to return here."

He turns on his heels and looks back at me, "I look forward to seeing you around, Madam."

"Please call me Saskia." I call out, as he walks off smiling.

He has a point, I think about the song lyrics of 'Somewhere Over The Rainbow'. The skies in Cancun are bluer than blue. I've left cloudy, rainy, depressing Manchester where the sky is grey and dismal and flown high over some rainbow to Mexico, where skies are blue. The clouds are far behind me for now and I can only hope that my dreams and aspirations start to come true, just like in the song.

A porter approaches me. "Your room is now ready for you and your luggage is waiting. May I escort you to your suite?"

I've never had first class treatment like this before. I think that I shall always book 5-star hotels in the future. They are certainly worth their price tag.

I have a deluxe sea-view suite, number 1818 (my lucky number double) on the tenth floor. Luckily not the 18th floor with the Chinese theory that floor 18 must be avoided, because there are apparently18 floors to hell. I would have had to request a floor change otherwise, especially after what the spirit warrior said to me on the plane. She is unfortunately still on my mind.

Due to the fact that I feel that number 18 has some relevance in my life, I once looked into its meaning. Apparently lucky numbers represent certain vibes or essences of your life. In the Chinese culture, there is a saying that good things come in pairs and they believe that number 18 is lucky. They interpret the number to mean that one will prosper. The Hebrew word for alive is Chai and this is given a numerical value of 18. Jewish circles give monetary gifts and donations in multiples of 18. They believe that this is a blessing for a long life. Arabs believe that the number 18 is on the right palm of every person's right hand. I was amazed when I came across this and found it to be true. I did have to look for a long time before I found it though.

My lucky suite has a lounge area and a stylish step-out balcony with fantastic views where I plan to be able to unwind and watch the sun sink into the ocean in the evenings with a glass of Sauvignon Blanc. The floors are beige marble and the walls are painted plain crisp white, decorated with framed ocean paintings. There is a queen-size bed that has been draped with burgundy silk sheets and scatter pillows. It is decorated with pink and cream rose petals and there's a towel made in the shape of a swan. It's so pretty that I don't want to use it.

I pour myself a gin from the liquor dispenser optics and add some tonic water from the minibar, whilst I unpack. This should help me relax and recover from the long flight, whilst the large round hydro massage bath is running ready for a good long soak before dinner. There is even an option of four different bubble baths to choose from. I am feeling perfectly pampered. This is just what I would expect from a 5-star hotel - pure luxury.

Whilst my bath is running, I phone Catherine. I want to let her know that I've arrived safely in Mexico, and that Daniel and I are no longer together. Her phone only rings once and she is talking before I even have chance to say a word. She is talking so fast that I can hardly make out anything that she is saying.

"Saskia, I'm relieved you are ok. I know about everything that's gone on. I hate that bitch."

I can only presume that she is talking about Sarah, and now knows that Daniel was having a fling with her. Daniel probably wanted to inform her of the situation before I did, knowing that she is a typical fiery red head and will be annoyed with him.

She carries on, "That pathetic excuse for a human being has visited my house today and given me bags upon bags of your belongings.

Catherine obviously knows more than me and I am confused with what she is telling me.

"Catherine, please just calm down and slow down. Has Daniel brought everything of mine to your house?"

I know that it was an amicable break up, but I didn't expect for him to be moving my belongings out the day after.

"No, that silly bitch Sarah brought all of your belongings round in black bin bags and she said that you aren't welcome at their house any longer."

"Their house?" I query as my eyes widen in shock.

"She told me that you have run off to Mexico, because you couldn't face the fact that Daniel loves her more than you, and she said that Daniel had asked her to move in with him."

I am a little baffled and confused.

She carries on, "I stormed round to your house to give him a piece of my mind. Sarah was there with a van and two meathead bodybuilders. They were unloading a van full of her things into your house. I asked Daniel what the hell he was playing at, but he was busy trying to carry the things out of the house that they had just carried in."

"What do you mean by that?"

"Well, he doesn't want her living there. She saw you moving out as the green signal that she could move in. She had decided that she was going to live there without consulting Daniel. In fact, he had to eventually tell her that their relationship meant nothing, and that he didn't want to see her again."

"What did she say to that? Did she move everything out?"

"Well at first she didn't. She told him that he had made his bed and now had to lie in it, with her."

I couldn't contain my laughter. No doubt Daniel will have given her some flannel at some point. Sarah was usually a logically-minded person. I really couldn't imagine her imposing herself on Daniel, not if she didn't really think that she was wanted.

"Is Sarah now living there then?" I ask, still giggling.

"No. She eventually got the message and kicked Dan in the balls, accusing him of having used her for sex. I watched the performance and listened to her screaming like a fishwife. Dan was bright red with embarrassment, spitting and spluttering. whilst crossing his legs in pain."

"Poor Dan" I remark, feeling guilty for finding his situation funny. "I suppose that may put him out of action for a while."

We both laugh.

"Don't feel sorry for him, Saskia. He deserves everything that he gets.

"Well, perhaps he has learnt a hard lesson from his actions."

"Saskia, Be honest with yourself. He will never learn, although I think it has taught Sarah a lesson."

"Why do you say that?"

"The cheeky bitch has more front than Blackpool. She came around to my house this evening to say sorry for her actions. She wanted forgiveness and asked if she could stay with me. She had apparently given up her flat to move in with Daniel."

"Did she have nowhere else to go?"

"One of the meathead removal guys had offered, so I think she was going there. I just hope he knows what he is getting himself involved with."

I find myself laughing out loud with Catherine at the events of the day. I am a big believer of what goes around, comes around, and I think that Daniel and Sarah have both had their dose today.

I fill Catherine in on the actual facts, why I have left Daniel, and how I am really excited about being in Mexico. I also tell her about meeting Hania, the Spirit Warrior.

"You must be careful, Saskia, I believe in all of that kind of psychic stuff. Promise that you will keep in touch. I'm going to be really worried about you."

Catherine is everything that you would want from a best friend. She is caring and considerate. I know that if she says she will be worrying, she certainly will.

"I promise to keep in touch, even if it's only to keep your mind at rest."

As we say our goodbyes, I blow little Joshua a kiss over the phone. I'm missing them both already. It would be nice if they were here with me.

Following my long relaxing bubble bath soak I feel really tired. I think that the travelling and the events of the day have eventually caught up with me. I had planned to get dressed up and have dinner in one of the hotel restaurants, but to be honest, I just feel like lounging about in my nightwear, watching some television, ordering room service and then having an early night, ready for whatever tomorrow may bring. I lie on the bed and close my eyes. This bed is so comfortable.

I awaken fresh and breezy with the sun shining brightly and strongly through the window. It is casting dancing shadows around the room that make me want to get up and join the fun. I have slept really well in the queen-size bed with the silk sheets and feather-filled pillows.

Following a quick shower, I tie back my hair, and cover my body in sun protection factor. I am hoping that as long as I am careful and keep applying this regularly, my skin shall turn a nice golden brown without going through the bright red cooked lobster stage first. I've been there before, and it wasn't nice, believe me.

I have decided that I am going to have a lazy day by the side of the gorgeous pools that I saw when I first arrived yesterday. I wear my new bright yellow bikini and matching sarong and I place my book, sun cream and some other accessories in my beach bag and head down to breakfast.

There is everything that you could possibly dream of eating being offered for breakfast, all served buffet style. There is the typical American full breakfast, pancakes, freshly baked bread that is still warm and soft from the oven that smells heavenly, omelets cooked to your liking, cereals, fresh fruit and yoghurt. They even offer a full salad bar for breakfast with a selection of cooked meats. I've never really been a breakfast person and I'd just planned to have a cup of black coffee but the food smells so good, and I am really tempted, so I decide to have a little bit of everything and then swill it all down with a fresh berry smoothie. I suppose that's the only problem with all inclusive, you end up eating more than you ever would at home. I feel like a bloated whale. If I get in the pool today I will do one of two things, either float or sink. I don't think that I would be able to swim.

The pool area is just as I remember it from yesterday, more beautiful than I remember it actually. There is decking around the pools and Indian stone crazy paving surrounding the haven garden areas. The gardens are filled with tropical plants and palm trees that are decorated with small twinkling lights. It is only 7.30am and everything appears still and quiet, apart from the sea which has gentle waves caressing the sandy beach shore. The waves sound like relaxing therapeutic music. I place my beach towel on a cushioned wicker sunbed that is next to the pool. I slump down and close my eyes. I'm not tired, but after all of that food I just want to close my eyes and rest, whilst my poor intestines work hard to cope with my overindulgence.

I feel myself doze off. I am feeling that I am awake and asleep at the same time. I try to move but feel like my body is paralyzed. I could swear that there is someone stood over me and I can see someone, almost a reflection of myself, but the person's not really there. It is a strange place to be and I feel like I am in a dream state not connected to others, existing apart and alone from all other living beings. I feel that I am in a complete delusion from consciousness. I can still hear the gentle caressing of the waves in the background and I intuitively feel that I am experiencing a realization of the truth, of my being or of my past soul. I am still feeling…half awake… half asleep, still unable to move despite trying. I am in a dream state…a state of consciousness characterized by a pervasive sense of individuality, a sense of 'me' as a separate self. I feel like I am on a roller coaster ride where I have moments of utter clarity and can see things, hear things, feel myself move, followed by moments of delusion.

My consciousness then returns to a clear clarity, a cleanness that is no longer deluded or confused, but I feel sickness. I look around me and the pool area is no longer a tranquility of calmness like when I arrived this morning. It is now busy and there is music playing and hotel guests are soaking up the rays of the Mexican sun and enjoying the various pool and beach entertainment. I have no idea about time, but I know that lunch has been and gone because there are plates around that haven't yet been collected by the waiters. I must have been in an unusual place to sleep through all of this. It was the most unusual dream, or perhaps experience that has ever happened to me. Perhaps Hania's theory has been subconsciously playing games with my mind for me to experience this illusion.

I feel like I am burning up and sweat is literally pouring off my face. My yellow bikini is sticking to my body and I have turned into a lobster because I haven't been applying my suntan lotion regularly like I had planned. I shall now have to apply lots of after sun to stop myself peeling. I am really annoyed with myself for going asleep.

There is a fabulous round pool bar positioned in the water with seats around the bar area, so I decide to cool off and go for a drink. I plan to just sit and chill for a little out of the sun. I've obviously had too much sun and it's caused me to hallucinate. That's what has happened to me. I am sure, positive in fact, what else could it have been?

I am pleased to see a friendly face serving behind the bar. It is Alonso who greeted me with a drink when I arrived yesterday.

"Saskia, it's nice to see you again," he says in a cheery, welcoming voice. "Have you come for one of my famous cocktails?" I am amazed that he has remembered my name. What lovely customer service.

He is already juggling bottles and mixing various drinks before I even have chance to answer.

"Just for you," he says slamming a glass on the counter with a large grin. "You seem hot and flustered and look like you need this. The heat of Mexico must be getting to you," he teases.

"Thanks for the compliment," I joke back. "I've just had a weird sensation where I was awake and asleep at the same time. I woke up really hot and bothered."

A gentleman who is sat at the bar joins in with our conversation. He has a very deep American accent. He is in his fifties with a head of grey hair and there is something unusual about him, but I'm not quite sure what it is.

"That is a common phenomenon and it's caused by one part of your brain being awake, while the other parts are asleep."

Alonso chuckles, "You should get an early night tonight, rather than partying all night in Cancun."

The American interrupts. "Sleeping in the sun won't help. Eating too much for breakfast won't help either. Your plate was overflowing this morning." He laughs, but I don't.

I am embarrassed. The American gentleman obviously saw everything that I had piled up on my plate for breakfast. He must think that I am a right pig, but I can't believe he is rude enough to mention it.

I decide to ignore the comment about the food and speak to Alonso. "I didn't go out last night. I was tired after the long journey and travelling, so I was tucked up in bed early."

Alonso smiles, "Well then, your brain needs awakening so do go out and party all night. At least you will have an excuse for sleeping in the sun."

"Ok then, where would you recommend for a single girl to go, where it's safe and friendly." I enquire.

"There are lots of leaflets in reception which may give you some ideas," Alonso informs me.

"There is a Pirate Ship trip which would be suitable," the American suggests. "There's lots of food there for you too." He winks.

He is really annoying me. I roll my eyes in frustration and Alonso intervenes, "If you come to the piano bar this evening, Saskia, I shall introduce you to Scotty who deals with the Tequila Pirate Ship sail. He's a great guy and will tell you about the trip."

If I wasn't embarrassed about having eaten so much this morning, I would give the rude American a piece of my mind. I mean, he hasn't exactly got a body to die for. He has a beer belly as evidence of overindulgence. I really can't believe his nerve.

I notice the American messing with his right eye. He then splashes something into his beer glass and pulls a black patch over his eye.

He winks at Alonso with his left eye. "EYE really enjoyed the pirate trip" he says.

Alonso and the other bartender laugh, but I don't get his joke, if it was one. He obviously has a weird sort of humor.

"I'm going for a swim now. Don't move my drink because EYE will be watching you and EYE will know."

Alonso rolls his eyes as the American disappears from the bar.

"What's all of that about?" I ask, puzzled.

"Look in his glass," Alonso instructs me.

I lean over the bar and nearly fall off my stool.

"It's a glass eye and it's staring back at me. That's disgusting. Is it real?"

"It's his party trick," says the other bartender. "He's been coming here for years on and off, and I've just got used to him doing this. I thought it was a joke at first, but it is a real glass eye. We have to be polite to him and pretend to laugh along with him because he's a guest."

Alonso interrupts, "We even have a special glass that we keep especially for him and his glass eye."

"Thank goodness for that. I wouldn't want to drink out of a glass that had previously had his glass eye in it. I'm feeling sick just thinking about it."

"We give him a green glass, so we don't accidently throw it away by accident. Can you imagine trying to find a glass eye in the rubbish?"

We all laugh together.

"He doesn't by any chance work on this Pirate Ship, does he?

"No. They are nice people. You will be fine with them," Alonso reassures me.

I see the American swimming back towards the bar and decide to make my excuses, and a quick exit. I don't think that I could stand seeing this man put his glass eye back in its socket.

It's been a really weird day. I've probably had enough sun on my head and skin, so I return to my suite. It would be nice to have a rest before I go out this evening.

CHAPTER FIVE

I am ready to go out for the evening. One last look in the mirror, and I pour myself a gin and tonic to boost my confidence. I haven't been out alone for a very long time. In fact, come to think about it, I have never been out to dinner on my own. More G and T or just G would be better. Gulp.

I am feeling a little nervous thinking about the situation. Maybe I should just ring room service and order burger and chips, but then again, I have got myself all dressed up now, and for once I feel quite good about myself. A far cry from where I was a couple of months ago, with panda eyes, feeling depressed and down in the dumps. I used to look at a reflection in the mirror that I did not recognize, whilst popping more anti-depressants than prescribed, to help myself get through the day without crying. After meeting the man with one eye, an attitude and a weird sense of humor, I actually feel quite normal.

I am wearing one of my new gorgeous cocktail dresses and it would be such a shame to waste it on burger and chips. It's rose pink, strapless and is fitted to the waist but has layers of netting that flow out to my knees. It's very *Sex and the City* style, especially with the matching three-inch heel shoes and the matching handbag.

I sit on the edge of the bed deep in thought. I can't hide in this room for the next two weeks, nervous of the outside world without Daniel. I am no longer with him and I need to go out and meet new people, have new experiences and move on. Besides, Daniel hasn't really been part of my life for a long time now with the way that he has been behaving. I've said goodbye to the anti-depressant pills and I will survive without them, and I can survive without Daniel. This is the new me, I just need to find myself. I need to enjoy what Cancun has to offer and have some fun, just like Alonso suggested.

I wander down to the piano bar. The pianist appears to be a drifting character and he is relaxed and lost in his melody and harmonious sounds. The music is peaceful in sound and I immediately feel relaxed in the fluidity of the atmosphere. All of the tables are taken by families and couples, so I decide to sit on a high stool at the bar and stuff my face with the little bowls of chili peanuts and nachos that are there. Alonso acknowledges me with a wave and a smile, even though he is busy serving guests. I've noticed that he works very long hours at the hotel. He seems to always be around.

Typical Mexican beers are listed on the bar menu along with champagne and various wines, but I am slightly confused with the cocktails. There are numerous cocktails but when you actually look at the ingredients of each, they all contain tequila, tequila and more tequila.

Tequila is Mexico's national drink, and an icon synonymous with Mexico. It is promoted very well at my hotel. It can be drunk straight, or with a variety of mixers, and there are some wonderful cocktails on the menu. There are different combinations and they all sound quite appetizing. Perhaps I should try one of each and decide which I like the most.

The options to mention just a few are Tequila Sunrise, The Bull, Black Turncoat, Tequila Sour, The Giraffe, The Margarita, and Cocktail on The Attack.

I think that I shall opt for The Margarita. It contains Tequila, Triple sec and lemon juice served with salt on the glass rim. I know this drink and it is famous in New York.

I've always wanted to go to New York. I have fantasized that when I eventually get to the skyscraper city, that I will go on the 'Sex in the City' tour and drink Margaritas in every bar. Well, I'm not in New York, but I am on holiday and I can still drink Margaritas in my Sex in the City style dress, somewhere sunnier and warmer.

I am distracted as I hear an abundance of noise coming from the other side of the room. All the guests in the piano bar hear the noise and turn to look at who is drowning out the pianist's harmonious sound with loud jokes and laughter. Three men, a similar age to me, walk through the glass doors leading from the beach, unaware of the chaos they are creating.

The pianist suddenly gets louder, playing more like a jazz pianist, competing against the racket, and I can't help but smile. I instantly recognize one of the guy's accents. He must also be from Manchester like me, because he has a Mancunian accent and a dialect specific to that area. He also has the most infectious insane laugh. I could listen to that laugh all day. It's the kind of laugh that makes you feel that you have something to laugh about, even if you don't, if you know what I mean? You laugh at his laugh. It's like the laughing clown at Blackpool, if you have ever been there and seen it. The laughing clown laughs so much that you laugh. It's funny. If you haven't seen or heard the laughing clown, then you should. You leave feeling happy but haven't a clue why. This guy's laugh makes me feel happy. It's strange but so real.

Alonso observes my reactions and leans over the bar looking in the same direction as me, towards the Mancunian.

"He has the same effect on every woman that meets him, or that even sees him."

"Pardon," I ask, looking away.

"The tall guy that you are looking at with the dark shiny hair, the glistening suntan, the toned body and the beautiful straight white teeth that people would pay a fortune for at a dental clinic, the man with the Colgate smile."

I turn to look at the three men again. To be honest I hadn't really noticed what any of them looked like. They had only stood out because of the noise they were making and the laugh.

"Actually, I wasn't checking any of them out. With the distraction that they were causing, I was just trying to work out if they were the three amigos or if they were three desperados."

Alonso laughs. "I don't believe you, but your secret's safe with me." He winks and turns to serve a customer who has appeared at the bar. I observe that the Mancunian could be a heartbreaker. I see the heads of women turn, as he walks in my direction with his group of friends.

The three men appear at the bar talking and laughing amongst themselves, but not as loud as previously, and fortunately the pianist has now returned to his harmony. Alonso serves drinks to them and looks like he is in deep conversation with the kind of good-looking one. To be honest though, I don't find him that attractive, he's not my type. Everyone has a type that they go for and he doesn't really tick any of my boxes in the looks department. I can understand why a lot of women would be attracted to his laugh though.

A bartender approaches. "Have you decided which cocktail you would like to try?"

Before I have chance to answer, I am interrupted by the tall tanned Mancunian.

"I'd recommend a Tequila Sunrise if I was you. It will put a bit of sunshine in your life. You'll need it if you've come from Manchester."

He approaches me and shakes my hand, "I'm Scotty. Alonso's just been telling me that you are here on holiday and need somewhere fun to go."

I glare at Alonso giving him daggers. He must think that I'm a single boring desperado and can't organize my own fun. He's only spoken to me a few times and certainly doesn't know me, so what right does he have to mention me to a total stranger?

Alonso rushes over, "This is Scotty who is organizing the pirate cruise trip. You said that you may want to go on it. We talked about it this afternoon."

I feel really embarrassed and don't know where to look, so I just give Alonso a sympathetic smile. I don't think that Scotty or his friend have noticed because they are busy lighting their Cuban cigars that apparently some bar in town has given to them, or so they say. Scotty takes a puff of his oversized stinky cigar and starts coughing. Alonso rolls his eyes and passes him a glass of water.

"Drink this. You'll spoil your reputation, mate, not being able to smoke a Cuban cigar."

Scotty's two friends laugh at him and Scotty gives them a sarcastic smile. Whilst he is still recovering from choking, Scotty's friends Johnny and Rick introduce themselves to me.

Johnny is very well-spoken and comes across very professional. He is well-dressed and groomed, and I can tell that he takes pride in his appearance and attitude. He leans and kisses me on my cheeks in a Mediterranean fashion. He looks Mediterranean with his black hair, dark brown eyes and olive skin. "It's lovely to meet you, Saskia."

Rick has blue eyes that glisten with mischief and his floppy blond highlighted hair falls into his eyes. He informs me, "I'm shy on the inside but a little crazy on the outside. Once you've got used to me you will get over me." His friends inform me that he is telling the truth and to never be alarmed by his actions or words especially when he has had a few drinks.

In a croaky, husky voice whilst still coughing, Scott says, "So tell me why you've flown over a rainbow and come to sunny Mexico."

I smile. Over the rainbow is obviously a phrase used between Alonso and Scotty.

"I've come here on holiday, just like everybody else has come here."

Scotty looks around the room observing the couples and families, "Yes, but everybody else has come with somebody. You've come on your own. Are you travelling?"

I feel like I am being interrogated by a bunch of strangers, but in a fun way. Scotty, his two friends and Alonso are all leaning on the bar looking at me, waiting for an answer. Nosy sods! I slide off my chair placing my sunglasses on top of my head.

"Ok, I am going to tell you all and I want that to be the end of it. My husband was shagging my friend and I have left him and come to Mexico, but I had already fallen out of love with him before he did this."

Their mouths hang open in astonishment at my revelation to them. I don't think that they can believe that I have just confessed something to them so personal. Neither can I. At one time I wouldn't have done this, I would have lied and made up some amazing fantasy about travelling the world, or something, but my time at rehabilitation has taught me to speak openly, and I feel confident doing this. It's great to just get things off your chest and be honest and open.

"One Mancunian can tell when another Mancunian is lying," I say to Scotty, "I therefore thought that I would just tell the truth."

"The bastard," Rick states, "Get this lady a strong drink. Get me one too."

"So is that why you've come to Mexico," Johnny enquires, "to get over your ex, have some fun and decide what you want in life, going forward?"

"I guess that sounds about right." I answer.

"Well, you've come to the right place," Johnny confirms.

"We'll make sure that you have some fun," Rick nods, "We will look after you."

Scotty informs me, "I came here two years ago to get over my ex. I fell in love with Mexico instead, and decided not to go home. Perhaps you'll do the same."

This suggestion actually sounds quite appealing. "I am going to take things one day at a time."

I sit at the bar for a while drinking one, two, three Margaritas talking to my newly found friends. They are really interesting characters and have welcomed me into their friendly circle.

Scott disappears for a while and looks busy talking to one of the barmaids who is enjoying his flirty behavior, leaving me to talk to Johnny.

"What jobs do you all do?" I enquire. "Are you in entertainment, with organizing this pirate trip?"

"No, Scott and I work for a Tequila distillery. I suppose you could say that Rick works in entertainment because he helps with all of our big projects, like this."

"What is it that you do for the Tequila distillery?" It's my turn to be nosy now.

Scott's the Marketing Manager for Disruption Tequila, a leading Tequila distillery. I work with him helping to promote the brand. The spirit is distilled in just a small number of locations now and we are well-promoted in this region, by ensuring that we are stocked in all of the hotels, bars and clubs."

"That's why all the cocktails here have Tequila in them, is it?" I suddenly realize.

Johnny nods in agreement, "Where the brand chooses to be and how it chooses to be there is really important, so we put great emphasis on visiting the locations where it is sold and ensure that everything is how it should be. It needs to be presented correctly and served in a professional manner in order to not cheapen the brand, but it's also our job to keep the consumer happy."

"This sounds an interesting job."

Johnny nods again, "Getting through to the consumer means creating involving experiences. Tonight, we are holding a party to promote our brand. We hold a lot of events and parties. We are expecting quite a lot of holidaymakers, but we have also invited some of the owners of the bars and hotels that promote our brand. It's a thank you for their custom and loyalty to the brand."

Scott rudely interrupts loudly, "This is new marketing and our motto is 'Disruption, Bring Tequila to life in Cancun.' It will be one big party and we have arranged for some of our best customers and their guests to sail the high seas, enjoy a Caribbean sunset and drink lots of Tequila cocktails with our compliments, on board a Pirate's 90ft Spanish Galleon."

Rick glances at me from across the bar looking anxious. "Saskia, I presume that you will be coming along, but I must warn you that it isn't like Scott's described and I wouldn't want you to be under any false delusion based upon his description. The Pirate cruise is more a night of eye patches, peg legs, squawking parrots and crazy pirate antics and lots of drinking. It's actually Pirate Hell!"

We all start to laugh. I am not sure what to expect, but I'm on holiday and what the hell! I just hope that the guy with the glass eye and pirate patch doesn't turn up.

Before I know what is happening, shot glasses of Tequila are lined along the bar in front of where we are sitting, but my Tequila shot is a different color. "Why is my Tequila pink?"

Alonso smiles, "Scott says that you are a lady, so I had to add grenadine to the Tequila which makes it pink, but you must still drink the Tequila in the classic manner required. He is such a perfectionist on how we serve this brand."

Johnny comments, "He has always been a perfectionist for as long as I have known him. His mother used to complain about how he always insisted that all of the tins faced the right way in the kitchen cupboard, so that you could see the front labels, and that towels in the bathroom were always hung in a straight line. I once went to collect him for a night out and had to wait twenty minutes. I thought that he was getting ready, but his mother advised me that he was pressing his trousers because he wasn't happy with the way she had ironed them. He wanted every single crease removed. I wouldn't have minded but the trousers were linen and were creased again within minutes of him being sat in the car. I feel sorry for whichever woman he ends up with. Living with Scott would be like living with that guy out of the film *Sleeping With The Enemy*."

It becomes clear that Johnny and Scott have known each other since they met at university many years ago. They appear to have lots in common and seem to be close friends, laughing and joking between themselves.

Scott places a pinch of salt on the back of my hand, "This is how you drink Tequila in a classic manner. On the count of three I want you to do the following, Saskia. Lick the salt, raise your glass above the table, slam the glass down on the bar, but not too hard else you'll break it, and then drink the entire contents of the shot glass in one gulp!

"I'm counting - one, two and three." Thump!

I hear a clatter before I have even licked the salt and can't help but burst out laughing. Scott's face is a picture of dismay as he stares at Rick, unimpressed. His look is transfixed in disbelief at the ruckus that Rick is creating. He had licked the salt off his hand, banged down his Tequila on the bar breaking the shot glass, fell off his stool and managed to squirt the lime in his eye, and is now tipping his head back using somebody's glass of water as an eye bath.

"If that's what your Tequila does, I don't think that I want any, thank you," I remark.

"Well, I said that the brand would be disruptive, but I didn't have this in mind," Johnny states.

I feel that we may have a long night ahead of us as we set sail on the galleon. Upon boarding we have all had our photograph taken with the pirates of Mexico. Rick was right, they all had eye patches, peg legs, squawking parrots and were shouting, "Sailing high seas, ship wreck and sinking ships," before we even left the shore, but it is all light-hearted and fun.

Tequila with champagne is being served to the guests by the pirate's pretend hostages. No salt or lime required this time, thank goodness! Johnny is demonstrating how this new drink should be served and drunk and all the guests raise a toast to 'Disruption.' Everyone appears to be having a wonderful time as the party moves into full swing and cocktails are flowing. People are dancing on the decks with the pirates and there are lots of silly games, including spin the Tequila bottle (of course) and a treasure hunt.

We have been at sea for half an hour now and we are approaching a small enchanting island, where apparently there is only a small community. I stand on board looking at the distant view and watching the nearby yachts and boats bobbing in the breeze. I have a sense of familiarity but also a sense of eeriness, strangeness and weirdness. I feel like I have been there before. It is a strange feeling of déjà vu, but I also feel really relaxed, like I should be here.

My thoughts are interrupted by Scott, "Sorry to disturb you, but would you mind if I join you?" He has been busy entertaining for most of the journey and I haven't really seen him, so I don't mind.

"Not at all, I was just deep in thought, Scott."

"I could tell. What's on your mind? I hope that you're not thinking about your ex-husband?"

I shake my head, "I sometimes feel like a lost soul drifting through life uncertain of whom I am, dreaming of what my perfect life would be."

"Saskia, you're a free spirit. You're friendly, honest and humorous." He pauses, "You are simply suffering from the pain and misery that we encounter when we are unable to have the love from the person we need it from the most. Years fly by and relationships come and go. One day you will meet somebody who will set your heart on fire and you will know that it is true love."

Scott looks like his mind is elsewhere as he stares over the water towards the island.

He frowns, "I used to believe that the definition of love was the same as the definition of hurt. I used to think that it was a painful sensation or a mental suffering. I now think that love isn't an ideal thing, but it is a special friendship set on fire, and if there is something, anything special, then you shouldn't let go of it." He turns and looks into my eyes, "I am going to ask you a question that could change your life forever, some of us never hear one and others ask them too much. Is the love you had with your ex-husband worth fighting for?"

This question isn't even worth thinking about. I never loved Daniel.

"The marriage was possibly the biggest mistake of my life. I never loved my ex-husband, I just needed him. I tried to love him, but in essence he was just a passing fancy, somebody to fill time and a gap in my life. I really hope that he meets somebody who he does love and somebody who loves him back, but that someone isn't me. The relationship that we had wasn't worth fighting for. He didn't fill the gap in my life. Perhaps, one day, I will meet the right person for that gap."

We both watch the dolphins that have suddenly appeared swimming near the galleon and we both say together, "Dolphins swimming near a ship will bring good luck."

I laugh because he is superstitious just like me. He places his arm around me and gives me a big friendly hug. His body is lovely and warm, and I sink into him enjoying this mystical moment. The world suddenly feels like my oyster without any worries. I have my life, health and freedom and this is like a ticket to the world, but for now Mexico is the right place for me. It feels like the right place to be at this time in my life. It feels like home.

CHAPTER SIX

As the galleon reaches the shore, some of the passengers choose to walk the plank and jump into the sea, whilst others just clap and cheer them on. "Walk, walk, walk the plank," They chant.

I spot Rick in line to walk the plank. "Looks like your mate's going for it," I joke.

Scott turns to look, "Thank goodness that they've put swimming bands on him. He would probably drown otherwise, considering the amount of Tequila that he's had to drink."

I hadn't even noticed the bright orange armbands. It's really funny seeing him wearing these, but I think it is all part of his act to entertain the guests. He starts to walk the plank and puts on a performance for the spectators by drawing a cross on his chest with his finger then clasping his hands together, looking up to the heavens and starting to pray. A pirate pushes him off and we suddenly hear him shout, "Shiver me, shiver me timbers," as he plunges into the cold water. Scott starts laughing. I can't help but laugh myself, not at Rick, but at Scotty's incredible laugh.

The sky that was bright and blue is now turning darker. It is the beginning of darkness in the evening when the surface of the Earth is neither completely lit nor completely dark.

The galleon has now docked in a half-moon bay and the guests are starting to vacate the decks. They follow a pathway that is lit with candle torches that release an aromatic scent of citronella, which naturally repels any insects. The torches are set alight on silver stems positioned firmly in the sand. The flames lead to an archway in the cove that takes you through a dark passageway lit with glass jar candles that are positioned on the jagged crags of the caves to guide people's steps.

I recognize this perfect bay. It looks busy and enchanting tonight, but my mind recalls it as a tranquil quiet place. It feels memorable to me, as though I have been here before. I think long and hard about it, and I wonder if I have been somewhere that looks very similar. I have never been to Mexico before, so couldn't have visited here before.

"Are you ready to get a passion for partying by the sea?" Johnny asks, as he approaches Scott and me, who are staring down at the beautiful decorative bay from the galleon.

For some reason I feel nervous, and even though it is still warm, I feel a cold chill go up my spine. Both Johnny and Scott detect this and look concerned.

Scott takes off his jacket and puts it around my shoulders. "Holiday parties can be intimidating if you have never done anything like this before; especially on your own. Don't worry; we are here for you."

Johnny interrupts, "Learning to be less shy is scary, and learning to meet new people is work, but it will be fun; believe me."

Scott agrees, "You will soon have more friends than you know what to do with; we promise."

I'm not a nervous person at all, and I really don't know what has just come over me, but I am keen to know where the candlelit path leads that the guests have been following. I am intrigued.

"Let's go and find out what's in store then," I say.

I remove my three-inch high heels. These won't be any good for walking on the beach.

The white sand is warm from being sun-drenched throughout the day and spreads between my toes. It feels comforting.

As we head towards the end of the narrow cave, I hear music start to play. It's not the type of music that I would expect from a beach party. I was expecting dance music, but instead I hear something that sounds similar to live folk type music.

"What's that unusual type of music I can hear?" I ask both Scotty and Johnny.

Johnny replies first, "It is Mariachi music. It's the only thing more Mexican than Tequila. It's a shame to have one without the other, so we thought that we should bring them together tonight."

"Mariachi music will be in your heart and flow through your veins by the end of the night. It encompasses the essence of Mexico," Scotty says.

At the end of the cave we are welcomed by a vast tropical beach lined with palm trees and filled with people partying.

A Mariachi group of six men greet us playing live music. I realize that Mexican folklore music is distinguished from other types of folklore music by the instruments and the attire of the musicians.

They are all dressed like Mexican cowboys wearing large brimmed sombreros and tightly fitted wool pants which open slightly at the ankle. Their waist-length fitted jackets are finished with embroidery, intricately cut leather designs and silver buttons. Each outfit is finished with a wide belt that defines what they wear, and a shirt with a large bow tie. They wear differing footwear. Some are wearing ankle boots and some wear sandals. They all have the traditional Mexican moustaches, and I wonder if these are real or have been stuck on. I can't help but smirk to myself thinking about this.

The group has an integration of stringed instruments. The six musicians have a violin, a harp, a classical guitar, a vihuela which is a high-pitched five-string guitar, and a guitarrón which is a large acoustic bass. Somebody shakes a maraca in my face, suddenly grasping my attention.

The sound is harmonious and for some reason my imagination transports me through Mexican towns and villages. I've never visited these places, yet my mind seems to know what these places would look like. I feel that time has stopped, whilst I cease moving and listen to the songs speaking about love, life, betrayal and death, but they are vibrant, colorful and cheerful sounds. They sing in Mexican but somehow, I understand what they are singing about.

I can see sadness, happiness, celebration and mourning expressed on the musicians' faces and in their eyes, as they sing each song. I feel like I know these people and look forward to spending the evening in the company of their beautiful music. The musicians perform with a passion and energy that doesn't fade. I can feel the music running through my veins just like Scott warned.

As we walk on, I see numerous other mariachi bands playing along the wide strip of beach where this tropical beach party is being held. They all play the same music in symphony together. There appears to be a lot of guests attending; hundreds. Some have arrived by boats, others by coach. They all wear colorful costumes and beachwear. Some are wearing grass skirts, necklaces and some hula kits.

There is a large wooden dance floor that has been erected on the sands. It has a roof made out of a net of sparkling multi-colored small lights, similar to what you put on a Christmas tree. People are already in the spirit of partying by the sea and are dancing their hearts out under the stars. I can hear the sound of their feet driving and pounding into the wood as they dance to the mariachi music. The waves lapping against the shore add to the ambience.

There are numerous Caribbean palapa huts with palm tree roofs, where chefs are cooking on open flame fires made with mesquite wood, ringed with stone. The smell of fresh fish, steak, lamb, chilies and natural sea salt fill the air. It smells beautiful and I am starting to feel hungry.

Scott kindly points out to me, "The first ingredient for the food is the mesquite wood which the chefs are using. It adds the most delicious flavor to the food. It also goes very well with Tequila." I can't wait to try it.

We spot Rick sat around a crackling bonfire with six other people who were on the galleon. They are all drinking Tequila cocktails out of half coconut shells. They appear to be playing a game and are all laughing and making lots of noise. I am suddenly becoming aware that wherever there is Rick, there is noise and commotion of some kind, but in a nice way.

"My friends are here at last to join us," he shouts, pointing towards us. "We are just playing a game of…of…." he stammers. "I can't remember but you have to ask a question, and everyone has to answer it honestly, and we get to know about each other."

"We are playing a game called 'Blowing your own trumpet'," a girl with long blonde hair sat around the fire informs us, "Come join us; it's fun."

Rick points over at a man sat around the fire with long dreadlocks, "This is Anthon and he showed us how to play. He has been backpacking around the world and he met a guru who showed him how to play."

We shake Anthon's hand and introduce ourselves, "Was it a guru in Hinduism that you met whilst backpacking?" I ask.

Anthon speaks in a posh voice, "The guru that I met was one who was regarded as having knowledge, wisdom and authority to guide others. I learnt from a personal confidence guru. He helped people acknowledge and appreciate their own positive qualities."

This sounds quite interesting, so we sit down on the picnic blankets that have been positioned around the fires to join in. Scott, Johnny and Rick are all off duty now. Others are now looking after the guests, so they can relax and enjoy the party themselves.

"We are playing a game called 'Blowing your own trumpet'. Your friend Rick is very good at it," Anthon informs us. "He is very funny."

"I can imagine," Johnny remarks sarcastically, then throws a cheeky glance towards Scott who just smiles.

Anthon nods, "I have just asked everyone to describe their friends and Rick said that his friends are random, funny and optimistic so how would you describe Rick? It would be interesting to hear your description and opinion."

Scott smiles, "How about drunk?"

Everyone laughs.

Anthon raises his eyebrows. "That's very good, Scott. I have learnt that to describe accurately usually takes a lot of effort. We need to be honest with ourselves. You did well then."

Scott, Johnny and I all burst out laughing. This must be some kind of wind up. It was easy for Scott to describe that Rick is drunk, because he simply is. Rick gives us a glare of disapproval.

Anthon carries on, "The guru always asked people how they would describe themselves and the most common response that he got was, 'I don't know'. Apparently describing yourself positively is one aspect in the journey of learning how to find your true self. Let's play the game and see what conclusion you come to."

We now join in with the game called 'Blowing your own trumpet'. We all have to take it in turn to ask each other questions, to try to find out about each other. We ask about celebrity crushes, dream vacations, foods we like, etc. It is quite fun, and I have been asked questions that I have never really ever thought about. There are some funny answers and there's lots of laughing between us. I am actually finding this quite fun but then one question springs up. It is the last question of the game and I can't ignore it. It is difficult to answer.

Anthon asks the question, "I would like you to now describe yourself. Do not describe any physical features and only describe your inner self."

There are lots of different descriptions from the others, like funny, loving, considerate, impish, good listener, but this isn't what Anthon meant, so he asks everyone to stop.

He corrects everybody, "The guru told me that the most beautiful trait anybody can have is to know exactly who they are and what they are about. He said that you need to feel comfortable in your own skin. Let's try something else that he showed me."

I can't help but worry if he knows what he is doing, but we carry on.

"I want you to all stare into the fire and pretend that it is your heart aglow. I then want you to close your eyes and think about yourself for a minute, think deeply about your inner self and then you should all be able to answer the question."

It's hard to think with the distraction of the mariachi music and the crowds partying in the background but I do try hard. As I stare into the crackling hot fire, Julia from the rehabilitation unit comes to mind. I remember her once saying to me, "Everything happens for a reason. Sometimes people come into our life and we know that they will affect us in some profound way, almost to serve a purpose. The people that we meet on the path of life help us to create who we are and who we become." I was a little anxious about coming to Mexico on my own, but I have met some good friends and I am enjoying myself. Perhaps Anthon will now help me to find out who I am, so I don't feel like a lost soul any longer.

I close my eyes and think hard. Our minds are compacted with mysterious thoughts and feelings that overwhelm our senses, and I have often wondered where these come from. Tonight, I am thinking deeper than I have ever thought, and I realize that there is information missing that I need to know. I still need lots of answers to questions about my life.

Anthon claps his hands and we all open our eyes. In turn he asks us, "Describe oneself?"

I am quite impressed with everyone's answers. One person says, "Genuine and caring." Someone else says, "Optimistic and at the same time analytical."

Scott describes himself, "I'm logical and focused."

I can't help but think that he is quite a deep character and I have still a lot to learn about him.

Johnny describes himself now, "I am direct and vibrant."

This doesn't surprise me at all.

Rick claims with a straight face, "I am rebellious and upbeat."

Everyone laughs. I think everyone knows that this is an understatement.

I then find that it's my turn to confess and you may find this really strange, but I am scared about my answer, probably because I don't feel that I know myself. There is a long silence, and I feel a moment of disconcertment before I speak, "I am an open-minded person and curious."

This is the most honest answer that I can genuinely give. I am curious to find out who I am, and I will stay open-minded until I find out. This is the best I can answer, because I honestly don't know.

Anthon speaks, "The guru once described himself as being a good listener and communicative. He told me that I should look deep into my soul to find out who I really was. He said that you should follow your natural impulses and instincts rather than your reasoned thoughts because they are the essence of your spirit and will help to direct you."

"Have you kept in touch with the guru?" the girl with the long blond hair asks.

"I hope to visit him again one day, depending upon where destiny takes me. I should be returning home to the United States, but I have decided to carry on travelling for a little while. I have met the most wonderful people whilst backpacking around the world and I feel that I don't belong in one place. I am going to stay in Mexico for a little longer. For some reason I like it here."

I see him wink at the beautiful looking girl, and she timidly smiles at him with a twinkle in her eyes. I can't help but wonder if she is the reason why he plans to now stay in Mexico for a while. They are obviously attracted to each other.

For some reason I feel for him, but in a way, I also understand him. He turns away from her and stares blankly into the crackling fire. I can see that Anthon is like me; he is a lost soul. He is looking for a piece of jigsaw missing from his life. Perhaps he hopes that she is it.

Scott shakes his head in disbelief at Rick who is lying on his back staring up at the stars. "You are going to have a terrible hangover tomorrow, mate. You need to stop drinking and eat some food." He hands him a glass of a drink called sangrita. It is tomato juice flavored with chili and other seasonings. It is a customary partner to a shot of Tequila, but also it should help to sober you up. Going by the smell of it I would prefer a hangover the following morning than to drink that.

We join the queue at one of the palapa huts where the chefs are busy cooking on their open flame fires, offering tender delights from the ocean below. They are looking after every request from the Disruption Tequila guests and are serving Tequila Shrimp, blackened fish, juicy filet mignon and red snapper squirted and cooked with lime juice and garlic. Both Scott and I opt for the juicy filet mignon, smoked with mesquite wood, served with beans, spicy rice and tortillas. It is served on banana leaves and the presentation is perfect. The taste is even better. It melts in your mouth.

Johnny has visited an alternative chef and has returned with a large steak that has been cut into slices and marinated in Tequila and secret spices. It is again served with tortillas and apparently some fiery red sauces that should have warning labels on because they are so hot, or, according to Scott they should. "Try some, Saskia, it will blow your head off. You'll end up wanting to drink the sea," he claims. I laugh but I don't think that I shall be trying any.

There is a marquee that is serving drinks, all Disruption Tequila based I must add. Johnny kindly goes to the bar and returns to the fire where we are all sat, "Disruption champagne," he tells us upon his return, as he holds up a bottle.

"Let me guess? Champagne with a dash of Tequila?" I query.

"Can you keep a secret?" Johnny asks.

"Yes, of course," I reply.

"I've managed to get us a full unopened bottle of champagne so no Disruption. Don't tell any of the guests though, because they have to have it with Disruption." He laughs, as he pops the cork.

I must admit Disruption Tequila does taste good, but it will make a nice change to drink something without it added, especially champagne.

Scott stands, "Disruption Tequila is about new possibilities and visionary ideas that bring mystery and intrigue. Let us raise a toast to our friendship and a prosperous life with Disruption."

"Here, here," we all shout as we all clink our glasses together.

I believe that dreams are like champagne. The smaller the bubbles the better the champagne but my dreams have previously been a cava wish with no sparkle. Tonight, it seems different though…. I feel like a magic wand has been waved and my dreams will come true. I can taste the prosperity in the fine bubbles as they sparkle in my mouth, before the fizz goes to my head.

Mariachi music is pounding through my blood. I feel like I have escaped and changed, I am feeling totally relaxed and ready for whatever adventure lies ahead. Whilst I look out at the ocean daydreaming, Rick suddenly staggers to his feet and slurs, "Where have those horses come from?"

Lots of people are pointing in the same direction as where Rick is looking, with the same confused look.

I stand and see two spotted horses galloping across the sands. They are white with grey spots. "Spotted horses possess magical abilities, so make a wish," I instruct everyone.

I close my eyes tightly, "I wish, I wish." I hope it comes true.

When I eventually open my eyes, the horses are gone. Scott, Johnny and Rick are all looking at me.

"That was a long wish, Saskia. Did you have a wish list as long as your arm? What did you wish for that took so long?" Rick asks.

I didn't realize that I had been so long, but I don't intend telling anybody my wish.

I answer Rick, "You are not supposed to tell people your wishes, because otherwise they won't come true."

Rick sighs, "Well, to be honest, I think that all of this superstition stuff is a load of nonsense."

Scott interrupts, "I'm superstitious to a certain degree. I mean, I'd never walk under a ladder."

"I wouldn't walk under a ladder either," Rick confirms in a strong tone. "There might be a window cleaner at the top who drops his bucket and you end up drenched wet through, wearing a bucket on your head."

We all laugh. It's not that funny, but I think that all the alcohol is going to our heads.

I know a lot about superstitions and I decide to set the record straight, "Actually, a ladder on a slight slant forms a triangle with the wall and ground and the triangle represents the Holy Trinity. If you walk through this, it puts you in league with the devil."

"How come you know so much?" Rick quizzes me.

"A lot of what I know has been passed down from my grandparents," I reply. "They were very superstitious."

"I believe a lot of what is said," Scott says. "My aunty once said that she had seven years bad luck because she broke a mirror."

"I've never really ever thought about it," Johnny remarks. "I don't really think that you should believe in things that you don't understand."

"Well, I'd rather have good luck than bad luck," Scott replies.

"I once wanted a snake as a pet," Rick comments. "I nagged my Mum for it, but she wouldn't get one. My grandma came to visit, and she was superstitious. She told me that if I plaited a horse's tail and then put it in water, after a while it would turn into a snake. I really believed her, so I ran to the local stables and did just what she said. Turns out that she just wanted some peace and quiet and the only thing I got was a limp from where the bloody horse kicked me." We all start to laugh, apart from Rick.

He carries on, "She visited another time and took me to the shop to choose some sweets. She said that I could have a cheap mix bag, but I really wanted some strawberry Hubba Bubba, so I could blow big bubbles, just like the older kids used to. She wouldn't let me have any and I ended up crying. She told me that if I put a bit of hoof in the microwave, that it would turn to chewing gum that would last forever. I went to the local farm and got butted by a bull. I didn't listen to her again after that."

We are all laughing at Rick's story. In fact, I have tears rolling down my face.

"No wonder you don't believe in superstitions, Rick," Johnny comments.

"No, I just think that superstitions are an illusion of control in an uncertain world. Some of the stupid things I have heard like…like inhaling horse breath will cure whooping cough, and if you eat a hair from the forelock of a horse, it's a cure for worms."

"Did your grandma tell you to do that too?" Johnny asks seriously.

I'm laughing so much that I have had to wipe away tears and my right eye starts to tickle and itch to the point that even rubbing it doesn't stop it.

"Have you got sand in your eye, Saskia?" Johnny asks.

"No. It is just tickling and itchy."

"My goodness," Scott says, before announcing another superstition, "If your right eye tickles it is supposed to be lucky, and if your right eye itches you are supposed to see your love."

Rick stands, "I'm going to get us some more drinks. You lot are talking a load of nonsense, in fact, forget champagne, you need some sangrita."

He walks off to the drink marquee. He must be sobering up, as we get drunk.

Somebody sat around the fire starts to sing aloud to the Mariachi music and we all join in.

"This isn't music to be sung, it is music to be danced," Scott declares.

Johnny joins in, "You are right. Music and dance are a big part of cultural identity in Mexico. Let's get up and dance."

I didn't really think that men like dancing, so I am surprised when they both stand and grab hold of my hands, pulling me up from the sand, obviously keen to hit the dance floor.

I pull myself away. "No way am I dancing and embarrassing myself. I'll just sit here and observe. I see dancing more as a spectator sport."

"Sorry, Saskia, but you don't go to a Disruption party and not dance," Scott shouts above the music.

"There will be a disruption if I get on that dance floor. Not only have I been drinking too much Tequila and champagne, but I also have two left feet. I have no coordination at the best of times. I'll stay and watch and perhaps join you when I have sobered up a little, after my sangrita."

Rick returns with the drinks at the right time. I slowly sip the sangrita and pretend to be enjoying it. If nothing else, it's a delay tactic. It tastes bloody horrible and I think that I would rather have hair of the dog than face this really hot, spicy, tomato-flavored drink. I think the only reason that it sobers you up is because you have to drink a gallon of water afterwards to stop your mouth feeling like it's on fire.

I watch as Johnny and Scott let loose on the dance floor and I must admit that I am quite impressed with their moves.

"They are dancing the huapango dance," Rick informs me as their feet move to the music.

They have obviously made an impression on the dance floor as they don't seem short of women to dance with. I watch Scott and Johnny both hold their upper body erect and still. Their feet perform rapid, intricate, shuffling maneuvers at the same time.

"It looks complicated. Can you dance, Rick?" I ask.

"Not as good as Scott. He's had dancing lessons. Wait to see what he does next."

I watch in amazement as he puts a glass of water on his head at the same time as dancing. I expect it to fall but it doesn't because of his incredible upper-body muscular control.

The people dancing clap and cheer and he laps up the attention. He is such a show off.

"He's not as good as some people at dancing," Rick informs me. "Mexico has its own official dance called Jarabe Tapatio. None of us can dance to that."

"Why's that then? Is it hard to learn?" I enquire.

"Not if you've learnt it from an early age. It is taught as part of the curriculum in Mexican public schools. Traditionally, the dance tells of love and courtship between two people. Young members of opposite sexes were once kept apart in society, but the Mariachi participated in the rite of courtship. They sang and played the Jarabe Tapatio in secret locations and brought young lovers together."

Rick isn't the best at telling a story, but it still sounds really romantic.

The cha-cha-cha starts to play and I know that this is music that I can dance to. A friend once taught me how to cha-cha-cha when the Mexican Salsa disco version first started hitting some night clubs when I was eighteen. I also used to watch my grandma dance to the cha-cha-cha in a traditional style. I am sure that the Mariachi music moves will be very similar, perhaps a combination of both. If I am going to dance, then this is the music for me to try to dance to. I suddenly get the urge to dance. I have to dance.

"Let's dance, Rick", I scream excited, getting to my feet and pulling him up as the music fills the air. "I can't usually dance but I am willing to give this a go."

We join Scott and Johnny and we are all swinging our hips and dancing to the music whilst repeating the words, "One, two, cha-cha-cha." We laugh to each other, "Three, four, cha-cha-cha." More and more people appear on the dance floor to samba, mambo and rumba under the starlit sky and the party is in full swing. It appears that everybody likes to cha-cha-cha in their own unique way. Some dance using small gliding steps and some use more intricate footwork, but the sounds made by the bare feet and shoes on the dance floor all make the sound cha-cha-cha.

Different music comes on and I carry on dancing. I feel that my body is being swept away by the powerful rhythms and my feet won't stop moving, this feels natural to me, but I don't know why. Here, I don't need to worry about anything because the music and movement wrap away all of life's stresses, but then I see something that stops the movement of my body.

I recognize the man stood casually at the side of the dance floor. Do I recognize him, or does he just look familiar? This is causing confusion in my mind. He stands out amongst the crowds, wearing a linen suit with a casual dressy open-necked shirt. It suits him, and I feel some attraction towards him. Across the crowded dance floor, he looks in my direction and smiles. I quickly look away.

I realize that it's the eyes…I recognize the eyes, the beautiful ocean blue eyes. I know those enchanting eyes, could never forget them.

I suddenly feel dizzy remembering where I know him from. He is the man who is in my repeated nightmare. In my dream, I am staring into his eyes as we drive down the steep cliff road. That's it. He is the man who is driving the car in my dream. He is definitely the man in my dreams and nightmares.

"Oh my god," I stop in my steps…What is he doing here? I can't believe this is happening. He's a real person, not just a figment of my imagination. This is a serendipitous moment. I am being presented with the truth of my imagination.

I move to the furthest part of the dance floor where I can observe him from a distance. There have been many memorable people in my life ranging from obvious choices to the obscure. This man, though, is the most memorable person to ever cross my path. Somehow, I know that this man's impact upon me is directly related to who I am, to my emotions and to what I am doing. "What am I doing though?" I have to ask myself.

I am standing at the edge of a dance floor staring at a man who I don't know, but for some reason I think that I do know.

I think hard and talk to myself, "I have certainly never met him, I certainly don't know him." My mind is confused and all jumbled and I feel like I am claiming a part of myself that has been left behind at some point. This is complete madness. Perhaps it was too early to stop taking my tablets. I have gone from being depressed to crazy.

I have heard that some people report having experienced some form of déjà vu, having experienced coincidences and familiarities coming out of nowhere, the feeling of having had been somewhere or done something before, or the feeling of knowing a complete stranger. Some people believe that every attribute, belief and feeling of déjà vu in life comes from somewhere in our mind. The compelling sense of familiarity and strangeness feels as though an event has happened at some point in the past.

It's hard to explain the feeling but you just know when it's happening and it's happening to me right now.

I stamp my foot on the floor. "Oh golly gosh! What shall I do?"

My grandma believed that we have all been here before in a past life. Could I know him from a past life? If I do know him from a past life, does he recognize me? Do I recognize him because he looks the same as in a previous life? Or, is this just a feeling of familiarity that it is the same person? I have an overwhelming sense of familiarity with something that should not be familiar at all. My head is spinning, and I blame the Tequila and the champagne. I must think rationally.

I am burning up and feel like I am going to faint. I run away from the dance floor, along the sand, through the crowded beach to the seashore, away from most of the people and the noise. I bend down and splash the cold waves on my face, and I take a moment to recollect my thoughts and gain clarity of this situation.

Now and then, we all meet people who could end up as friends or lovers. Some people just pass us by and it feels that our soul recognizes them. We meet people where there is an instant connection, like you know that person even though you have never met them before. This is just a coincidence. The man on the dance floor just looks like the man in my dreams. It is a coincidence, that's all.

I return to the edge of the dance floor looking for Scott, Johnny and Rick. I feel a close familiar presence and turn to find the tall dark stranger standing behind me. He smiles and something in his smile brightens up my heart. I feel my heart unexpectedly start to race and pound, and there's a hiccup in my heart's rhythm like it has just skipped a beat. I have never experienced anything like this before. It is one of those impossible to explain how I feel moments. His eyes reflect me and all I can see is him, no one else. I feel that there is just the two of us present. For a moment, I stop breathing and can't help but blush. My heart goes even faster and my hands start to tremble. He is my fantasy, the one that I dream about, definitely, no doubt about it. I am being presented with the truth of my imagination.

"Hello, am I right in presuming that you are English?" he asks with a foreign accent.

"Yes," I answer, wondering how he knows. I can't find the courage or words to say anything else. He takes my breath away.

"I heard you speaking with your friend in the marquee earlier. That's how I know," he says.

He had obviously noticed me earlier in the evening, before I saw him. I watch his lips as he talks. I would love to kiss him.

"I speak many languages a little, but fortunately I can speak English fluently. Would you like to dance with me?" he asks, pointing to the dance floor. "I have just requested a song and the Mariachi have agreed to play it next. It's the hat song and it has a really romantic story behind it."

This is the second time this evening that I have heard about a song having a romantic meaning.

"Traditionally, the dance tells the story of love and courtship," he tells me.

This sounds familiar. "Is this the official dance of Mexico? My friend Rick told me about a dance called Jarabe Tapatio that is taught as part of the curriculum in Mexican Public Schools. He told me that it was a really hard dance to learn."

He nods. "This is the same dance. It is a difficult dance but if you dance with the right partner it is easy, I promise. Come and dance with me, please. Whether you are the belle of the ball or have two left feet, I believe dancing the Jarabe Tapatio is a great way to get close, have fun and check chemistry."

I haven't agreed but he holds my hand to lead me to the dance floor and as our fingers entwine I feel thousands of butterflies fluttering in my stomach. It is a fluttering sensation that I have previously heard about, but never experienced until now, and I don't just like it, I love it.

The dance floor starts to clear, leaving me with my tall dark stranger and a few other couples who all appear to be Mexican. They all look like professional dancers judging by their clothes and shoes. People surround the dance floor and start to clap. I spot Scott and Johnny in the crowds. Scott has a silly smirk on his face as he stands folding his arms and raising his eyebrows at me. Johnny is glaring at me with a look of horror, probably wondering what the hell I am doing. I wonder what the holy hell I am doing, too.

I start to wonder how I have managed to be so stupid to have got myself into this situation. I mean, Scott can dance but Rick told me that he wouldn't even attempt to dance to this. I look for a gap in the crowds contemplating running off and pretending that I was never in this situation, but there are no gaps in the crowds. There aren't even any legs open wide enough that I can crawl between them. The nice butterflies have disappeared now, and my stomach has been replaced with knots. Horrible, tight, cramping knots.

I feel his hand stroke my cheek. "It is fine, baby. Don't be worried. Please just follow my steps and everything shall be ok. I have seen you dancing earlier, and you are good."

Did he just call me baby?

"How can I follow your steps when I don't even know the music?" I ask, worried.

He gives me a reassuring smile as the music starts to play. "Zapateado," he says, "footwork."

I look at the other dancers. The ladies are all facing their partners with their feet together and arms down by their sides. I copy their actions. We all kick our heels out three times, alternating our feet each time then clap twice. We repeat this eight-times and then the chorus comes and starts to play louder. I link elbows with my partner and skip around in a circle staring into his eyes all of the time. We circle once and then circle in the opposite direction. The compelling sense of familiarity and strangeness make this feel as though it has happened at some point in the past. I am conscious of my memory conforming, knowing how to dance. I know exactly what is going on around me as it happens.

The music gets faster and faster and we repeat these steps, starting with a different foot each time. I feel like a lovesick teenager drawing hearts and roses in the sky as I dance. We are both laughing as we spin around focusing on each other, but we then spin in opposite directions ending up on opposite sides of the dance floor. The other couples appear to have left the dance floor, leaving just the two of us. The crowds are all cheering.

He skids on his knees towards the middle of the floor and I stand with my feet a width apart and march in place to the beat of the music towards him, grasping my skirt in either hand at knee height. I feel like a bird flying through the sky in his direction, as I am caught safely in his arms. We stare into each other's eyes and but for the crowds cheering and coming towards us, I am sure that he would kiss me.

"We string together like daisy-chains and charm bracelets," I tell him.

He looks at me like I have said something that I shouldn't.

"Have I said something wrong?" I ask.

"I haven't heard that saying before, but for some reason it sounds familiar. It's just a strange feeling, that's all." He nervously smiles at me.

A Mariachi musician approaches us, introducing himself and congratulating us before placing us on a wooden stage in front of the crowd.

"I would like to crown this couple, Miguel and Saskia, the Mariachi couple of the year."

I wonder how he knows our names. Perhaps Scott's informed him. I can't help but be happy as the crowds throw their arms around us both, and place flowers around our necks and tropical flowers on our heads. To congratulate us, the crowd lift us up in the air and pass us over them like a 'Mexican wave'. I go in one direction and Miguel is passed in the other.

That's the last that I see of my tall dark stranger. I am left with just a name, Miguel. I look for him amongst the crowds, but I can't find him. There's no denying that he set my temperature rising. He made me feel alive again, but now he has gone, and I can't help but wonder where and why.

It's getting later and some of the crowds have now disappeared but there are still a few people wanting to party until the sun rises. I am happy to stay; I am tired, but I don't want to go back to the hotel where I will feel lonely. I'd rather be surrounded with people. At least I don't feel alone here. The music is still playing, quieter now, and some couples cuddle up in front of the fires that are still alight across the beach. The air has a chill to it, but it disappears as dusk turns to dawn and the sky is painted red, as if on fire.

I walk along the beach alone, whilst the sea caresses my feet and I wish that Miguel was here with me. I didn't know him for long. I didn't know him at all. I only know that he can dance, and he showed me how to dance with him. I suppose that it was better to have met him, than to have never met him at all. At least I am left with the memory of him, even though I feel sad that he has gone.

I see a horseshoe on the beach and remember the spotted horses that I saw earlier in the evening. As I hold the shoe in my hand, I hear a voice.

It's Scott. "Like a rabbit foot, a horseshoe is well known as a good luck charm."

I smile, "I really need some luck."

"I don't think that you need any luck, after seeing the way you danced tonight with that great looking guy. Where did you learn to dance like that and where is he?" He looks around for Miguel, "The man you were dancing with?"

I feel a pang of emptiness, "I don't know; he's gone. He came into my life, made a memorable impression and now he's gone. I don't know why he went or where he went. I don't know why I am so bothered by this." I shrug my shoulders. "I think all of the alcohol that I have drunk has gone to my head and it is making me emotional. It may sound stupid, but I just felt a connection with him, like I have never felt before with anybody. I feel like I know him or should know him."

"I know what you mean. I've been there myself in the past, but that's what it is, just the past, we all have to learn to move on. As the saying goes 'It is better to have loved and lost, than to have never loved at all." He smiles sympathetically.

Did I love him? Is there such a thing as love at first sight? I feel myself hiccup and then I carry on hiccupping.

Scott laughs and passes me some of his drink. It happens to be sangrita and Scott smiles as I screw up my face. The chilies in it are red hot.

He jokes, "I believe that horseshoes also possess healing powers to cure a case of hiccups, but you must remember to keep the ends of the horseshoe facing up."

I smile because my horseshoe is upside down. How stupid of me. I quickly face it the right way up. "The luck will pour out if it's the wrong way," I observe.

Scott nods agreeing, "Don't need any more bad luck."

I smile, "What would I do without you, Scott? I'm happy that I have met you."

He holds me in his arms and gives me a friendly hug. "Keep hold of that horseshoe. Hopefully it will bring us both some good luck."

We both hear a load of commotion in the background.

People are singing, "What shall we do with the drunken sailor, hammered in the morning," and carrying Rick towards the galleon.

"It's time to leave now. The pirate ship is waiting for us," Scott confirms.

CHAPTER SEVEN

Through life we have lots of opportunities to grow as a person and gain greater awareness and understanding of ourselves, the people we know and the world around us.

I have learnt that our relationships, friends and family are things to be thankful for each and every day. Although my grandparents are now only carried forward in mind and heart, I am lucky to have Catherine and Joshua in my life, and I would be lost without them. They are my family and friends rolled into one. Having someone who can give me support and allow me to experience love and affection is a blessing. Our relationship will never be taken for granted.

Following last night, I need to confide in someone, and that someone is Catherine. She sounds tired when she answers the phone. I am conscious of the time difference, so I have been careful not to phone when she would be asleep.

The phone only rings twice and Catherine answers. She sounds weary.

I speak quietly, "Hi honey, were you asleep? I didn't mean to wake you up."

"No, I just haven't had much sleep, that's all."

"Have you got a man there with you?" I tease.

"Trust you to think that," she giggles. "The only man in my life is Josh, and you know that. I don't have time for any other male. He hasn't been very well so hasn't been sleeping like he should. It's totally knocked our sleeping pattern."

"What's wrong with him?" I fret.

"Calm down woman, it's not serious and it's nothing for you to be worried about. He has just had an upset stomach. I have taken him to the doctor, who has prescribed him some medicine. It seems to be doing the trick. Anyway, how's your holiday going? Have you met any tall dark strangers yet?"

"Catherine, my head is spinning. I went out last night and I have met someone called Miguel."

"Wow, I was only joking when I asked. I didn't expect you to move so fast," she laughs, "What's he like?"

"He's just like you described. He's tall, dark and handsome." I feel butterflies in my stomach just thinking about him.

"I am really jealous," she jokes. "Are you seeing him tonight?"

"No, I'm going out with some guys that I have met who are from Manchester."

"You're a fast mover," she teases.

"No, it's not like that. I was out with the guys from Manchester, when I met Miguel. He is just perfect. I think it could be love at first sight."

"Now I am worried. Have you had too much sun on your head? You should wear a sun cap."

I laugh, "Well, I drunk a lot of Tequila, but do you think that there is such a thing as true love at first sight?"

"I wouldn't like to comment, I suppose only you will know that depending on how you feel. When are you seeing this Miguel guy again?"

"Well, that's the big problem. I was only in his company for about an hour. He danced with me and we won a Mariachi dancing competition, but then he was gone."

"Hang on… let me get this straight; you won a dancing competition?" I hear her laughing. "Saskia, you can't dance. You have no coordination at all. We went to step aerobics and you fell off the step and knocked three ladies over. On the rare occasion that we persuade Daniel to babysit and we go out clubbing, you won't dance because you can't, and if you did you would probably stand on people's toes."

"Catherine, things are really different here. I have the strangest déjà-vu, like I have been here before, and I know that I have no coordination, but honestly, I could dance last night."

"You are such a liar, Saskia, but ok, I will believe you, but many wouldn't. Anyway, more importantly, did you kiss him?"

"Well, I wanted to, but we didn't. To be honest, I would have done anything with him. I honestly think that he is the man in my dreams."

"The man of your dreams, you mean?" she corrects me.

"No, the man IN my dreams."

"Hang on Sas. Is everything ok?"

From her serious tone, perhaps she thinks I am having another cuckoo moment.

She sighs, "You have just made the strangest comment."

"Catherine, I'm ok, I promise. Do you remember me telling you about my dream, where I am in a car with a man who has the most beautiful ocean blue eyes?"

"Yes, of course I remember. You have told me about it loads of times."

"Well, Miguel has the same eyes. He looks like the man in my dreams."

"Sas, because he looks like the man in your dreams, it doesn't mean that it is him. Anyway, you said he drives off a cliff with you, so I'd keep out of his way if you do think it's him."

I can detect concern and sarcasm in her voice, so I just decide to agree with her. I don't want her thinking that I am going cuckoo, even though I thought so myself last night,

"Yes, you're probably right. I have probably just had too much sun on my head, just like you said."

"You're really lucky, Sas, having your own free will."

"What do you mean?"

"Well, it's an amazing thing to have free will. You can make choices to better your life without having to consider anybody else. You have control over your own destiny. I mean, you just went to Mexico with no planning."

"You have the same options, Catherine. What is all of this about?"

"Well, I am always rushing everywhere. I fill every waking moment with things to do. I always have places to be and people to see. When I'm not at work or attending a child group with Josh, there is always something else to do. I never seem to get any time to myself. Someone from work recently said that time to think is a wonderful thing, and it suddenly dawned on me that I am always up against time, and never get chance to enjoy it. I am so emotionally drained that I don't even take time out to think."

"You're tired, honey, that's all. Why don't you take Josh to Daniel's?

They both love to spend time together, and you could have a rest. Have some time to yourself."

"Yes, you're right. I think that I just need time alone to reflect on my life. Time to think is a wonderful thing that I really enjoy, when I get the chance, and I used to get the opportunity to do it, but don't now. I used to be able to always come up with ideas and answers to questions that I couldn't previously answer. Thought and time out will perhaps provide me with a new beginning and a fresh perspective."

"Why do you need a new beginning and a fresh perspective? What's wrong? I'm worried about you."

"Well, I love Joshua to bits, don't get me wrong, but I sometimes wonder what things would have been like but for having him. I really loved my ex and I think about him a lot. For some strange reason he has been on my mind continuously for the last week. If I hadn't been stupid that one night of my life and had a one-night stand with Daniel and got pregnant, then we would still possibly be together now. Life could have been very different. I have so many regrets."

I hear her sniffling starting to cry. She is obviously feeling very down.

I patiently wait for her to stop. "Well, for my own selfish reasons, I am happy that you did meet Daniel and that you did get pregnant. If it hadn't happened, I wouldn't have you or Joshua in my life now, and that would be devastating."

Catherine's voice softens then she says emotionally, "Saskia, you're my rock and I am so happy that you are in my life, thank you."

I smile, "We all have a fear of the unknown, and we all have a fear of change, but change is inevitable in all circumstances. I'm coming to learn that after everything that I have been through. We just need to learn to adapt and I learnt this at rehabilitation. I will always be here for both of you, whatever the future may bring."

It's nice to know that I am someone's rock. I will always be here for her through thick and thin.

"I think that you just need some sleep," I advise her.

"Perhaps I will look at things differently when I have had a few winks. I just feel really low at the moment. Perhaps I just need time to develop a new philosophy about who I am, what I am capable of and my ability to shape my destiny. If I was supposed to be with my ex, I would be with him, wouldn't I? He wouldn't have left me like he did."

I think about it. "Perhaps he is somewhere thinking of you and regretting leaving you. If you are supposed to be together, I am sure that destiny will make it happen."

"Thanks, Sas, love you."

"Love you too. I will call you soon."

I hated the thought of my best friend being at a low ebb. I just wanted to give her the biggest cuddle in the world.

I wander down to the pool. Alonso is at the pool bar and greets me with a large grin. "Morning, Saskia. It's nice to see that you have a spring in your step this morning."

I don't feel like I have any spring in my step this morning. I feel tired and hungover. I think that it's time for hair of the dog again. It might perk me up.

"Morning, Alonso. Please may I have a bottle of lager?"

"You want a lager? Not a cocktail?" he quizzes, shaking his head in disagreement.

"Yes, please," I nod, "I would like a large bottle of lager. I think that I drank enough Tequila last night to last me a lifetime. All of your cocktails have Tequila in them, so I don't want anything fancy, I just want a plain old bottle of lager, but please don't tell Scott and Johnny that I have said this."

"Your wish is my command," he says placing the bottle on the bar. "Talking about Tequila and last night, Scott has been looking for you this morning. He said something about some guy you danced with or something."

I'm defensive. "Has he been gossiping? What did he say?"

Alonso has a blank look upon his face, "Sorry, I can't remember now. I was busy with a guest. He also said something about a picnic at lunchtime or something."

"A picnic?" I query

"I think he said that there was a picnic at lunchtime and he would collect you." Alonso starts to laugh, "Disruption's probably planning something, and he is inviting you. I suppose that you shall be drinking more Tequila after all."

"Great," I reply, raising my brows.

It is quiet by the pool today and it is nice to get some peace. Apparently, there is a coach trip to some Mexican ruins. I have read about them in the book that Martha gave to me and but for Scott inviting me to the Disruption picnic, I probably would have gone along. It is lovely to just lie on a sunbed and close my eyes, doing absolutely nothing apart from recover from my hangover though.

Following my conversation with Catherine, I have decided to use this time to relax and take time to think. Thought is creative because I think that it is the consciousness of what you really want in life, and it is probably the key to addressing your inner life purpose. My grandma used to say, "Everyone has a purpose. It just needs to be discovered. When you uncover the purpose of your life, it brings a whole new outlook on life."

I think that a lot of people don't take time to reflect because they don't like to be alone. I like my own company, but I prefer to fantasize rather than reflect. I fantasize about the life that I would like to have, rather than the purpose of my life and how I can improve it.

I can have any life that I want when I fantasize, but when I reflect it is not possible to control my thought patterns. It is real and there is no denying the truth. When I do try to reflect, and I have really tried, I uncover lots of the negative feelings in my life that I don't like. I find skeletons in the cupboard that I didn't know were there. I start to criticize myself rather than learning to uncover what is causing these feelings and dealing with them. When I fantasize, I feel happy because life is how I want it to be. I wish that I could reflect upon life and make myself happy in reality.

I know deep down that I shouldn't deny my thoughts and feelings, and that I should acknowledge my anxiousness and fearfulness. Perhaps I would then recognize the message or meaning behind my life. I thought that I had resolved this problem at rehabilitation, but it appears that the skeletons are still in my cupboard, and they are coming back to haunt me. My grandma once said, "Beliefs are such a big part of who we are as people."

I need to stop fantasizing about my future and get on with the reality of it. I need to think straight, fear less and do more. I ask myself the questions, "What do I believe about myself? What do I believe about the world? What do I believe about the future?" I close my eyes as the sun is bright.

I feel half awake and half asleep, as I lie on my lounger. I am almost in a daze, deep in thought looking for answers to my questions. The sun is burning on my face. I am awake and asleep at the same time, and even though my eyes are closed, I see darkness with a glimpse of a yellow dot moving left to right, then right to left, almost hypnotizing me. I try to move but my body feels heavy, so heavy that I can't move. I am fully conscious but can't move my limbs. I feel scared. I feel like I am experiencing something paranormal. Someone is stood over me, but I don't know what they want. I suddenly realize that it's a reflection of myself, but then the reflection disappears and the yellow dot returns, burning in my eyes.

I am now drifting lazily through a hazy dream thinking of the past. I am a little girl, running along the beach with my grandparents and we are flying a kite. It is flying so high, so high. It is touching the clouds and we are laughing. My grandma takes me by my hand and I suddenly see the kite disappear and scenes from my life flash across the sky. My grandma's hand grip gentles until she disappears, and I realize that I am on my own, I am a lost soul. They have passed away and left me, but they are still with me in my mind and emotions.

I abruptly become aware of my surroundings, "Saskia, Saskia, come on and wake up. You are going to be late." I feel cold water on my face and Scott is gently shaking my body. "Here is a glass of water. That must have been some dream. You were talking all sorts of gobbledegook in your sleep."

Golly gosh, how embarrassing! I rub my eyes, I didn't even intend to go to sleep, I just wanted to close my eyes and reflect. I have all sorts of weird experiences when I sleep. Perhaps it would be best for me to never close my eyes, ever. Just stay awake forever.

"Sorry, Scott, What time is it? Alonso said that Disruption was having a picnic. Is it time for you to collect everybody?"

"No wonder you look as rough as you do. I can only presume that Alonso hasn't given you the full message?"

"Gosh, you know how to make a girl feel good, don't you?" I reply sarcastically and grumpily. "Just for reference, I didn't get in until the early hours of this morning after being slaughtered on Tequila, as you are fully aware. I was then awake with a dicky tummy after drinking some concoction that I was told to drink called sangrita. I've now been woken up, when I was just trying to get some sunrays to cover my pale sickly complexion through no sleep. No wonder I look rough, and for reference, you don't look that great yourself."

Scott looks alarmed then his straight face breaks into a smile and we both start to chuckle.

He jokes, "Well, I wouldn't have woken you up if I had known you were going to be such a grumpy cow."

"I am sorry, Scott," I apologize, "I just have my grumpy head on. I had a really good night last night, despite having a dicky tummy and hardly any sleep. Just give me five minutes to get changed and I will be with you to go on this Disruption Tequila picnic, but please tell me I don't have to drink more Tequila. I really couldn't face it today."

"I am afraid that I can't control what you are drinking today, since I'm not going on the picnic."

"Why aren't you coming? What do you mean?" I ask, screwing up my face due to the sun shining in my eyes, "If it's a Disruption picnic then surely you're coming. You'll need to look after your guests."

"Saskia, I don't think that you understand. I left a message with Alonso this morning which is the reason why I am surprised to find you asleep at the side of the pool. I thought that you would be dressed up to the nines by now."

"Scott, why would I be dolled up to the nines for a picnic?" I sigh.

"Well, did Alonso not tell you who was going on this picnic?"

"No, but I presumed you would be going."

He sighs. "That explains everything." He looks disappointed, "I wasn't sure if Alonso was listening and my instinct was right. He was with a customer and I was rushing off back to work."

I'm puzzled, "Right, can you stop talking in riddles. I have just woken up and you're not making any sense."

"Take a deep breath, Saskia. You have a date with that guy."

"Which guy?"

"I am referring to Miguel. The guy you danced with last night and won the dancing competition with."

"What?" I remark, looking at the state that I am in. I'm sweaty and look as rough as hell. "Is Miguel going on this Disruption picnic?"

"There is no Disruption picnic. He has invited YOU to go on a private picnic with him. You should be meeting him in an hour and I offered to drive you to meet him. I presumed that you would want to go. I was right, wasn't I?" he is frowning at me not getting all of this.

"Yes, of course, follow me to my room quickly and tell me all about this whilst I get ready. I can't believe that Alonso hasn't given me the correct message."

"I left a note for you at reception too. I tried to ring your room but there was no answer. You've still got time to get ready if you are fast, and you can probably make yourself somewhat respectable if you try," he jokes cheekily.

"Ha, ha," I say sarcastically, as we enter my room.

I exit the bathroom looking and smelling more respectable.

"I didn't think that you knew Miguel. You never said anything last night," I query.

"Well, I didn't. I received a call today from the Palm Wellbeing Resort, a holiday complex. We have been trying to persuade them to stock Disruption Tequila, and we invited them to our beach party last night. Miguel decided to take up the invitation and he placed an order with me today, because he had such an enjoyable evening and thought our Tequila was wonderful. I decided to personally deliver the order. I thought that it would be nice to introduce myself. It was really strange though, Saskia."

"Why was it strange?"

He frowns, "I recognized Miguel straight away and he also recognized me, and instantly asked about you. He remembered that I was with you last night and wanted to know all about you. Obviously, I couldn't tell him much, but I think that he really likes you, and he asked me to invite you on a picnic with him this afternoon. I just presumed that you would want to go after what you said about him last night."

"If he does like me, why and where did he disappear last night?"

Scott shrugs his shoulders. "He seems keen to see you now."

I sit on the edge of my bed looking down at the floor whilst I fasten my sandals.

Scott sits down at my side. "You will just have to ask him why he disappeared. He may have a genuine reason." He lightens the conversation detecting my nerves, "Following all of the alcohol you drunk last night, I just hope that you still like him when you meet him today. You might think that he's really ugly when you see him again."

I look up and smile, "Why? Do you think he is ugly?" I'm amused by his comment.

He shakes his head, "No, I think he is really good looking, but if you don't fancy him, will you please be polite to him."

"Why?" I query.

He smiles then jokes, "I don't want him cancelling his Tequila order that he has just placed and would like to keep him as a customer."

I laugh.

I wonder why Scott has kindly arranged this on my behalf, and agreed to take me, so I ask, "Just out of interest, why have you agreed to take me to this picnic? I mean, you hardly know me, but you have been really nice to me."

"I'm a nice guy and like to help people, besides I really like you, and you are from my home town of Manchester. You seem a nice person, who needs a bit of help. I consider you a friend now, and friends should help each other out."

"Thanks, for being my friend." I'm grateful.

I am pleased that he considers me a friend. He seems a really nice person and I feel comfortable in his company. We also seem to have a lot in common.

He smiles, "It appeared that you really like this guy and I want to help you to be happy. Perhaps you can help me to be happy too, one day."

"Why? Are you not happy?" I ask concerned. "I thought that you loved your job and living in Mexico."

"I do, but there is something missing in my life or should I say someone. I once had someone special in my life that I loved. I worshipped her, and she meant the world to me, but she betrayed my trust. I have felt an empty hole in my heart since we separated."

"Scott, that's terrible," I say. "My friend has had a difficult time recently. She separated from her boyfriend a while ago and hasn't really ever got over him. I was talking to her about it earlier today and sometimes a listening ear can help. I'm here if you ever want to talk about it."

He nods, "Yes, I will fill you in at some point. It's hard to talk to Johnny or Rick about it. They would just think that I was some kind of pussy cat and laugh at me. They think that I should just be living the single life in Mexico, but the thought of her stops me. Don't get me wrong, there are lots and lots of beautiful women here and some literally throw themselves at me, but I just can't go out with them. None of them interest me. My thoughts are always with my ex because deep down I still love her."

"There must be hundreds and thousands of people out there who are in the same position as you and my friend. Perhaps your ex still feels the same way about you. Could you not just phone her or write to her?"

"I tried. I called her mobile phone, but she must have changed her number because there was no ring tone. I did write, but I didn't get a response. She obviously doesn't feel the same way about me as I do about her, otherwise she would have been in touch. I suppose that I just need to learn to move on without her in my life. It's hard to do that though, when I believe she was my soulmate"

There was a connection between Scott and me, similar to that between a brother and sister. I almost felt the pain that he was going through. He is a wonderful man with a lot going for him. He is generous, good looking, kind hearted and considerate. He appears to be everything that every woman in the world would want. Why do some people have to be selfish and screw things up? How could any woman want to betray this lovely man? She must be stupid to have thrown away someone so perfect.

I can't help but think how Scott would be perfect for my friend, Catherine. I think that they would get on great and have a lot in common. They are both good looking, have a great sense of fun and would be compatible in lots of ways. I wish that Catherine was here, so that I could introduce them to each other. They could help each other with their heartache. It sometimes helps to speak to somebody in a similar situation.

"Anyway, we need to go now," Scott says as he starts to walk out of the room. "Miguel might cancel his order with me if you're late or stand him up."

"I hope that you are only joking and not being serious, Scott," I reply, as we walk out of my room together. "I think you've only arranged this date to get a good order for your Tequila."

"I'm only pulling your leg," he laughs, as he jokingly elbows me in my side.

CHAPTER EIGHT

Palm Wellbeing Resort is nestled in a tropical jungle by the sea. It is away from the hustle and bustle of the main resort and is very tranquil. Scott informed me on our way that it is an alternative vacation experience where you are unplugged from civilization. I wondered what he meant by his statement but didn't ask. In fact, I didn't talk much because I was feeling nervous.

Apparently, the clientele includes celebrities and highly-stressed city workers looking to release all of their worries. My understanding of Palm Resort is that it is a retreat that offers a world of wellness. Here, only the guests and their peace of mind matter. Guests can release all of their worries and let the sun, sand and sea awaken their senses. It sounds wonderful.

Scott pulls up at the entrance to the long drive. "I am going to drop you here. I'm not able to go any further due to not being a guest. Palm Resort respects their clients' privacy. I think that a walk down the drive might help relax you though and could help you to get your thoughts together before you meet Miguel." He stares into my eyes, "You seem really on edge."

"I'm just nervous, Scott. I felt a real connection with this guy yesterday and I am unsure what to expect today."

He gently holds my hand and gives it a tight squeeze. "There is nothing at all for you to worry about. Miguel is a reputable guy who also happens to like you. Just go along to the picnic, enjoy the food and company and then decide if you want to see each other again. It's simple as that."

I shrug my shoulders. I know that he is right.

"Would you like for me to pick you up later?"

I am grateful for him bringing me and offering moral support, but I don't know if I am going to be here for 10 minutes or a few hours.

"No, don't worry about collecting me. I can call a taxi."

"I will catch up with you tomorrow to check out the gossip on how the big date went then." He winks and starts to laugh his mischievous laugh that suddenly makes me feel at ease.

"Get lost and I'll see you later."

He drives away.

I was expecting a luxury resort, but Palm Resort looks similar to something out of Robinson Crusoe. It's not totally distressed but certainly shabby chic. Everything looks handmade and hand built to last. The reception area is basic but beautiful. It is filled with quality authentic wooden Mexican furniture, rustic home furnishings and handmade pottery. There is a mix of sofas made out of leather or pigskin and they are decorated with various-sized scatter cushions embroidered with traditional Mexican designs. Everything looks like it has been here for years and will be here for years to come. Everything is good quality and made to last.

There is a large reception desk that has been hand carved out of wood and waxed. Some sections of it have copper embellishment and other areas of it are painted in bright green and red. On the wall behind the desk are Mexican Fiesta Banners and photographs of Mexican bullfights. It's totally different from where I am staying where everything is new and gleaming. This hotel gives a true impression of Mexico and its traditions. It has authenticity.

There was nobody at reception when I first arrived, but a beautiful lady in her late thirties has now appeared. She has long crinkled hair and is wearing a seventies style embroidered tunic dress. It is a mixture of vibrant colors and really suits her. She has a hippy chic look to her.

"Hello," she greets me and kindly smiles.

"Hello, I have arrangements to meet a gentleman called Miguel."

"Ah, you must be Saskia," she says cheerfully. "You match his description. He said that I should expect you. Please take a seat and make yourself comfortable while I go and get him."

I sit on one of the larger leather sofas and sink into the large soft cushions behind me. There is a beautiful bouquet of freshly cut tropical flowers on the table in front of me. I delight in the aroma of their breathtaking fragrance and exquisite beauty. They are a collection of bright shades and original shapes. Nothing like I have seen before.

There is some literature on the table about Palm Resort and I decide to pass time reading it. It describes Palm Resort as being a rustic ecological hotel with basic services that is looking to preserve nature and the environment. Apparently, due to its remote nature it has no gas or electric. There is a solar power system to provide the electricity in the main reception, but according to the literature, after sunset all other areas are lit with nothing but candlelight. I find the idea of this quite nice but probably not practical.

I am distracted with a noise and wonder what it is. It sounds like somebody sneezing. There is nobody in reception apart from me. I hear it again, a louder sneeze, it is closer this time. I look all around me, then my eyes are attracted to the movement near my feet. There is something that I can only describe as looking like a gremlin. It is green, and it is staring at me and sneezing. It looks like a punk rocker with a row of spines or spikes running down its back and tail, and it has a third eye on the top of its head. It swishes its tail and looks angrily at me. I've done nothing to it, but I am afraid that it might bite, so I quickly move my feet and jump to stand on the sofa. I watch it petrified, trying to keep as still as I can.

"Are you ok?" I hear Miguel's voice behind me, which I recognize from last night. It's deep, sexy and echoes a gorgeous foreign accent when he speaks in English.

"Sorry for standing on your sofa," I stutter. "You have a gremlin running around the floor swishing its tail at me and making hissing and sneezing noises."

"What is a gremlin?" His face looks puzzled.

Miguel looks alarmed and walks to the front of the sofa. He might want to face this creature but I'm staying put right here. It's not getting me. That 'Gremlins' film gave me nightmares. I thought that it was fiction, but in Mexico, gremlins are for real.

"It's an iguana," he laughs. "It's a lizard native to tropical areas of Central America and the Caribbean. Palm Resort is nestled in a tropical jungle and we experience sightings of many different creatures, but none of them will hurt you, Saskia."

I feel really stupid. This isn't how I planned for us to meet each other again. He must think that I am really stupid.

He stamps his foot and the iguana runs away. Holding out his hand to help me down, I climb from the sofa.

"Nature provides the most beautiful surroundings, Saskia, and I would like for you to feel totally relaxed whilst you are here with me. You have nothing to worry about. You are my guest and I will look after you." He laughs, "I'll even protect you from gremlins."

I find his voice both calming and reassuring and his eyes…well, I could just gaze into them all day long.

"I shall try to relax." I hesitate. I can't help but wonder what other wildlife or creatures I am likely to see while visiting this lush paradise though. My skin feels itchy just thinking about it.

He still hasn't let go of my hand since helping me off the sofa and my hand fits perfectly and comfortably into his. I don't see any reason to let go. I don't want to let go. Butterflies are fluttering through my stomach with the connection.

"I have made us a picnic. I hope that you are hungry. Are you happy to eat at the beach?" he asks.

"Yes, I'm starving. The beach sounds good."

Actually, I can't think of anything more romantic than to lay down a blanket on the beach and share a picnic together.

He tells me, "The picnic is ready. We just need to collect it on the way."

The beach is a short walk through the greenery and he talks to me about Palm wellbeing Resort on the way.

Palm Resort is built like a tiny village that's private, warm and friendly. Various-sized cabanas made of wood with bamboo roofs are located along the pathways throughout the jungle. Miguel refers to them as stylish jungle chic lodgings, where you can stay and connect with nature.

We pass a lady sat cross-legged on a wooden deck area. She seems switched off from what's going on around her. She doesn't even notice us walk past her.

"Is she ok?" I ask Miguel.

"Yes, she is meditating. Palm Resort offers meditation and healthy lifestyle classes where we aim to help guests refresh, renew, revive and, in some cases, find their soul."

"Find their soul?" I am alarmed. "Do your classes actually work?" I'm intrigued.

"It can work if the guests immerse themselves in explorations of their body's wisdom. In this chaotic world it's easy to get lost and many find that they have to reconnect and rediscover themselves. This is the perfect place to do just that.”

“That’s an interesting thought, but I wouldn’t have a clue where to start. Do you show your guests how to do that?”

“It’s easy to disconnect from the world but it’s important that you know yourself. There is nothing closer to you than your own inner voice. If you listen to yourself you will gain guidance, direction, insight and clarity in your life. We have classes that help guests trust their own inner wisdom and this helps them connect with their spirits.”

As interesting as all of this may sound, I am not totally sure if I believe it.

“I find what you tell me interesting, Miguel, but to be honest, sometimes my head is in the clouds on a massive scale. When I am blissfully ignorant of reality it can feel beautiful and exhilarating. I can’t see any reason why I should want to connect with myself.”

“Clouds are beautiful, Saskia, but sometimes it helps to have your feet on the ground. It’s important to reconnect with your body when you feel lost. It is important to take full responsibility for your peace of mind and happiness. We help our guests to bring their full attention to their feelings, thoughts and behaviors and to be aware of how to manage them.”

I have been deep in thought listening to Miguel and have been following the pathway not really taking notice of where I am going. My breath is suddenly taken away as the tropical jungle flows into a sea of green. I am surrounded by pure white sand and a sea of calmness. There are also a few brightly painted wooden houses right on the beach. Some have sea turtles only a few feet away from them. This is definitely what I would describe as connecting with nature.

“Do you like?” Miguel asks.

“I am lost for words, Miguel. This is beautiful.” It really is. It is the most natural and beautiful beach I have ever seen.

“Let me show you where I live. We need to collect the picnic from my home.”

He points down the beach to what I would describe as a luxury beach shack. It is built of wood with a thatched roof but somehow looks elegant, painted white. It has a private beachfront terrace with a hot tub. It’s the ideal place for stargazing with a glass of champagne. I can’t help but wonder how many women he has shared the experience with. I feel a pang of jealousy thinking about this and try to put it to the back of my mind. I mean, I'm not even dating him. He's just invited me for a picnic and here I am letting my imagination run wild yet again.

We enter the shack and it is immaculate. I half expected it to be untidy. Most men that I know who live on their own usually don't clean up. Not properly, anyway.

"You are very tidy." I observe.

He laughs. "I wouldn't be if the hotel cleaner wasn't good enough to tidy up for me, she is very good."

"Obviously," I remark.

He walks into the kitchen area. It is like a long corridor fitted with modern units and appliances.

"Our picnic is in the fridge. It contains a lot of fresh food and I didn't want it to be compromised with the heat. I shall just sort it and we can go."

The kitchen connects to the lounge area where there is an oversized corner sofa. I even notice a plasma television on the wall."

"I didn't think that you had electricity or gas here. I read your literature in reception telling me that."

He looks up for a moment. "The guests come here for short periods of time and appreciate connecting with nature. They don't want gas, electric or televisions. They want to connect with the properties of earth, wind, fire and water, because they are combined to purify the mind, body and soul. I live here full-time, not just for a couple of weeks and I like my necessities and luxuries. I like Sky television and lights at night. Living under candlelight is romantic but not practical, not all the time."

I notice a door off the lounge area that is slightly open and can't help but nosy. I stretch my neck to try to see more. I always have been quite nosy. My grandma used to say that I could eat corn on the cob through a venetian blind. I prefer to just consider myself inquisitive.

"Would you like to take a look around my home?" Miguel asks.

I jump. Gosh, I thought that he was busy with his head in the fridge.

"No, I'm fine, thanks. I just thought that I heard a noise?" I have to make some excuse and it's the first thing that comes to mind. I don't want him to think that I am being nosy. I mean inquisitive.

"I had better check that out then." He smirks at me as he walks past and opens the door.

The door leads to a large bedroom featuring a queen-sized bed, draped with luxurious bedding. It looks so comfortable that I could just climb in it and sleep, with him. There is a large fan over the bed and mosquito nets surrounding the sides. It's nice to know that no creatures can join you in there.

As I see him standing in his bedroom my mind suddenly runs away with itself and fills with filthy, flirty thoughts that are totally inappropriate. I would love to share his hot tub, then later roll between the covers with him. There is no denying that he sets my temperature rising, and it's not the heat of Mexico, it's him. I can't help but crave the company of this gorgeous man. I fancy him like no other man that I have ever met. Golly gosh, thinking like this makes me such a bimbo. I have never had a one-night stand or even ever thought about it, but here I am in a stranger's house contemplating taking him to bed. What has got into me?

"Stop it, Saskia," I suddenly find me saying to myself aloud.

"Pardon," he looks through the door. "Did you say something?"

I must be going crazy again, talking to myself this time.

"I just asked if everything was ok," I say quietly.

"My window was open." He informs me, "Maybe there was a slight breeze that disturbed something or perhaps some wildlife entered."

"Yes probably," I answer, trying not to sound guilty.

"Shall we eat now?" he asks. "The picnic is ready."

I can't think of any nicer way to spend an afternoon than having a picnic in a beautiful spot, with a gorgeous man who makes my heart race. Looking at all of the fantastic food that he is unpacking out of the picnic basket makes my stomach rumble. I skipped breakfast this morning due to feeling a little rough, well a lot really, but I am hungry and have gained my appetite now.

I haven't got a clue what most of the food is, but it smells appetizing. There just appears to be a lot of it. I mean…I have been eating quite a lot whilst I have been on holiday, but even with eyes bigger than my belly, I know that we won't be able to eat all of this between the two of us. Perhaps he has a healthier appetite than me.

"I wasn't sure what you like and dislike, so I wanted to give you lots of choice," he says.

"That's very considerate of you. I'm not a fussy eater though. All of this looks and smells good."

"I visited Merida market this morning to buy the food. Have you been there yet?"

"No, I can't say I have. Should I go?" I enquire.

Merida market does sound familiar. Perhaps it was mentioned in the book that Martha gave to me.

"I truly think that you would enjoy the experience. It is a huge bazaar packed with stalls that sell everything that you could possibly ever want in Mexico. There are stalls piled high with chilies, fabulous fruits and various foods. Crowds of people travel there, not only for the food, but also for clothing, sandals, embroidered items and panama hats. It is known to be one of the world's greatest markets. It is the shopping hub of the Yucatan."

I can picture the market in my mind, like I have been there previously, and I feel the buzz that he describes in my bones.

"It sounds great. I need to buy a couple of presents and it sounds like the place I should go."

"I can take you if you like?" He looks up from serving the food for a response.

I can feel myself blush. He obviously wants to see me again. I have that fluttering feeling in my stomach again and feel like I am on cloud nine, wherever cloud nine is. It's just a term that I have heard.

He carries on. "I know my way around the market and might be able to help you find whatever you look for. There are a number of very good stalls that have high quality local work, with many beautiful things. I know a man who sells hammocks of every size and color and there are large hat stalls, with friendly owners who have lots of panamas in various styles. I am sure you will find something for presents."

"That sounds good." I smile.

Miguel has set out all of the food in little dishes on our picnic blanket and he has put up an umbrella to shade us from the sun whilst we eat. He has put lots of effort into this and I really appreciate it. Some men would struggle to pack a picnic with sandwiches, let alone all of this choice. It looks amazing.

He talks me through the various Mexican dishes and the ingredients included in each. He even feeds some of the food to me.

"You should be adventurous," he tells me.

I don't feel adventurous when some of it runs down my chin, but he wipes it off with his finger and seductively licks it.

There is raw fish drenched in lime juice, a little like sushi, crisp fried tortillas that could be filled with 100 possible fillings. There are nachos and two little bowls of sauce. The red one is relatively nice but the green one is made with the strongest green chili and nearly blows my head off… honestly.

"I need a drink," I cough and splutter.

Miguel laughs, "Have some of this freshly squeezed orange juice to get rid of the taste."

It goes down well. "I haven't been running but feel like I have done a mile. That stuff makes you pant and puff." I joke.

The most pleasurable dish is made of chopped hard-boiled eggs in a sweet pumpkin sauce served with a spicy tomato sauce. The dishes seem endless, but all taste delicious. I am now full and totally bloated.

I am amazed…not only has he packed a picnic, but he also cooked all of the food. They say that the way to a man's heart is through his stomach. I think it's the other way around. He has definitely won me over, as long as he doesn't give me any more of the green sauce. I just hope that I don't need to cook for him, as I will have to see if there is an M&S alternative at this Merida Market.

I feel really comfortable in Miguel's company. Conversation flows and we laugh and joke with each other. I feel like I have known him forever. In fact, I don't think that I have ever been so naturally myself, with anybody. We both talk about our childhood and our past. There is chemistry between us despite coming from different backgrounds and cultures. You would think that we had known each other forever.

Miguel spent two years in England which explains why he speaks perfect English. He was sent to boarding school by his parents, due to their work commitments. They owned hotels and had busy schedules, so when he returned from England he lived with his grandma.

"My grandma literally brought me up and is one of the most important people in my life," he informs me. "I wasn't happy at boarding school and she stepped in and offered to look after me. I owe her a lot."

"Do you see her often?" I ask.

"Quite regularly," he replies. "She doesn't live far away, so I visit at least twice a week. She is getting older now, so I take her shopping and sort any jobs that she needs doing. My parents live far away, so I make sure she is looked after."

I get the impression that Miguel is a beautiful person – both inside and out. He seems really caring and considerate.

"I really miss my grandparents," I inform him sadly. "I wish they were still here with me. I don't understand why we are born to live and love, then die, leaving our loved ones behind. It's not right."

He frowns, "Sometimes, life isn't fair, Saskia, but we need to deal with it the best we can."

For some reason, in this relaxed environment, I feel like I can open up and talk about my feelings with Miguel. I look out at the calmness of the sea and push my feet gently into the sand with my heel. It is warm on the surface but as I push my feet deeper, I feel the coldness of the ground. The coldness of where I think we end up when we die.

Miguel watches me. "Death comes to all of us, Saskia, but you shouldn't be sad. Your grandparents have now gone somewhere special."

My grandma always said she was going somewhere special when she passed away.

"How do you know that?" I ask, intrigued.

"Many civilizations and cultures have created rituals to try and give meaning to human existence. In Mexico, death is considered to be the passage to a new life. Just like a caterpillar has another life when it turns into a beautiful butterfly.

"So, do you believe in life after death?" I question.

"I believe that you live again in some form, but I don't know all of the answers. I think that you possibly get to put right everything that you may have done wrong in a previous life. Just like a caterpillar turns into a beautiful butterfly, we come back more beautiful having learnt from previous life mistakes."

I think about it. "I suppose that anything is possible?"

"In Mexico, we bury our deceased with many of their personal possessions because we believe that they will need them in the hereafter. Each year families celebrate the belief that death is a transition from one life to another."

I am surprised by his credence. I am quite upset that death is celebrated and I think Miguel detects this. I loved my grandparents and I mourn them. Unfortunately, I am left with just their memories and unforgotten love.

My feet feel really cold now, pushed as far into the ground as possible, without literally getting a spade and digging. I feel connected with the earth beneath my feet. The coldness smothers my feet and flows through my veins making my body feel cold.

Miguel stares at me, "Sorry if I have upset you, Saskia, but I don't think you understand. Sometimes, when people of other cultures hear about the celebration of death, they mistakenly think it is horrible. In essence, it is a special ritual to happily remember our dead relatives, and give meaning and continuity to their human lives. It is a celebration of their life, not of their death. Thousands of people travel to Mexico from all over the world each year to witness and take part in this beautiful rite."

I now understand that it is a special ritual with a pleasant meaning. "When do you celebrate this?"

"The 1st of November is set aside to commemorate the deceased infants and children, while November 2nd is set aside to commemorate deceased adults. Perhaps you would like to come with me and see that it isn't sinister at all. I celebrate with my grandma and I am sure that she would like to meet you."

I reluctantly agree, as I suddenly recall my conversation on the plane, with Hania, the spirit warrior. She had told me about this celebration in detail and what it meant to me; I didn't believe her.

She had told me, "Communication exists between the living and the dead, Saskia. Your soul from your previous life is being called for Dia de los Muertos (Day of the Dead) and this is why you are on your way to Mexico. Your soul from your past life is in the background of your present life. There are issues that need resolving, and this is something that you and your past have to do together before you can move on."

I ask Miguel, "Is this celebration called Dia de los Muertos?" I need clarification.

He nods, "It means Day of the Dead. Have you heard about it before?" he asks.

"Not until recently," I proclaim.

He looks at me for further clarification, but I am too worried to say anymore.

A young boy and girl have appeared on the beach. They delight in building the most magnificent sandcastle that looks like it's been designed by an architect. It is a large complex construction with towers and arches. They sculpt their design effortlessly and happily using buckets, spades and imagination.

"Would you like to become a bucket and spade superstar and build a sandcastle too," Miguel jokes.

He has obviously observed my quietness and interest in their creation. Watching them takes my mind off what the spirit warrior told me.

"The only sandcastles that I can build are in the sky. I was never very good at building real sandcastles as a child, and the ones I built never lasted. The sea always found their weakness and washed them away."

I smile remembering happy times spent at the beach with my grandparents and carry on. "I always preferred to fly my kite. We flew our kite so high in the sky that it became invisible, but I always knew that it would come back, and not disappear like a sandcastle always did."

He stands and wipes the sand from his shorts. I feel that there is a tension between us since our discussion about death. Perhaps he is going to walk off and leave me. Perhaps he has had enough of me. I have screwed up again. Why can I build the most beautiful sandcastles in the sky, in my mind, but not build them in reality, with real people. Why can't I have happiness? It's all that I have ever wanted. Until I find happiness, I will be a lost soul, just like the lady who used to mumble to herself at the rehabilitation unit. There is something missing in my life that I need to find.

Miguel looks down at me and holds out his hand. "Let's go for a walk along the beach. I know of a little beach bar where we can get a coffee or maybe something stronger."

I hold out my hand and he gently helps me to my feet. As I rise, he draws me close to him and holds me in his arms for a time. I feel the warmth of his body press against me and it feels the safest place in the world. As we pull apart, he kisses me on my forehead, in a reassuring, comforting manner and my insecurities start to erase.

We walk along the edge of lapping sea waves in silence, hand in hand, leaving our footprints behind us in the sand. I expect that they will wash away, just like my sandcastles did as a child. Nothing is forever - sandcastles, footprints, love, life. It's what I have come to expect now.

Miguel breaks the silence. "My parents used to tell me that there are no limits but the sky. I therefore used to build lots of sandcastles in the sky, but like your childhood sandcastles, I realized they were only temporary. When I built something temporary in the air, I was trying to create something that couldn't exist. There were no foundations for my thoughts."

"What did you do about it?" I ask.

"I put all of my energy into making my dreams and aspirations come true. I created Palm Beach where other people could also find their dreams and aspirations through wellness. Palm Resort made me realize that the aim of life is to live, and to live means to be aware. Daydreaming only covers the cracks in your life. When you address the gaps you find hope and achievement that enriches the world."

"I wish that I could be like you. I worry about the future and mourn for the past. Building sandcastles in the sky helps me to cope with day to day life though."

"Your mind, body and heart carry your personal history that you will never forget, but you need to live in the present moment. It's your journey, Saskia, and only you will know how to get where you want to be."

I agree with what he is saying but it is hard to face the truth when it is being presented to me clearly.

"My grandma used to tell me that my heart and mind were a compass that would help me navigate my life."

"Perhaps it is time to let your heart, mind and soul navigate for you then; our minds are powerful beyond measure, and sometimes thought can overtake all other feelings. You also have to remember to listen to your heart and soul otherwise the compass won't work."

"Does your compass work?" I have to ask.

"I face challenges and ask myself questions, as we all do, but I will work them out. Not everything in life can be straightforward." He smiles at me whilst nodding.

I can't help but wonder what challenges he might face.

After a short stroll, we arrive at a small beach bar with a palm roof. There are a number of chopped tree trunks placed in the sand, creating tables and chairs for the guests visiting to relax and enjoy their drinks at. I take a seat under a softly swaying coconut palm, whilst Miguel goes to the bar. The heat under here is gentle and it is a great place for people watching. I see Miguel laugh and joke with the bartender and some people at the bar. He is so handsome and obviously known here.

He returns to the table. "I have ordered us both an Americano coffee."

"I love Americano coffee. I like it strong with no milk." I inform him.

"Good choice. That is exactly what I have ordered."

"Perfect." I am surprised that he hasn't needed to ask. Perhaps it is the only coffee that this place serves.

The bartender brings our coffee and a large bottle of chilled white wine in an ice bucket.

Miguel smiles, "I thought that you may like something a little stronger too, so I have ordered us a nice bottle of chilled white wine for afterwards. You do like white wine, don't you?"

"I like Sauvignon Blanc, but anything chilled is nice." I comment.

The bartender smiles as he reveals that the wine in the ice bucket is Sauvignon Blanc. He is very friendly with Miguel, and they appear to get on very well, laughing and joking. "You must be psychic, Miguel, ordering for the lady before asking what she drinks," he jokes.

Miguel winks at me.

The barman pats me on the shoulder in a friendly manner, "Miguel is a great friend of mine. Please take good care of him and don't hurt his feelings, I think that he likes you."

Miguel blushes with embarrassment and I feel for him.

I shrug my shoulders, "Well, I must like him too, because I am here on a date with him, and where else would I find a man who knows exactly what I drink without asking me."

The bartender holds his thumb up at Miguel. "Well, enjoy the rest of your time together my friends." He walks off smiling and Miguel chuckles shaking his head.

I am intrigued, "I presume that you know each other?"

Miguel nods, "We have known each other since childhood. He is a good friend."

"And do you bring many ladies here?" I have to ask.

He shakes his head, "No, I have never brought any lady here before. That is why my friend is trying to embarrass me. I always come here alone, it is a special place and I wanted to share it with you. I have been too busy building a business to share much female company, and until recently, I didn't even know what I was looking for in a woman."

I don't ask any questions but smile and feel myself blush.

I take a sip of my white wine. It is cold, refreshing and fruity. It is the perfect tonic for the end of the day. "This wine is lovely," I remark.

"Good choice then?" he asks.

"Perfect."

He smiles at me. "I am pleased that you like it."

"I presume that you are experienced in choosing wine with owning a hotel."

He shakes his head. "I once visited a local winery with one of my buyers for wine tasting. To be honest, I struggled telling the difference between Cabernet and Merlot. I was taught how to look, smell and taste the different wines. It all just tasted the same no matter what I did with it. I am not a wine connoisseur, but I just like drinking one of life's true pleasures."

"I totally agree," I remark.

We clink our glasses together, "To life," I say.

"And to life's true pleasures," he adds.

As we walk back along the beach towards Palm Wellness Resort the sun has gone down and the stars have started to come out, even though the sky is still quite blue. I am feeling totally relaxed after spending a day with Miguel. He has a way about him that brings calmness to me that I have never experienced before. We talk about anything and everything. He is really easy to get along with and we are both content in each other's company. You would think that we had known each other forever.

"I wish that I could wake up every day and see the clear blue skies and shimmering tropical waters," I say, "It is really beautiful, here."

"Life can be like that for you if you really want it to be," he replies, "You could just stop dreaming and make it a reality."

As we arrive at his home, he faces me and kisses me gently on my lips before gently pulling away. He advises me, "The pulse of life slows down at Palm Resort and the gulf between thinking and doing drifts so that all that is left is contentment. You should stay here and try it for yourself. You won't need to build sandcastles in the sky then and could find what actually makes you happy."

"What do you mean?" I ask.

"You tell me that you daydream about unattainable goals. You should try dreaming of something that you want to do and make it a reality."

We look into each other's eyes for a moment before he breaks the silence. "I shall make us some coffee and then I can arrange for one of my drivers to take you back to your hotel, or alternatively, you are welcome to stay and find yourself."

He leaves the terrace, walking into his house and leaving me in thought.

I am unsure if that was a proposition. I am uncertain if he has asked me to stay the night or if he actually wants one of the hotel's drivers to take me back to my hotel. This requires friendly advice and I need Catherine. I wish she was in Mexico. It's costing me a fortune to keep calling her in England. I rummage through my bag to find my mobile phone. It has a signal, thank goodness, which is amazing in this remote place.

I walk down to the shore where the waves are gently lapping and try to dial Catherine's number. I don't want Miguel to hear our conversation. My hands are shaking but I don't know why. I nervously drop the phone in the wet sand and have to pick it up and start dialing again.

I am relieved to hear a friendly voice at the other end. Catherine sounds really excited.

"Ah, Saskia, glad you phoned. Did you get my message?"

I can hear her jumping up and down on her bed screaming, giddy with excitement. I haven't heard her sound so happy in a long time. I hadn't checked my messages all day.

"No, what message? You sound really excited. What's happened? Have you won the lottery or something?"

"No, but I am coming to Mexico. I am flying tomorrow night from Manchester. I told Daniel that I was tired and needed a holiday and he suggested that he pay for Joshua and me to join you at your hotel."

"Honestly?" I ask surprised. I am amazed at Daniel's generous offer. Perhaps he is changing for the better; I would like to think so. I always try to think good of people.

"Yes. Great news, isn't it? He received a bank statement or something and it detailed the travel agent that you used to book the holiday. He took me there and he booked it with a nice lady called Martha. Apparently, she used to go to school with you."

I smile, "Yes, I know Martha. I am still confused by Daniel's actions. Why is he being so nice?"

Catherine laughs. "Don't knock it." I hear another excited scream, "Sorry, I can't help myself. I am really excited about joining you in Mexico."

"I know. It's brilliant news and I can't wait to see you both," I reply, still trying to absorb the news. "Call me the minute you arrive in Cancun and I will be ready to meet you at the hotel. I shall also be able to introduce you to all the new friends I have made."

I am sure she will like them.

"I will. I am just on with our packing now."

I can hear her throwing things into the suitcase. She isn't methodical.

I am looking forward to Catherine coming to Mexico. I have thought about her and Joshua lots whilst I have been here, and I've wished that they were both here with me.

I suddenly remember my reason for calling. How could I forget?

"Catherine, I really need your advice."

"I am all ears. Go ahead," she replies joyfully.

I pause for a second, "I have met somebody really nice and I am contemplating spending the night with him. It's the guy that I danced with, that I previously told you about. Do you think I should stay the night with him?"

"Gosh, Saskia, I can't answer that question. It's for you to know the answer to that question. Is this the guy who you thought looked like the man in your dreams?"

I decide to ignore that question because I seriously believe that he is the man in my dreams, and I don't have time to have that debate.

"I really want to stay the night with him, but I am scared."

"What are you scared of?"

"I am scared of what he will think of me in the morning; that I am cheap and easy." I pause, "At the same time I really want him, like I have never wanted a man before. I don't think I have ever felt like this about anybody. He is special to me, he has special qualities and I want this to be special to him, like I feel it would be for me. I want him to respect me."

"This sounds hot, babe. It sounds serious."

"Yes, it is, but I don't know if he has actually invited me to stay the night." I explain how he worded his proposal.

"Oh, Saskia, you are so strange at times. He has invited you to sleep with him. It's as simple as that. He has offered you the choice of staying or going. The choice is up to you, and how you feel. I think that he wants you to stay, but he is being polite and offering you the option to decide if it is what you want too."

"Well, no. Gosh, I don't know," I say flustered. I am confused and only have the wine to blame.

"Well, you could ask him, Saskia?" She bursts out laughing, "You could say, 'Considering you are insanely good looking and I'm on holiday, I think we should have sex, if you want?"

"I didn't mean like that and I wouldn't want it to be like that. This is important. I feel like I have known Miguel forever, we just seem to click. I want to spend the night with him, and will have regrets if I don't, but I want it to be special and I want him to respect me."

"Saskia, I haven't a clue what you are going on about but listen to me. There is no reason to walk away from a holiday romance if it feels right. Just go with the flow, but don't make the same mistake that I made in the past. You know what I mean by that, don't you?"

I knew what she meant. She was referring to having had a baby with a man she didn't love. My situation was different; I only wanted to sleep with Miguel because I knew that I had feelings for him; I loved him.

She carries on, "Look, I'll see you very soon, babe. We will talk about it then."

"Ok," I reply reluctantly, "have a safe journey."

"Bye," I hear her scream with excitement again as she cuts the call and I can't help but smile.

I walk back up from the beach to the house. Miguel is lying chilling in a hammock on the decked terrace staring up at the sky.

"There is enough room for two if you wish to join me," he says.

I join him and cuddle into his soft skin.

"I would like to stay the night," I whisper in his ear. I feel butterflies in my stomach.

He kisses me on my cheek. "I can arrange for you a room in the main hotel if you like, or you are welcome to stay with me."

Of course, I don't want to stay in the hotel. I want to share his bed with him. I want to carry out all of the dirty, guilty thoughts I had about us this afternoon when I saw him in his bedroom. I want to make this fantasy a reality.

"I am scared of the dark and want to be with you," I reply.

I feel myself nervously shake. I have never felt or done anything like this before. It is so out of character for me. This could be a one-night stand, or it could be forever. Whatever it is, I want to spend the night with him, more than I have wanted anything in my life before.

He lights a cigarette and puffs a circle in the air. I haven't seen him smoke all day.

"I didn't know that you smoked," I remark.

"I gave it up two years ago but needed this tonight."

"Oh, right," I just nod. I am really tired and close my eyes.

He hesitates, "I don't want to rush this thing between us. I want to spend quality time with you and get to really know the girl," he pauses, "that I think I already know. Does that make sense?"

"Yes, I know," I reply sleepily. I do know what he means. I feel like I have known him forever.

He holds my hand and leads me inside.

In the bedroom, there is no resistance, I rejoice at his tender touch as our hearts and pulses beat together as one. Could there really be such a thing as real love? I suppose only time will tell and time goes really slow at Palm Resort. The pulse of life really does slow down, and I orgasm like never before.

CHAPTER NINE

The Mexican Yucatan Peninsula is home to an amazing diversity of tropical birds and animals. I slowly waken to the sounds of twitters and screeches coming from the nearby jungle. This is juxtaposed with the relaxing sound of the ocean gently caressing the golden sands. The natural sounds, although very different, touch and stroke each other lovingly under the warmth of the sun rays and for a moment I forget where I am. I haven't woken up properly, I am still in a daze, half asleep and half awake.

A shadow appears over me, invading my personal space and blocking out the ray of light coming from the roof window. I suddenly jump, startled like a deer in front of a gun, moments before death. The ray of light suddenly appears again, brighter than before and common sense suddenly prevails. I come to my faculties as I slowly but fully awaken and turn to Miguel who is also awake and is watching me closely. His presence eases my scattered mind and relaxes my anxiety and frazzled nerves.

"Good morning," he greets me.

I sit up and rub my eyes. "Hello. What time is it?" I ask.

"It's quite late, about 10am, but I didn't want to wake you. You didn't sleep very well during the night."

"Did I not?" I ask, baffled. I felt like I had slept great. "It must be linked with being somewhere strange, perhaps being in a strange bed," I joke.

Miguel doesn't laugh. "You tossed, turned and shouted in your sleep. I was really concerned about you." Anxiety and a look of worry are displayed on his face.

I feel myself drain. I know exactly what he is referring to when he tells me that I was tossing, turning and shouting in my sleep. I know because

I have been in this situation many times before. The same happened on the plane. Witnesses of my recurring nightmare have described exactly the same as Miguel, with apprehension.

I have been told that it is like I am fighting for my life, as I throw out my arms and legs unaware of anybody around me. Usually though, I am fully aware that I have experienced the nightmare. At the point of my nightmare where the car descends off the cliff edge, I have an unusual feeling that my soul has left my body. I wake up with the sense of falling at this stage, and my sleep leaves my body. I am then left wide awake with a fearful anticipation of the future. I am left a troubled spirit, anxious to understand the dream.

This time, I am really concerned, because I have no recollection of having had the dream. I didn't waken knowing that this had happened, like I usually would. I don't know which scenario is more frightening, the nightmare or the not knowing. I am confused as to what has happened.

In the past, I have pleaded for an answer from the God of heaven concerning this mystery. I still wait in anticipation for his answer. Until then, I suppose life goes on and time will tell. I just need to remind myself to be patient.

Miguel is looking for a reaction from me, so I reply, "I am sorry if I stopped you sleeping. I must have been having a bad dream. It happens sometimes." I yawn, stretch, then smile, trying to make light of the situation.

He gently runs his finger down my face. "Don't worry about keeping me awake, baby. I was just worried with the things that you said, because you said things that I have thought in the past."

Strange thing to say, perhaps it's just his translation. "What do you mean?" I ask, puzzled.

"Oh, nothing," he replies. "We all have nightmares, but as long as you are ok, that's all that matters." He changes subject, "Anyway, I've made fresh coffee and pastries."

As we eat our breakfast on the veranda we watch a group of men and women taking part in a yoga session on the beach. They all appear to be concentrating intently and this appears to bring calmness to their bodies and minds.

Miguel observes my interest. "I would like nothing more than to spend the day with you today, but unfortunately I have to work. Please will you meet me for dinner this evening when I have finished work, and we can then spend some more time together?"

"I would love to," I answer without even thinking about it. It would have been nice to spend the day with him, but I understand that he has commitments.

He smiles, "You could take part in some of the activities and classes today that Palm Wellness Resort offers. I could visit you at points to see how you are doing."

It's a kind offer, but I'm not sure it's for me. I don't know what classes are on offer, but, for some reason, I don't believe that a yoga class or any other class will have the same effect on me as I see it having on the people participating on the beach. I just can't relax like they appear to be doing. Besides, I quite like my own company and my own space to think.

"Thanks for the offer but I am considering visiting some archaeological sites that I have read about."

The book Martha gave to me makes the sites sound quite interesting and it would be nice to visit them.

"I believe that the sites are somewhere near here," I state.

Miguel nods, "You are referring to Chichen Itza. It is one of the most visited archaeological sites in Mexico. An estimated one to two million tourists visit the ruins every year."

"Yes, I believe it's a major tourist attraction," I agree.

"There are some other ruins that you can visit nearer to here that aren't publicized and don't get as many tourists. If you go to reception before you leave, they will provide you with a map and information."

I am quite looking forward to visiting one of the new seven wonders of the world, Chichen Itza, but I also quite like the idea of visiting the ruins Miguel has informed me about.

The receptionist is extremely helpful. She gives me literature on nearby tourist attractions, Chichen Itza and other ruins.

She also advises me on transport, "Few people in Mexico have cars and therefore the buses are heavily used."

"Is there a bus to Chichen Itza?" I query.

She smiles and nods, "There are many buses available to most destinations, including where you want to go, but there are different classes of bus, depending on schedules."

"I'm happy to catch any bus, as long as it gets me to my required destination," I comment.

She smirks, "There are several classes of buses in Mexico, from third class to luxury. Some of the buses are brand new luxury vehicles with reserved seating, there are modest converted VW vans, pickup trucks with canopies and then there are rickety jalopies."

"Which shall I be catching?" I ask enthusiastically, as she looks at a bus timetable.

She screws her face up, unsure how to break the news, "Sorry, you shall be catching a chicken bus."

I'm not sure what quite to expect, but I will keep an open mind and remain optimistic.

I stand by the side of the road to catch my bus. The receptionist at Palm Resort has informed me that there are regular chicken buses running past the site. The chicken buses also head to and from rural locales and regularly host an animal or two, however they are cheap and pretty safe. I really want to experience the true Mexico, so I suppose that this is a great way to travel.

I see my rickety chicken bus approaching. It's probably better described as a shed on wheels. I raise my arm and it pulls over sharply, throwing dust up from the road into my eyes. I enter the vehicle with care and pay a few pesos for travel, unsure what to expect.

I guess you get what you pay for and I can't help but laugh to myself. I am seated next to a family of Mayas dressed in traditional brightly-colored clothing, who are on their way to a festival. They do nothing but argue and shout at each other. There is an old lady sat in front of me with a chicken under her arm that keeps clucking like it's about to lay an egg any minute, and there's a man with a goat on a lead that appears to be a pet. It decides to urinate, and the fountain is heading towards my feet, but nobody seems to bat an eyelid. This is just normal to them. I'm glad that I have noticed and lift my feet just in time to prevent a drenching.

The bus starts and stops continuously along the journey. It calls at more places than you could possibly imagine. Due to the fact that there are no bus stops, people just stand at the side of the road all along the route and wave to stop the bus. You can stop, start and then stop again within two minutes. It's like being in a bumper car being thrown backwards and forwards. I am relieved to eventually get off the bus and get some fresh air. I must admit that the journey has made me feel nauseous.

I have eventually arrived at one of the seven wonders, Chichen Itza, and I feel fortunate to be here. I feel that this is an experience of a lifetime. I used to dream about visiting places like this. I have to nip myself to check that I am now actually here and not dreaming. I am excited to be visiting the mysterious temples and pyramids of the Maya.

I queue for entry, pay my pesos and buy a map of the ruins. As I proceed into the site there is a representative informing guests about the history of the Maya city.

The man addresses the public with a loud speaker and I listen attentively, "The Mayans constructed vast cities with an amazing degree of architectural perfection and Chichen Itza is one of the largest Maya cities, covering an area of many miles."

The people look at each other in amazement and some say, "Wow," as an expression of their wonder.

The speaker carries on, "The site contains many fine stone buildings in various states of preservation. Some of these have been restored to a fine standard."

I study the map and look at all of the places that I would like to visit, whilst I hear the speaker talking about the temples, buildings and pyramids. I am pleased that I am wearing comfortable shoes. I get the feeling that I will be doing a lot of walking.

It appears quite commercial and there are tourists all around. The heat and humidity are unbearable. I am feeling dehydrated, so I approach a stall and buy a bottle of water. There are hundreds of stalls. The local people are selling handcrafted souvenirs made out of limestone and wood. The stall holders are lovely people and their prices appear very reasonable, however, I still hear many tourists haggling for a better price.

One of the stalls attracts my attention. I see skeletons that are dressed in elegant dresses made out of satin and lace. My grandma once gave me a porcelain flamenco doll when I was younger. She had bought it when she visited Spain and it was dressed very similarly.

I once asked my grandma, "Why is it called a flamenco doll?"

She told me, "Flamenco is a genre of music, song and dance from the Spanish region of Andalusia that dancers move to. The dancers are beautiful and dress in satin dresses with ruffles down to the floor that are trimmed with ribbon and fine lace. The dancers move like no other dancers, bringing the music and atmosphere alive."

One day I accidently dropped my flamenco doll and it smashed. I had loved that doll with all my heart and used to often daydream about being a flamenco dancer myself one day. I was distraught that it had smashed, and in my eyes, died. Now I see one of the skeletons dressed in a beautiful dress like my doll used to wear. My doll was beautiful and alive looking. I am confused as to why you would dress a skeleton like a flamenco doll. A skeleton is not living; it's dead, isn't it?

I approach the stall with curiosity and apprehension. There is a young boy trading and he welcomes me with a larger than life smile.

"Hello," he greets me.

There are other people looking at his souvenirs. He sells crosses, religious emblems, copal – a native incense, candles, skeleton dolls, paintings and artisan-handcrafted bracelets. The bracelets are loaded with various colored glass beads and silver charms that include skulls, flowers, religious pictures, crosses, skulls and heart lockets. I delicately handle one and look at the intricate detail.

"Do you like the bracelet?" the young boy asks.

"It is very unusual," I answer.

"It is a shrine bracelet," he explains, "to remember your dead."

I look up and he shows me, "You can put pictures of your deceased relatives in the heart lockets and when you wear the bracelet they will always be with you."

I place the bracelet back on the table and look at all of the other items on the stall. I have always been interested in art and study the paintings on display. The paintings include skeletons in various situations, such as dancing, getting married, cycling, etc. I don't find the paintings sinister because the skeletons are smiling in all of the scenes. In fact, some are funny.

The young boy informs me, "The artwork is not meant to be scary. It is meant to celebrate the spirit and honor the memory of those that have left us behind."

"What about the doll?" I ask, picking up the skeleton that first caught my attention.

"I call it a living-dead doll, but its real title is La Calavera Catrina. It's the skeleton of a woman and one of the most popular figures of the Day of the Dead celebrations."

"Day of the Dead," I repeat quietly, looking at the skeleton doll and remembering my smashed doll. "It's a day to remember the people that have left us behind?"

"Yes, that's right."

I buy the doll and head into the site where many souls have journeyed through the cycle of life and death. A large Mayan community once thrived here between 700 AD and 900 AD. Its history appears clouded in mystery.

I visit the Pyramid of Kukulkan. It towers above the other architecture at 98ft high. My leg muscles ache as I climb to the top where there is a terrific view of all the ruins. I can see elaborate and highly decorated ceremonial architecture, including temple pyramids, palaces and observatories. They are set near a jungle that stretches out over the horizon.

I have climbed 91 steps and am slightly out of breath; well a lot really. I am panting and puffing. It's got to be this heat to blame, not the fact that I am unfit. Having said that, there must be lots of unfit people here, because they all look out of breath.

There is a platform that is reached via one of four sides. Each side has 91 steps, totaling 364 steps. The top platform makes the 365th step.

I hear a tourist guide speaking to a small group, "The Mayans were masters of mathematics and invented the calendar we use today. The 365 steps represent a step for every day of the year."

I hear a gentleman reply to the guide and group, "The Mayans must have been very clever. I believe that they used to be able to know the date and time, depending upon where the sun was shining on the steps."

I feel happy to have a watch and a diary. The Mayan method sounds far too complicated for me.

I sit on one of the steps for a rest whilst watching and listening to the guide and escorted group.

One lady comments, "The pyramid has a structured feel about it."

The escort agrees, and points out, "Two sides have been restored and two left to show the condition before work commenced. Also, if you look closely, the Mayans developed hieroglyphic writing and there are Mayan symbols inscribed in the temple that represent sacred gods and spirits."

The group move on and for some reason I feel a need to close my eyes and take a moment to honor the gods and spirits. I feel my heart pound loudly and a magical energy flows through my body and over the steps.

When I open my eyes the shadow of the sun is playing on the stairs, causing the illusion of a snake processing down the pyramid.

I don't know why, but I keenly follow the illusion down the temple, across the grass and to an area where there are no tourists. I am directed to a hidden vertical hole with narrow stairs leading downwards. I follow the steps in darkness, holding on to the walls for guidance. I can feel Mayan carvings etched into the walls pass under my fingers. I reach the bottom of the stairs and now that my eyes are used to the dark, a bizarre world is brought to my attention. A beautiful green pool of unknown stretches out before me with steam rising from it. I can hear a commentary coming through the speakers positioned throughout the underground. I have apparently reached a natural sink hole, called a cenote. It is also known as a sacred well or a well of sacrifice.

In the dark, I can vaguely see the outline of other people, but for some reason I can't hear them speak. I can only presume that this is because the air is thick and musty.

I feel a chill run up my spine as I listen to the deep-voiced commentary.

"Pre-Columbian Maya sacrificed objects and human beings into the sink hole as a form of worship to the Maya rain god Chaac. Gold, silver, jade, pottery and human remains are believed to have been found in here. A study of the human remains show evidence of wounds consistent with human sacrifice."

I feel a chill run up my spine and my body feels cold.

The musty smell of the past that is still present after over 1000 years, is suddenly replaced with a strong smell of incense.

I hear my name being whispered, "Saskia, Saskia."

I turn but there is nobody there although I feel a presence. I walk back towards the steps to exit, but a sudden strong wind holds me back and it feels like someone is in front of me, blocking my way. There is a barrier preventing me from leaving no matter how hard I try, I am pushing with all my force to escape. For a moment, I feel a tingling sensation go through my body and it feels like someone is passing through me with incredible sadness and desperation. I feel pale and fragile as an overwhelming fear creeps through me. My body starts to shake and my teeth chatter as I feel my body turn even colder, ice cold. There are two shadows a short distance away from me that look like they are dancing from side to side and slowly heading in my direction. The shadows disappear then return, disappear then return.

I feel that death is waiting in the shadows, but I don't want to be taken to a place of unwanted souls. I want to live, as life is for living. A flash of something lights up the underground. There is nobody else here, but me and the darkness.

I hear a scream and I feel a body brush past me but when I turn, no one is there. All I want is to get the hell out of here. I manage to run, feeling a presence like I am being watched. I am relieved as I approach lightness at the top of the steps, leaving a very dark place behind.

I know too well about dark places. I was in a very dark place when I suffered from depression. I used to feel sadness and desperation, just like whatever passed through my body at the well of sacrifice. It was the same feeling, a feeling of being lost. I also know that depression is accompanied by paranoia. I just hope that I am not heading towards that dark place again. I wipe tears away from my eyes and cheeks. I have got myself worked up and know that I should take some of my mood stabilizers. I don't want to believe what has just happened, it must have been paranoia. I will believe that I was just frightened in the dark. I will be fine.

I take a sip of my water and pour the remainder over my face. I must have had a moment of madness. It was probably the darkness frightening me. When I was little I insisted upon sleeping with my light on. I used to think that there were demons that would come into my room. I don't like the dark and in the light of the day I now have clarity. My mind was playing games again.

I walk towards El Castillo. Tourists are standing facing the foot of the temple and shouting their own names as instructed by the guides. As they shout, their echo comes back as a piercing shriek and I have to cover my ears. It sounds like their voices screaming back.

I shout my name, releasing any tension accumulated from the cenote.

I shout, "Saskia." My name echoes back, becoming fainter and fainter until barely perceptible, "Saskia, Saskia, Saskia."

I am contemplating going inside the temple as a lady comes out and tells me, "The guide takes you down dark, humid corridors and chambers."

I decide to pass on this one. The thought of darkness scares me.

I study the map and decide to visit the Great Ballcourt that is totally open to the sky. I need some fresh air and lightness in my life. There are raised temples at each end of the ballcourt, where Mayans used to watch the ball game. I am not quite sure how the game was played, but from reading the provided literature, I believe it was a blood sport where the winning captain would have his head presented to the losing captain. The Mayans believed this to be the ultimate honor, because the winning captain got a direct ticket to heaven instead of going through the thirteen steps that Mayans believed they had to go through in order to reach heaven. Perhaps the Mayans believed that you had thirteen lives before going to heaven, just like we believe a cat has nine lives. Strange thought!

I walk through the Temple of Warriors. There are hundreds of columns carved with reliefs. A vibe of sadness comes from within this space and I feel the urge to leave. As I walk away the sun breaks through between the columns, leaving a warm glow on my back.

I find the Nunnery quite interesting. Every wall has reliefs and paintings decorating it. Some of the paintings look sad, some joyful, some stand out more than others. I am sure that the Mayans that added to these over the years were trying to tell us something in their own unique way. I only wish I knew what they were trying to say. As I stand contemplating this thought, a furry creature runs past my leg making me jump back to my own century.

I visit the observatory and the El Caracol. I like the look of these locations and am pleased that I have left the best to last. I find the El Caracol very interesting. The Mayans developed astronomy and they built a tower that was used entirely for this. Its windows are aligned with the four cardinal directions, north, east, south and west. It was built so that these windows align with the equinox sunsets.

Apparently, according to an information board, there are sun signs and moon signs which both depend on your date of birth and the life you lead. I study the signs but find the information confusing. The signs advise me that I am living in the past, although I am here in the present.

I refer to a female member of staff and query, "What did the Mayans mean by this?"

She tries to help and looks at my date of birth, the signs and tries to understand the life I should lead.

"How strange!" she frowns, "There are two contradictory propositions and I am unable to assent to either of them."

"What do you mean?" I ask.

"Doubt brings into question some notion of a perceived reality. I suppose that reality is merely an illusion and your view of the world may not be as accurate as you think."

I am unsure what she is talking about and would like to spend longer here, but I am conscious of time, as I have arrangements in place to meet Miguel for dinner. I want to go back to my hotel and get showered and changed. I leave the lady still looking at my sun and moon signs, scratching her head.

As I leave the site, I see the young boy who sold me my skeleton doll. He is packing away his stall. I wave to him and he smiles and comes running over.

"Wait!" he shouts.

"Is everything ok?" I ask, turning back.

"You forgot your living-dead doll's love." He hands me a skeleton of a man dressed in a suit wearing a top hat. "Your living-dead doll has a living-dead partner."

I look at the skeleton and think about what Julia told me at the rehabilitation centre. "Everybody has a soulmate," the boy advises. "Please take this so they can be together." He skips off.

It's been quite an emotionally draining, tiring day and I really don't think that I can face the chicken bus on the return journey, so I opt for a taxi and relax as air blows through the open window on the way back to my hotel.

CHAPTER TEN

Scott is in reception upon my return to the hotel. He is dressed very smartly, like he is going somewhere special.

"What's happened to you?" he asks in a joking tone, looking me up and down.

"What do you mean?" I query.

"You look like you have been dragged through a bush backwards." He laughs his cheeky laugh that makes me laugh too.

"You are so complimentary," I sarcastically observe. "I have been walking around Chichen Itza all day in the hot heat and my feet are killing me. I can feel the blisters developing, despite wearing comfortable shoes."

I take my sandals off to relieve the pain. The cold marble floor provides instant relief.

He smirks, "What you need is a Disruption Tequila trip to bring you back to life."

"I think that one of your trips would definitely finish me off," I laugh. "What I really need is a lovely hot bubble bath and an early night, but I have promised to meet Miguel later for a meal."

"Oh yes. How is the lovely Miguel? Is it still love at first sight?" He jokes.

I decide to change the topic of conversation because he is obviously in one of his silly moods, going by the daft large smirk on his face.

"Are you here to organize another trip?" I ask, lifting one of my feet and rubbing it gently.

"I'm collecting some of the hotel guests for a beach party. You are welcome to come with Miguel if you like."

"Thanks for asking, but I fancy a quiet night. My best friend is flying from Manchester this evening to join me, and I am expecting her to arrive in the morning. She is bringing her young son, so I am expecting to be rushed off my feet when they get here. After today, I think that my feet need plenty of resting ready for him. I think that an early night might be a good idea, so that I have lots of energy for them."

"Oh, sounds interesting." He raises his eyebrows and smirks, "Ricky and Johnny will be in their element when they find out that you'll be able to introduce them to a single Manchester lass. When will we all get to meet her?" he teases.

I smile and play along with his amusement, "Firstly, you mean to ask when YOU will get to meet her. Let's be honest Scott, you aren't really bothered about Ricky and Johnny meeting her. You want her all to yourself, don't you?" I laugh at my own joke.

He elbows me playfully, "Let's keep that little secret between us, shall we?"

I carry on, "Secondly, she isn't a beautiful girl from Manchester."

His face drops. "Well, if she isn't beautiful, introduce her to Ricky and Johnny then."

We both laugh at his cheek.

"She's beautiful alright, very beautiful," I tell him. "She just isn't from Manchester. She lives there but she's originally from Ireland."

I laugh but Scott doesn't. For some reason he goes serious on me.

"My ex-girlfriend was from Ireland. If your friend is Irish, I shall definitely be staying out of the way. Don't really fancy another broken heart."

I think for a moment that he is still joking, but his facial expression has turned to sadness, and his smile has disappeared. The atmosphere has changed. The woman that broke his heart obviously meant the world to him, and possibly still does.

I want to reassure him that he will find somebody nice one day, but whilst thinking what to say, he opens up to me, "I have to move on with my life and I will eventually find somebody, maybe a soulmate. Perhaps I will find somebody who makes my pulse race similar to the effect that Miguel has on you." He pauses for a moment, "I said that you looked a little rough after walking around Chichen Itza all day, but to be honest, really honest, you appear to have had a glow about you since you met Miguel, and I don't think that it's your suntan." He smiles and touches my arm. "I'm really happy for you."

I nod. It's nice to speak to somebody about how I feel and as Catherine isn't here, I feel confident confiding in Scott.

I hesitate, "Please don't repeat this, Scott."

"Ok, your secret is safe with me," he reassures me.

"Miguel and I have a magnetic connection that I have never felt before with anybody. I think that this could be the real thing."

He looks puzzled. "How can you be so certain? You hardly know him but seem really confident about this."

My mind goes back to the Psychiatric Rehabilitation Centre, and I think about Julia and Chang.

"A friend once told me that when you meet your soulmate, you will just know."

I suddenly remember the cherub that Julia gave to me.

"When are your guests due to meet you here?" I ask.

"In approximately twenty minutes. Why?"

I grasp his hand. "Great! You have to come with me. I have something to show you."

In my room, I open the front-zipped pocket of my suitcase and delicately present the little blue box that Julia gave to me. Scott sits on the edge of my bed, watching my actions.

"What are you showing me?" he asks.

"I was given this by a very dear friend. There is a crystal with a cherub shooting an arrow inside the box. Every time I look at it….it has an unusual effect on me." I pause and take a deep breath. "My friend Julia told me that when it didn't have the same influence anymore, then the cherub would have shot its arrow and I would have found true love."

"What are you waiting for then? Open it," he demands, "I can't wait to see this, you are crazy mad, in a nice way of course."

I close my eyes for a moment, take another deep breath and slowly open the box removing Cupid. I wait for that feeling but there is nothing, it doesn't come. The effect has gone. I look at Scott for his response but instead witness a magical glow coming from his body as his fingers reach out to touch the crystal.

"You are right, it's beautiful," he tells me. His mouth opens in amazement.

I know that it is having the same impact on him as it once had on me.

"It's yours. Please have it." I hand it to him with pleasure. I have a contented heart knowing that the time has come for Cupid to help someone else, just like Julia told me.

"I couldn't."

"You must, and you will," I insist. "Julia told me that when I had found true love I would know, and I honestly think that this moment has arrived. I believe that the time has come to pass it on to somebody else who needs Cupid's help, and I think that somebody is you."

"What about you? It's yours."

"I don't think that Cupid needs to help me anymore, I think he has helped me as much as he probably can." Scott slings his arms around me for a tight cuddle.

"Thank you. I will look after it with all my heart."

I know he will. He holds me tightly in his arms for a moment before leaving to meet his Tequila party guests, whilst I get ready to meet Miguel.

I can't help but think about what an unusual day I have had. There are still lots of questions to be answered in my life, but I also feel like I have found the part of myself that I was looking for. It's also lovely to have a true friend like Scott in my life. Sometimes it almost feels like he has come into my life to serve some profound purpose. He keeps finding missing pieces in the jigsaw of my life and I wonder if he will help me find the rest.

As I shower in the lovely coconut oil shower gel that the hotel has left in the bathroom, the anxiety of the day washes away down the plughole, right where it belongs. It appears that the cherub has helped me to find my true love and my heart feels a warm glow. I can't wait to see Miguel tonight.

When I arrive at Palm Wellbeing Resort, I find Miguel is pacing the empty beach in short distances, backwards and forwards. I observe his dark shadow against the sunset from a distance. He looks a worried man and I am concerned.

I approach him slowly and he looks in my direction but doesn't acknowledge me.

"Hello," I say quietly.

He stops pacing and looks me up and down. Only at this point do I realize that he has been crying. His gorgeous eyes look puffy and bloodshot, yet I still feel myself sinking into them. I feel his upset and walk towards him to try to hold him, but he doesn't want my comforting, he gently pushes me away.

"Don't Saskia," he says calmly, "This can't go on any longer."

I am startled so ask, "What can't go on?" I don't need an answer because I already know what he is going to say, due to the way that he looks at me. I feel that he doesn't want to be with me anymore.

"Is it us? Do you not want to see me again?" I feel my eyes start to fill.

I have got carried away dreaming again. This was probably nothing more than a holiday fling to him and I've made it into something that it's not. I am really stupid and annoyed with myself. I can't help how I feel though, I love him. I haven't known him for long, yet I feel like I have known him forever, and I have never felt like this about anybody. It's really strange.

I wish that I had the energy to fight for him, but I understand that if he doesn't feel the same way about me as I do about him, I would be fighting a losing battle.

As I turn to walk away I remember Julia once telling me that if something is meant to be then it will come together.

I stop in my path and turn, "You will always be with me, Miguel, even when we go our own separate ways. You will always be in my mind and I will never forget whatever it was that we had. It was special. I don't regret it, even if you do."

I start to walk away again but hear him shout, "Aren't you going to ask why? And what's happened between us?"

I stop but don't turn around. I don't want him to see tears rolling down my cheeks, and my mascara is probably smudged by now. I haven't even brought my sunglasses to hide behind.

He is close behind me and confuses me with what he says next, "I'd give up forever to be with you, and to touch you tonight, even if we were to die tomorrow. What about you?"

I need to tell him. I might not get another chance. "I love you and I want to be with you whatever it takes."

I turn to look at him and I shrug my shoulders, "If it's true what my grandma used to say, we are eternal beings in an eternal world, so I would be with you, even if we were to die tomorrow."

I look up to heaven and wonder if she is there, or if she is somewhere else, somewhere special like where she said she was going.

Miguel comes close and runs his fingers down my face. I close my eyes enjoying his touch.

"Do you believe?" he asks, "Believe in life after death?"

I gasp, then reply, "I feel disconcertment, an uneasy sensation of having done something or having been in an identical situation before, but I am unsure why. From the moment I arrived in Mexico, it has felt familiar. Maybe I have been here before in some life. Maybe I know you from a previous life. I believe I do."

He holds me from behind and wraps his arms around me whilst we face the ocean.

He suggests, "Perhaps you are feeling déjà visite."

"What's that?" I enquire.

He whispers in my ear, "It is when a person visits a new place and feels that it is familiar."

"Maybe," I remark.

"You could be experiencing déjà senti though, which is the recovery of long, sought after information."

His body is warm, but I feel a cold feeling suddenly run through my veins and body. I know Miguel feels it because he pulls away, and I feel lost in myself as my teeth start to chatter. He walks down to the sea edge and throws a pebble into the sea. I rub my arms to warm myself and approach him to stand by his side. It is still really hot so there is no way that I should be so cold.

"What's happening? I need to know," I ask.

He carries on throwing pebbles in the sea before answering. "I know what will happen next and it's not good. If I tell you what I know, it will distress you and I worry that you won't want to see me ever again, despite what you said."

I watch a pebble skim the water and sink. "If we are to be together, it's only fair that you tell me whatever you are keeping from me."

There is a long silence between us. "Please," I plead.

He nods. "I tried out a new meditation class today that was supposed to help you connect with your spirit and bring you peace. I couldn't concentrate because all I could think about was you."

"That's nice, isn't it? I've thought about you lots today."

"I spoke with the spiritualist who was running the class and she told me to go and get you. I travelled to the ruins, but I couldn't see you, instead I found the shadow people. The dark shadows scared the hell out of me making me feel insane."

I feel myself go cold again and I don't like the feeling. I want the coldness and the shadows to go away and never come back. I have been looking for excuses for them, but now I am hit with the reality of their existence. The shadow people are real, and they frighten me.

He faces me, "You know, don't you? You've seen them too, haven't you? I can tell by the expression on your face." He sounds angry.

I look down at the floor. "I don't know, I saw something, I saw shadows of people when there was nobody human in my presence. Please tell me who the shadow people are. I've never heard of them before now. I thought they were figments of my imagination today."

Miguel pauses then tells me, "A shadow person is when someone has passed away, but their soul is still earthbound. The soul is on earth as a shadow person."

"What do they want?" I ask concerned and worried.

"They are shadows of us. They are our lost souls from our past life. We are seeing them because we have been here before in another life. There's a time lapse when death has occurred, but the soul has survived. They want something but I'm unsure what."

I'm shaking, "How do you know?" I fear that I am asking questions that Miguel can't answer.

He shakes his head, "I didn't know that they existed, I thought that I had seen ghosts. All sorts of weird things have been seen at the ruins. I mentioned it to a spiritualist who is staying here, and she put me straight. They are here for us."

I feel ice cold, frozen in my tracks. "I have had dreams," I disclose. "No, I have had nightmares actually, bad nightmares." I ramble and come to my own conclusion, "We are going to die. I have dreamt it. We are going to die together in a car. This is their way of warning us."

My stomach cramps as I keel over and feel like I want to be sick. My world is spinning fast, faster than I can think, and I feel dizzy.

Miguel kneels at the side of me and puts his arm around me. "I know. I have had nightmares, Saskia. We are in a car travelling together and the car drives off a cliff."

He pulls a tissue out of his pocket and wipes his head. He is burning up. I don't know what is worse, the burning up or the freezing feeling.

I take a moment then stumble to my feet, "I need to go," I repeat, "I need to go now."

Miguel grabs my hand tighter than I like, "I love you. Please stay. We need to deal with this together."

I have to look away to stop myself crying, "When I saw you last, you told me that you believed the aim of life is to live and to live is to be aware. Life is for living, Miguel, and if I go now I can ensure you will live. I love you and this is my way of rescuing you and saving both of our lives. If I leave, we can't die together, and the nightmare won't happen."

We hold each other tightly, crying. I contemplate spending one more night with him, but I worry that it might have severe consequences, and it is now time for us to say our goodbyes.

I walk away from him heartbroken, unsure where life shall take me. Along the beach and the sea edge, there are only my footsteps trailing behind me, nothing lasts forever. I don't know where I'm going, and I feel in a time lapse, like I am capturing my life and reliving events and experiences. I have been here before but unsure when. I am at my nerves end and I feel jumpy. There is somebody with me but nobody in sight. It is a feeling that somebody is there watching me, walking with me, there all the time. I turn around and look but there is only my shadow at the side of me. My lonely depressed shadow, which is my reflection, making the same movements and being my life, without my heartbeat.

I walk into the calm sea to lose whatever or whoever is with me; the shadow. I once heard that water is a symbol of emotion and the subconscious, and I feel that it is calling me. I keep walking until the sea reaches my waist and I can swim. The water is slightly warm and there is a strong smell of seaweed which is messing with my thoughts. The flowing movement deals with my emotions and the stirring movements of my deeper mind. I'm not in control of my emotions or my thoughts, they are controlling me, and the sea is also controlling me. My clothes are feeling heavy, really heavy and the sea wants to take me to the dark beneath, like it took the car over the cliff edge in my nightmares. This is when my soul apparently survived and is now haunting me as a shadow person.

The sky is dark and there is a dark cloud hovering over me. I look up at the movement of the sky. Dark clouds are circling above, symbolizing confusion and clouded judgment. My time has come to let go. I can't fight life, shadows or obstacles anymore.

There is a flash in the sky, like lightning, and out of the mists of my deepest thoughts my choices become clear. What on earth am I considering doing? This is a message from my higher self and the universe. I see my shadow, my soul, waving arms in the air grasping my attention. I am here to live and see life through, no matter what it may bring. I will not be taken, not now, not again. I am prepared to fight for my life, love and soul.

I stumble out of the water, weighted down by my wet clothes and sit on some rocks at the top of the beach shivering, when I see something shining. Perhaps it's a penny? I need some luck. I lean forward to pick it up. It's not a penny, its Scott's cherub. What is it doing here?

I look up at a shadow covering the little light available from the moon. Scott looks down at me before seating himself on a rock.

"I am the messenger of important information," he smiles.

Despite being angry about him losing the cherub, I am pleased to see him, relieved to see him. He will keep me safe.

"Your cherub," I hand it to him and smile, teeth chattering.

"I was sat here thinking earlier today and it must have fallen out of my pocket. I should have taken more care."

"It's ok," I say, with my teeth chattering.

He explains, "Whilst out walking, I stopped here for a rest and was looking at it. I researched and found out that cherubs are symbolic of divine messages. This cherub was really glistening like it was trying to tell me something. I didn't know that I had left it here, but I think the cherub perhaps led me here to find you."

He takes his jacket off and places it around my shoulders to keep me warm.

"Have you been for a swim?" he asks, with a baffled look on his face.

I don't answer but instead ask, "If you weren't looking for the cherub, what are you doing here now?"

"Miguel is worried about you and he phoned me. The Tequila party is just a little further along the beach, so it was no trouble to have a walk down here and look for you. He said that he felt you would be heading back to the hotel this way, but he didn't want to upset you by coming after you himself."

"Thanks," I say with gratitude.

"I don't know what's going on with you and Miguel, but you need to talk, Saskia. The man's going out of his mind."

I know the feeling.

"I phoned him when I saw you from a distance sat on the rocks, so he knows you are ok. He said you probably need some time to think things through, but he's there if and when you are ready, whatever that's supposed to mean.

I look down, ashamed with my actions. "Thanks Scott. I appreciate everything you know?"

He nods, "I know. Now let's get you back to the hotel before you get a cold. Your friend is coming tomorrow, isn't she? You don't want to be poorly for her."

He holds out his hand to pull me up from the rocks and we walk together, talking about his Tequila party. There are four of us in total, including our shadows, which walk by our sides. Despite not ever taking notice previously, I now feel comfortable in the company of my own personal shadow, it's my soul. I think my now shadow is here to protect me. It's the other shadow people I have my concerns about. What does the soul from my previous life want from me?

CHAPTER ELEVEN

It is a pleasure to see both Catherine and Joshua. Catherine looks pale and tired when I greet them in the hotel reception and Joshua appears full of energy. He runs to me and wraps his arms around me. I bend and give him a big kiss on his head.

Catherine's mouth opens wide, "Wow, some hotel," she remarks, looking round the vast reception.

"It gets better," I tell her. "I've got the key to your room and your luggage will be taken there by the porter."

"Really?" she asks in disbelief and amazement. "You mean that I don't have to carry the cases myself. That's great!"

I don't think Catherine has ever stayed in a 5-star hotel before either, going by her expression. I'm sure that she will become accustomed to the luxury and care offered.

Alonso suddenly appears carrying a tray of drinks to greet the new arrivals.

"Would the beautiful lady like a refreshing cocktail following her long journey from sunny Manchester?"

Catherine looks at him eyes wide and laughs, "Whoever told you that Manchester was sunny. It was pouring down when I left. It's always grim and raining in Manchester at this time of year."

"I know. I am only joking," he says. "I know you flew over a rainbow to come here."

Catherine looks at him, clueless as to what he is talking about and I just smile to myself.

I introduce them to each other. "This is my friend Catherine," I tell Alonso. "Catherine, this is Alonso. He works in the bar and loves serving you Tequila."

Alonso laughs, "You know that the hotel has to promote it, Saskia."

"I hope there is some Tequila in this cocktail," Catherine interrupts. "I really need a strong drink to get over that flight."

"There most certainly is, Madam." Alonso smiles and hands Joshua a glass of juice. "No Tequila in this though."

I smile with gratitude. "Thanks, Alonso. No doubt you will see us about."

"Can't wait!" he says, then looks at Joshua, "Especially you, little guy." Catherine smiles and a look of relief spreads across her face.

"Are you ok?" I ask.

"Yes, I was just a little nervous travelling all this way with Joshua, but now I am here, I just feel that everything is going to be ok."

"I'm here to look after you, so everything will be fine," I remark.

We make our way to her room, so both her and Joshua can change into their swimwear, ready for some Mexican rays of sunshine.

It is busy by the pool today, but Catherine sleeps through all of the noise. There are clatters from the poolside bar and restaurant, chit chat from the crowds, music loudly playing from the entertainment team and a running commentary from someone on a speaker about who's playing and winning at volleyball.

I have agreed to play with Joshua, so she can have a rest. The long journey has drained her energy. Apparently, Joshua slept throughout the flight, but she had to stay awake to keep an eye on him, just in case he woke up. I thought that she looked tired when she arrived. She usually looks fresh-faced and young, but today she had dark circles under her eyes like she hasn't slept for days and her complexion looked a little blotchy. She doesn't appear to be her usual self. I am sure that a rest, sun and some good food will do her a world of good.

Joshua and I splash in the pool having fun. He takes my mind off the events of the last couple of days. He wears his armbands and thinks it is funny to keep trying to paddle away from me. I play along with his game, "Come here cheeky monkey," I shout. "I will tickle you when I catch you."

He laughs his head off and makes me laugh too. He has an amazing laugh. Come to think about it, it's similar to Scott's laugh, infectious.

I hear my name being called and look up. I am surprised to see Johnny and Rick heading in my direction. I wave at them from the pool and Rick starts to skip towards me in a silly manner, kicking out his legs as he moves along in tune with the music that is playing. Even Joshua stops playing our game and looks at him in disbelief, as do most of the guests. Johnny shakes his head like he normally does when he is in the company of Rick, obviously embarrassed by his actions and staying a few steps behind.

"Saskia, I've found you," Rick says.

"Yes," I reply, confused as to what he may want.

"Who's this little chap?" he asks in a friendly manner, bending down to tickle Joshua under the chin. Rick's eyes glisten with mischief and his floppy blond hair falls in front of them. Suddenly, his sunglasses fall from his head and drift in the water. Joshua starts to point at him and laugh. Rick being Rick starts to panic about dropping his glasses and leans to get them but loses his footing and falls head first into the pool, fully dressed in his chinos and sorrowful Spice Girls t-shirt. I hope he hasn't been drinking Tequila, because this is bringing back memories from the Pirate night. The crowds cheer and clap as though he is part of the entertainment and I laugh, despite getting a drenching from his large splash. Poor Joshua rubs his eyes where the water has splashed over his face and head.

"Please pass me that towel," I ask Johnny, pointing to my sunbed and beach towel.

Johnny rolls his eyes at his friend and obliges. I dry Joshua's face, but he doesn't seem too concerned. He appears to be fascinated with Rick, who is now pulling funny faces at him.

"So, what brings you here?" I ask Johnny.

"Scott told us that your friend was arriving today, and we thought we should call in to say 'Hello' with her being your friend," he smiles.

"That's really nice of you. She would appreciate that. Thank you."

Despite being a little crazy, these guys are really nice people who have gone out of their way to make an impression.

"Where is she then?" Rick asks as he pulls himself out of the pool.

I pass Joshua to him and use the steps to climb out of the pool. I wrap a towel around Joshua and he sits on the sunbed contentedly eating bread sticks, watching what's going on around him. I throw Rick a towel to dry himself off.

"She's sleeping," I reply.

"In her room?" he presumes.

Before I have chance to explain, we all hear a very loud blast noise. Even the people a number of sunbeds down the line look in our direction.

Rick pretends to jump then makes one of his scenes, "Was that you?" he asks loudly to play up to the crowds, whilst looking at me. "I thought that you were a lady."

I feel myself go bright red with embarrassment. "It certainly was not," I reply.

Johnny looks at me with disgust.

I insist, "It wasn't me. Honest."

Joshua looks at us, "It's M…Mummy," he stutters in toddler fashion.

Rick rolls his eyes at Johnny and then looks in my direction. "No wonder he wants his mummy. I would too. That was disgusting. I hope his mummy is more of a lady than you."

Joshua points at his mummy, Catherine, who is tossing and turning in the sun, and we all look in her direction. At the same time, we all hear a loud grunt from her.

"Oh my god, What's that?" Johnny looks in disbelief.

I can't help but start to laugh. Catherine has placed a soaking wet pink towel over her face and is snoring beneath it. The towel has clung to her face and it looks like a pig snorting. She lifts herself up slightly in her sleep, grunting really loud. Johnny and Rick take a step back, still looking at her like she is some sort of alien. I suddenly realize that she hasn't had her bikini line done and red pubic hair is streaming from her costume line. That's just not like her. She is usually so particular. I quickly take off my towel and throw it over the middle of her body, before Johnny and Rick notice. I doubt that she will live down the snoring with these two, never mind them spotting anything else too.

"Is she ok?" Johnny asks, "I mean …She isn't suffocating under her towel, is she?"

"She's just sleeping. That's all," I sigh. "I bet both of you snore in your sleep. It's only natural, especially when you are really tired, like she is."

They both shrug their shoulders together like something out of Laurel and Hardy.

Rick points at Joshua, "Well, little guy, if you want a break from these women, you can always come with us."

Joshua shrugs his shoulders copying them and Rick and Johnny laugh and carry on shrugging their shoulders making a joke of the situation, whilst taking steps back to go.

"Are you in the bar later?" Johnny asks.

"I'm not sure yet," I answer. "It will depend how she is feeling." I look over at Catherine.

Rick nods, "Ok, no doubt we will get to meet her soon enough, hopefully in less pig-like form."

We say our goodbyes and I lie in the sun wondering how to actually tell Catherine about what's gone on. I think I will also buy her a beauty treatment as a surprise. It might be easier than telling her that her bush is overgrown.

We decide to order room service this evening and share a bottle of wine. Joshua had some pasta earlier and is now content, fast asleep in bed, so it makes sense for me to go to her room. Despite there being lots of Mexican food on the menu, we opt for burger and chips, smothered in tomato ketchup and mayonnaise, and sit out on the balcony overlooking the dark ocean whilst we eat. It looks a different place to how it looks during the day. In the light of day, it is a nice place to be and is full of life but at night it looks dark, mysterious and a place of the unknown.

I would like to discuss my concerns about the shadow people with my best friend, but she may think that I am mentally poorly again, and I don't want her to be worrying. I therefore decide not to mention it. She appears to have something on her own mind anyway, without my problems. She has seemed a little distant since she arrived. She is a private person and I know she wouldn't want me to pry. I am sure that she will open up to me when she is ready.

"I was thinking about tomorrow," she says.

"Is there something that you would like to do?" I ask.

She leaves the balcony and shortly returns with a leaflet, "I picked this up in reception earlier. It's a trip to a butterfly kingdom," she says. "I think Joshua would like to go and I fancy getting out and about and seeing something, rather than just sitting by the pool all day thinking about things that are out of my control."

"Like what?" I ask.

"I've just been thinking about my ex. I need something to take my mind off him."

"It's a long time ago since you separated. Has he been in touch, or has something happened?"

"No, that's the problem. I think that the penny has now finally dropped that he's not coming back to me. I lived in hope, but he's probably happy with somebody else now."

She has tears in her eyes and I give her a tissue.

I try to reassure her but don't want to build her hopes up. "He might be somewhere now, thinking about you."

"Saskia, he could have got in touch but didn't. I don't know where he is, and I will probably never see him again. I just need to get over him, put him to the back of my mind and move on with my life. I don't even know why I'm thinking about him again after all of this time."

"Many thoughts suddenly appear from our subconscious minds. I've realized that recently." I have taken the time to ponder the situation.

Catherine looks at me intrigued and asks, "What do you mean?"

I think for a moment about how to explain what I have just said. "Well, our subconscious mind stores all of our previous life experiences, our beliefs, our memories, our skills, all situations that we have been through, and all images that we have ever seen, whilst our conscious mind is responsible for logic."

Catherine nods, "Yes, I suppose that our minds are split in two. Part is material that was once conscious but has been forgotten, whilst the remainder is our active consciousness. I suppose that our subconscious mind is like a storage room of everything that is currently not in our conscious mind. My subconscious mind is now playing games with me, creating false beliefs about my past relationship, and really my conscious mind needs to address this logically."

I sigh, "Gosh, we have been having some seriously weird conversations recently."

Catherine suddenly bursts out laughing and I join her. In fact, we laugh until tears run down our faces. It's lovely to have my friend back with me.

"So, are we off to the butterfly garden tomorrow?" I ask.

Catherine smiles, "Yes, I need to get to the beautician's at some point too, before I next go to the pool or beach." She blushes, "I need to get myself waxed. I've had that much on my mind that I forgot to sort it before coming away. I'm surprised nobody has noticed or said anything. I'm disgusted with myself."

I laugh, "Well actually, I thought it was pretty disgusting too, so I bought you a beauty voucher to use at the hotel." I hand it to her, "I was going to discreetly say something, but since you've brought it up, I don't need to."

We both laugh again. "Thanks, Saskia. I'll ring reception now to see if I can get an appointment in the morning, before we go to the butterfly kingdom. Hopefully the redness will have then gone down by the next time I put my costume on."

"You are so practical, Catherine," I roll my eyes and laugh.

CHAPTER TWELVE

Whilst Catherine is at the beautician's, Joshua and I enjoy a leisurely breakfast of croissants, orange juice and coffee. We sit outside on a veranda overlooking the beach, where a team of people play volleyball.

He is excited about going to the butterfly kingdom. He has never seen a butterfly before. I show him the pictures in the leaflet. "What is it?" he asks, innocently.

"It's a butterfly," I reply. "Isn't it beautiful?"

"It is. Can I stroke it?" he asks.

I hear a loud laugh and instantly know who it is.

I look up and greet Scott who is now looking over my shoulder at the leaflet, chuckling at Joshua's question.

"Good morning and hello little pal," he addresses Joshua. "Wow, you must be a lucky boy if you are going to see the butterflies."

Joshua nods at him.

"Do you have a pussy cat or a doggy at home that you stroke?"

Joshua shakes his head.

"Have you stroked a pussy cat or a doggy?"

Joshua nods. I look at Scott intrigued. He is a natural with children. He really has gained Joshua's attention.

"Well, butterflies are different. They are really tiny and really delicate. If you touch them or try to stroke them, you could hurt them. You can look at them and chase them, and it can be lots of fun, but never touch them because it can damage their wings and you wouldn't want to hurt them, would you?"

"I won't stroke them," Joshua states, shaking his head.

"He's never seen a butterfly before," I inform Scott.

He looks at Joshua, "Well, they are beautiful. They have lots of beautiful patterns on their wings and they are sometimes colorful. I think that they look like flying flowers."

"Flying flowers," Joshua repeats intrigued.

"Yes, flying flowers," Scott answers him then looks at me, "Anyway, I had best get going, work to do. I will catch up with you later, Saskia."

He waves goodbye to Joshua who gives him a beautiful big smile.

The butterfly kingdom is a large glass dome. A double entry door is used to ensure that no butterflies escape. We join the queue where we form a group of ten with some other visitors.

We are informed by a worker, "Once in the dome you can wander around at your own leisure, but we need to group you for entry. You enter the first doors and when they are closed the second set of doors slowly open so no butterflies escape."

We act as instructed.

Joshua jumps up and down, "I am excited, Mummy."

The dome feels larger inside than what it looks from the outside. There are sheets and sheets of glass that are penetrated by the heat from outside, and there are large trees that overpower my existence.

Millions of butterfly wings unfold in front of my eyes, as they lift their delicate bodies into the warm air. They first catch my eye as tiny ghost-like flashes. It actually takes my breath away. The bright colored wings with bold black markings look like vast stained-glass windows and at times block out the blue of the sky seen through the dome. They dip and soar, flitting between branches and sunbeams. Even the tree trunks are coated with butterflies resting their wings, from the bottoms to the highest branches.

I watch as visitors entering the dome look up, wide eyed. Their faces beam with excitement and at appreciation of this natural marvel. Cameras and phones emerge and are pointed in the air. Photographs are being taken for memories. I join in, taking a photograph with my phone, a photograph for my album, my memory, a record of a special moment and something important in my life.

Both Catherine and I smile as Joshua breaks into a sprint, joyously chasing butterflies that he has no hope of catching, but that's not the point, he is enjoying himself and it is a pleasure to see.

Catherine bursts with pride, smiling, "Well, look at my little boy. He is pretending to fly."

She walks towards him, picking him up tightly in her arms and spinning him around.

Joshua giggles with pleasure, "Look Mummy, flying flowers. They are flying flowers."

I watch with contentment, admiring their relationship and closeness, as they giggle together, holding each other tight. It's a bond that will never be forgotten or broken. I think about the bond that I had with Miguel. That will be remembered forever, but it has been allowed to be broken by the shadow people. I want to put the shadow people to the back of my mind today and enjoy my time with Catherine and Joshua. Unfortunately, they are still here haunting me in the subconscious part of my mind.

Streams run throughout the dome and there are little bridges and walkways taking you to different areas of the dome. The butterflies seem to really like Catherine as they choose to follow her and land on her like she is a tree.

"They flutter around me and keep landing on my head, hands and body," she says.

Both Joshua and I giggle, enjoying the moment, although I feel Catherine is getting a little frustrated.

She scratches herself, "They are making me itch."

A staff member approaches her, "Why are the butterflies landing on me?" Catherine asks him.

He pokes his nose in her neck and sniffs her like a sniffer dog. Catherine's face is a picture of both worry and amusement and I can't help but start to laugh.

"It's because you smell beautiful," he eventually answers in broken English, and then walks away.

"Looks like you have pulled there," I joke.

I don't think Catherine sees the funny side of it and is frustrated, "Why couldn't he just say it was my perfume, without sniffing and literally licking my neck. The butterflies made my skin itch, he made it crawl."

There is extensive butterfly education signage throughout the dome and the sniffer dog's comment is eventually explained. I see an information board advising that if you wear light floral perfume or white clothing, like Catherine is, it encourages the butterflies to land upon you.

Catherine reads the board and sighs with relief. "Thank goodness for that. I thought he was some sort of creep. He just must not have been able to speak very good English and therefore couldn't explain properly."

In a section of the dome is a tropical botanical garden with a waterfall. It splashes water in the air creating the effect of falling rain and makes small pools of water form on the ground. I don't see many butterflies in this area. The ones that I do see are hiding in the flowers and leaves with their wings closed.

I see my reflection in the water on the ground and feel like I am standing in a puddle of myself, deciding where I need to go and what I need to do with my life. Maybe that's how the butterflies in this area feel whilst they wait for the sun to return to aid their digestion and give them the energy to fly again.

I am distracted by my name being called and see Catherine and Joshua running towards me excitedly.

Catherine explains, "There is a little picture house further on showing a cartoon and documentary about how a caterpillar turns into a butterfly."

Joshua jumps up and down and informs me, "It's the very hungry caterpillar."

"Like the storybook, Saskia, you must have read it," Catherine quizzes me.

I had read the story about the very hungry caterpillar, a long time ago of course, and until this moment I had actually forgotten that a butterfly was once a caterpillar.

"Come on, it is about to start," she hurries me.

We enter a small oblong room with wooden benches around the edges and dim lighting. We take a seat and hear the noise of fluttering wings coming from the speakers situated around the room. They sound loud then slowly fade until they sound like a distant waterfall. At this stage a cartoon commences on the large screen and everyone in the audience goes silent.

The cartoon is similar to the story of the very hungry caterpillar, where a caterpillar eats his way through different types of food, eventually turning into a butterfly. At various stages of the cartoon the screen goes white and writing appears, providing educational information in many different languages. Catherine whispers in Joshua's ear to inform him what the writing says. I think that this is the quietest that I have ever seen him.

I have observed butterflies in the past and always thought that they were beautiful, but today I look at them in lots of different ways. I honestly didn't realize that there was so much to know about them.

A butterfly begins its life as an egg laid in a cluster of eggs on a host plant. When the egg finally hatches, the caterpillar starts its work and eats the leaf that it was born onto. It must weave a cocoon and live within it alone. I was alarmed when I heard that it prepares its cocoon as though it is dying. I thought that this was really sad, and I could almost feel the loneliness and fear of what it must be going through.

What the caterpillar thinks is the end of its life really is the beginning though, and this made me feel happier. It becomes a chrysalis and hangs from a tree branch or other support, always changing, waiting until the proper time to emerge as a beautiful butterfly. It's the happy ending to a beautiful story.

As the lights come back on for us to leave, I hear the lady next to me talking to her friend.

She says, "It's a very appropriate story for us mere mortals, many of whom are in transition. Change is mystical if you accept that it is a part of life and surrender to it."

I am intrigued by her comment and being inquisitive (not nosy, I must point out) I carry on trying to listen to their conversation.

Her friend replies, "Well you just have to understand who you are and know how to make positive changes in your life. Everything else fits into place."

I carry on trying to listen, but have to give up the effort, because there is too much chit chat drowning out their voices.

As we vacate the picture house a large bright yellow butterfly flutters in front of my face. It appears full of energy and captures my attention. It stands out from all the other butterflies that I have seen today, probably due to its color. It's bright yellow, like the energy of a bright sunny day, creating an intellectual energy within me. I once read that yellow symbolizes wisdom, means joy and happiness and also carries the promise of a positive future. As the butterfly starts to fly away from me, I am reminded to pause and enjoy the miracle of life and change, and to hope that my life changes for the better.

Joshua interrupts my thoughts as I watch the yellow butterfly disappear into the far distance of the dome. "I'm a hungry caterpillar and want to eat my dinner," he says.

I nod at Catherine, "I'm hungry too, if you could eat."

"I certainly could," she says, "There's a café near the entrance of the dome. We could go there."

"I want to eat a leaf like the caterpillar," Joshua states, "so I can change into a beautiful butterfly."

I have to ask, "Why do you want to be a butterfly, Joshua?"

I receive a simple answer, "Because I don't want to be a caterpillar. I am ready to become a butterfly and to spread my wings and fly." He runs ahead, lifting his arms up and down as though they are wings.

Catherine smiles at her little boy as he runs ahead, "I think that I would rather be a tadpole that changes into a frog," she states.

"Why is that?" I ask, already guessing her answer.

"Because when you are a tadpole you can swim all day, and when you eventually turn into a frog, you might be ugly, but you always have the hope that a beautiful prince might come along to kiss you and rescue you."

I smile at another one of Catherine's logical viewpoints. She usually does have an unusual way of looking at things.

As we walk towards the café we pass one more educational board. It informs us that for centuries, the local people have welcomed the arrival of butterflies in early winter, holding special celebrations in their honor. The Aztecs once believed that the Monarch butterflies were the souls of warrior ancestors who were unable to get to their afterlife. It was believed that the butterflies migrated through the forests on the way to the land of the dead.

"What does that mean?" Catherine asks me, puzzled.

I know intuitively, "The butterfly knows instinctively and in alignment with nature when the time is coming to attend the day of the dead."

"What are you on about, Saskia. You are going all weird on me."

I explain, "In Mexico, death is considered to be the passage to a new life. The Day of the Dead is a yearly tradition celebrated in Mexico, where families celebrate the belief that death is a transition from one life to another. They believe that departed souls return to visit on the 1st and the 2nd of November."

Catherine looks at the date on her watch, "That is in a couple of days then."

I nod, "I have been told that candles are lit, and incense burnt to help guide the returning souls. I believe it also guides the lost souls, including those that were unable to get to their afterlife, like the butterflies."

Catherine looks at the board reading it again and trying to understand it. "It's interesting but I am still a little confused by it."

"Me too," I reply, "but I really need to understand this," I frown.

"Why?" She looks at me intrigued, "Why is it so important for you to understand this?"

I would love to discuss the full situation with her, but what can I say without her thinking that I am insane? Nobody in the right frame of mind would believe the situation that I am in, unless they were facing the same issues. There is only one person who I know that is in this predicament and I need to see him. We need to face this together, no matter what the future holds.

"It's just something that Miguel said to me," I reply after a long pause.

"I thought that it was all over with him," she says.

"I think that I have made a mistake, Catherine. I need to see him. Do you mind if I skip lunch, so I can go and find him?"

"Well actually, I do mind you skipping lunch." She then smiles at me. "You will make yourself poorly not eating properly, so at least take a sandwich with you to eat on the way."

She hands me a sandwich from the refrigerator in the café. "You get off and I will pay for it. Take as long as you need with Miguel and I will see you either later or tomorrow."

"Thank you," I reply with gratitude.

"For what?" she asks, "I am only being your friend and want the best for you. Now go and spread your wings. Your time is now.

We give each other a hug and Joshua flaps over to join in.

"Group hug," he shouts.

CHAPTER THIRTEEN

iguel is standing at the entrance to Palm Wellbeing Resort as my taxi pulls up. He looks as though he is expecting me. I don't know why.

"Saskia, you are here." He looks pleased to see me and I am relieved. "I have been trying to contact you, but your hotel said that you had gone out on a trip."

He holds his arms open in apprehension. I look into his ocean blue eyes as though I am swimming in them and fall into his warmth, as he holds me tight in a protective manner.

"What made you come?" he asks.

"I've been thinking about our nightmares," I answer. "Life can end at any moment for anybody. It is how we spend our time here that really matters, and I want to spend whatever time I have with you. I want us to face the shadow people and resolve our past." I sigh in wonder, "We can then face the future, whatever it has to hold, life or death."

He nods understandingly, "I feel the same and I'm happy that you have returned. In fact, I have found somebody who I think can help. That's why I have been trying to contact you all day."

"Who can help us?"

"It's a guest who has been returning to Palm Resort at this time of year for many years. She claims to be a spirit warrior and comes to Mexico to help people like us. Apparently, there are a number of people in our situation. I found out about what she does by chance, just through talking to her in reception. She is a little weird and I worry about what she says, but she knows our situation, and I really believe that she can help us. I believe in her."

"Where is she?" I ask. I am intrigued to meet this person, especially if she can help.

We walk along the jungle paths in silence. The surrounding jungle is an explosion of hibiscus, orchids, birds of paradise and thickets of bamboo. Our fingers are entwined as we listen to the calls of nature, and rays of sunshine light our path amidst the haze.

I have come to the conclusion that Palm Wellbeing Resort is suited to unfussy travelers, who appreciate natural beauty and absolute privacy over the alternative option of luxury hotels. The emphasis here is on relaxation. I just wish that I could feel relaxed. I feel tense with worry.

Miguel breaks the silence, "This is going to be scary and what you will be told will be painful to hear and hard to believe, but I am right with you." He comforts me by holding my hand tighter. "I was scared when I spoke with this lady earlier, but what she has said does make sense, even though there is still a lot more to find out."

"Well, we can do that together." I reassure him that I am there for him too.

I wonder what I am going to see or be told, and I want to run away, somewhere far, but I know that my shadow from my past life will haunt me forever, wherever I am. I need to face up to whatever there is to come and look for clarity in my life. Once I have clarity, I may also have relaxation and happiness.

We eventually reach a section of the jungle which spills out onto the beach and contains what is like a treetop boutique hotel. I have never seen such beautiful sky-skimming treehouses, with decking verandas, which have views over the coral reef. I stare in amazement.

"Wow," is all I say, whilst I actually feel a moment of calm. Looking at the view, my mind is distracted from the dark thoughts of the shadows,

"This is totally different from the rest of the resort," I comment. "In fact I think I could live somewhere like this."

I am already fantasizing a Tarzan and Jane scenario in my head. Miguel could be my Tarzan and I would be his Jane. We could be at peace together here.

Miguel nods agreeing. "All the wood is sustainable too. This is the newest part of Palms Wellbeing Resort and lots of local craftsmen and artists contributed to the design. Their influence makes it special as each treehouse is unique in its own way. It's a part of them and what they stand for and will hopefully remain here forever."

I have always believed that nothing lasts forever, and I am thinking this over when I am distracted. I notice a woman cross-legged on a veranda meditating in the sun. I take a step forward as I am not sure, but then my doubt turns to certainty and I recognize that it is Hania. It's the crazy woman who was sat next to me on the plane. She introduced herself to me as a spirit warrior. Surely this can't be who Miguel has brought me to see? Golly gosh, I feel faint.

After fainting, I awaken inside a treehouse. Miguel must have carried me in. I hear the sea wash ashore and drift away again. It sounds like I feel, drifting through life, drifting with confusion. I am laid on top of a king size bed which is draped in white bedding with red cushions and there's a fan whirling above my head. There is a strong smell of cedar which I presume is the wood that has been used to build the treehouse, along with the smell of dope, that Hania said was white musk on the plane.

I lift myself up and observe what is around me. There is a small sofa in the corner of the room upholstered with white linen and there are black and white photographs of the beach in simple wooden frames on the walls. In the corner of the room is a vanity table with a large glass ball. Intrigued, I approach the table and see my reflection in the crystal ball, which makes me jump. I take a step back, unsure of the situation, because I suddenly realize that maybe I don't want to be confronted with my past or the future.

Miguel and Hania enter the room with a tray of tea, closing the door behind them. There is nowhere to run, and I need to face whatever is said to me. I sit on the edge of the bed and Miguel edges himself next to me. Hania places the tray on a small carved wooden table and starts to pour the tea. She hands both of us a cup and saucer and then offers me a biscuit from a small plate.

I observe her closely remembering how she scared me on the plane. She must have known my situation then, judging by what she said to me, but she didn't tell me everything because she knew that I wouldn't believe her. I thought she was weird and probably would not have believed her then, but she said enough for me to now realize that she knows something, and I am ready to listen to what she has to say.

She runs her fingers through her long black hair and places her hair behind her ears.

"You should eat," she insists. "The sugar will help you after fainting."

She picks a biscuit for me and hands it to me with a pleasant smile.

I gratefully accept and am actually tempted to dunk my chocolate chip cookie in the tea. When I was in rehabilitation, Julia's bad habit of biscuit dunking rubbed off on me a little, but I am going to resist temptation, as I don't want to offend the spirit warrior in any way. Also, she may want to read my tea leaves, and I don't want chocolate chip cookie crumbs to cloud her reading.

Hania sits down cross-legged on the small white sofa and sips her tea.

"Why are we here, Hania?" I ask nervously.

She stares at me, "I shall explain to you in as much detail as possible, but you will have to be patient with me because I don't yet know all of your answers. All that I can do is try to help and hopefully time will tell your story. You will also have to believe in me and what I say. You are facing the unknown and must overcome your own fears in order to proceed through your limitations."

"I am scared," I feel myself tremble.

Miguel holds my hand, "We are both scared, Hania, but want to proceed. Please just tell us what we need to do."

Hania nods and looks at me, "Miguel has explained both of your dreams in detail to me this afternoon and I have given this a lot of thought." She now speaks to both of us, "Dreams and self-knowledge are closely interlinked, and you need to put yourself in touch with the unconscious parts of your personality."

I don't understand, "The scenarios and situations that seem to emerge when we both experience these dreams defy explanation. Our dreams warn us of danger and difficulty, but don't present possible solutions."

She agrees, "Dreams often require interpreting to be fully understood. Our entire minds and bodies are interconnected and interdependent. The more in tune you are with your body, the faster you will recognize its needs. You need to deal with the problem that your subconsciousness has identified."

Hania closes her eyes and mutters to herself. She did this on the plane and I did not like it then and don't like it now.

She talks with her eyes closed, "Something has happened to you at some point and the memory has been buried deep within your consciousness. Only when a similar thing occurs, like you both meeting each other again, does that part of us know and remember everything. This then presents the original trauma for consideration.”

Miguel asks, “What makes you think that we have met each other before?”

Hania smiles and opens her eyes, “Because you are soulmates and have been brought together again.”

I look at Miguel who appears confused and then back at Hania.

“Again?” I query.

“Yes, it’s quite simple. You have been here together in a past life, before you both died.”

She looks at our facial reactions. Miguel looks like his chin is touching the floor, horrified, and I feel as white as a ghost. Perhaps that is what we are, ghosts speaking to a medium.

Hania stands and stamps her foot on the floor disturbing my thoughts and bringing me back to reality.

She raises her voice, “I did say that you would have to believe me in order for me to help you. Do you wish to leave whilst you collect your thoughts, or would you like to proceed? You will have to face this at some point though, this issue is not going to go away, and I am one of the few that can help you, but only if you want help and a future.”

I face Miguel. “We have come so far, and I think we should carry on. She may be our only hope.”

He puts his head in his hands and speaks quietly, “Ok, anything for you, but I am finding this hard to absorb.”

He turns to Hania, “You do seem to know a lot about our predicament, so we would like to carry on. Please help us.”

She sits back down, closes her eyes for a long moment and breathes deeply as though she is meditating. When she opens her eyes, she appears a lot calmer.

“I am pleased that you have decided to carry on.” Calmly she speaks, “Based upon your dreams, I believe that you were together in your past lives when you died. I understand this because you share the same experience when dreaming. Looking into your dreams, I believe that you both died in a car accident and that your souls did not leave earth.

“How can that happen?” Miguel asks.

“There can be many reasons for this, but I don’t know your reason. Like I said before, time will tell, time always tells, based on my experience.”

Miguel looks drained. I think that he could be taking this worse than me. He stands up and walks around the room. Hania and I watch him cautiously.

He runs his hand over the crystal ball as he talks, "I feel like I am in a state of transition, possibly moving from one state of mind to another or between two states of being. I feel that I am unable to make decisions, except to accept the inevitable."

I walk towards him and we both place our hands on the crystal ball. I am not sure what to say, but I need to say something, "I felt like I knew you from first setting eyes on you on the dance floor."

He agrees, "I felt the same and I now know that's because we did know each other. We knew each other from the past. There was a strong chemistry that couldn't be avoided."

He puts his arm around me and pulls me tightly into him and I am pleased that we are here to support each other in a time of need.

Hania looks on. "You probably felt like strangers to one another on the outside, yet there would have been an intensive attraction that could not be ignored. Inside you will know each other well from your previous lives. These feelings are being carried on between you now. Your lost souls have brought you together again and destiny cannot be denied."

Miguel looks like he is gaining some color in his cheeks and his body feels warm.

He whispers in my ear, "I am a believer. Do you believe?"

"Yes," I whisper back in his ear. What Hania is telling us makes sense.

Miguel gently pulls away from me, but he keeps hold of my hand as we walk towards Hania, who is still sitting cross-legged on the small sofa.

"We believe you," he confirms to her, "we just need to get used to the fact that there is a part of us that there is no use for. We need to come to terms with our feelings about our death, because we have died at some point in the past, after all."

I agree, "We do need to come to terms with our death and feeling of loss, but we also need to remind ourselves of our immortality, our immunity from death."

Hania seems frustrated and anxiously stands up, "You died in the past, so you are not immortal. You have been reborn, and you have been brought together because there was some unfinished business in your last lives that needs to be resolved in these lives."

This is all very complicated. Just when we think that we are starting to understand our situation, it seems to get deeper and more complicated, with more questions to ask.

Hania suddenly keels over holding her stomach. I let go of Miguel's hand and run towards her. She feels cold, ice cold, like I have felt in the past.

"Get the blanket off the bed," I shout to Miguel, panicking.

He wraps the sheet around her as she shivers, and I hold her tight in my arms. Her eyes seem cold, staring in one direction, towards her crystal ball. Miguel pours her some tea to try to warm her up, but she doesn't even acknowledge it when he puts it in front of her.

"There's something wrong," I inform Miguel, "we should get a doctor."

As I look at Miguel I realize that we have a serious problem. He stares at the wall behind the crystal ball and there are shadows. They are not our shadows from this life, they are the shadows from our past lives and they are dancing a circle around us. I feel myself go freezing cold and I shiver as I fall and kneel on the floor. Miguel is standing unmoving like a frozen statue.

I watch the shadows dancing around the room. I feel like they are dancing the circle of death, draining us of any life that is within us. I close my eyes and cover my ears. I can hear screams going through my head like the shrieks I heard at the ruins when people stood at the foot of the temple and shouted their names, and they came back as a piercing echo. This time the shadows are shouting our names. I feel my energy being drained away and feel one of the shadows pass through my body. A feeling of loneliness and neglect passes through every vein and nerve in my body. Everything goes black and I feel like I am flying through the air like a kite, or like in my dream, when my soul leaves my body when the car goes over the cliff.

I vaguely hear Hania ranting like she did on the plane. I open my eyes and see her playing with the beads and knots that are tied around her neck. "I call on the Moon, Earth, stars, Sun, water, air and fire. Priest and princess come bless this woman and man now."

I am confused as to what has happened, but both Miguel and I are side by side on the bed. Our own clothes have been removed and we are both wearing pale brown linen sheets tied around our bodies. Miguel rubs his eyes and shakes his head.

"What has just happened?" I ask.

"I haven't a clue," he remarks, "but it was weird, and where is Hania?"

We both climb down the tree ladder and find her on the veranda looking out to sea.

She appears frightened, "In all of my years as a spirit warrior, I have never experienced anything like that. You need more help than I ever anticipated."

"What happened?" Miguel asks. "Are the shadow people trying to hurt us?"

"No, they just need your help and are trying to grasp our attention. They have certainly achieved that."

"If they don't want to harm us, what do they want?" I enquire.

"Your souls have just passed through us, demonstrating that they are feeling neglected. You felt unsafe in your dream, which tells you that you want to escape the past. Your dream is trying to remind you of a difficult situation that you once had to deal with and this will bring you closer together when everything is finally revealed. In the meantime, your souls from your past lives are currently trapped by your physical bodies, so are looking for freedom. They need your help"

"How do we help?" both Miguel and I ask simultaneously.

"A candle has been lit by your past family, and incense burnt to guide your lost souls from your previous lives to the Day of the Dead event. The story of your past lives will be revealed to you on this special evening. I don't know any more, but I just need to ask you to attend. If you don't attend the Day of the Dead, your past souls and both of you will be lost forever in some form of purgatory."

"Hania, why are we dressed in these brown linen sheets? Do we need to wear these on the Day of the Dead? It's a couple of days off."

She shakes her head, "The color brown represents earth, death and promise. You are now on earth, you have previously died in a past life, but there is promise of a future in this life. I realized today that you need more help than most, so I consulted the gods of the ancient Maya. Until Dia de los Muertos, when your lost souls will eventually rest, if you do everything you are advised, a blessing will help you find inner peace."

"Who will provide the blessing?" Miguel queries, "I know a lot of priests and I would not want them to know about my strange situation."

Hania smiles, "I know and that is why I have arranged for you to go somewhere very special. You are going to be purified by an Ixmen that I know."

"What's an Ixmen?" I query.

"It's a female priest," Miguel informs me.

Hania smiles, "She is very special because she only blesses and helps people in your situation. She only holds three blessing circles every year which happen to be this month, with the Day of the Dead being imminent."

"When and where do we go?" Miguel asks. "The sooner this is all sorted, the sooner we can get on with our life together in peace, which is all we want."

Hania nods agreeing, "You will find inner peace, I promise. There is a full moon tonight so there is a blessing circle being held at the old ruins and cenote near this hotel. Just turn up in your brown linen sheets. To access the ruins, use the password 'earth, death and promise'. The Ixmen will be awaiting your arrival."

I can't help but feel that this sounds like some witchcraft plot and hope that we aren't sacrificed upon arrival, but having said that, all sorts of weird things have been happening and this may be our only chance of having peace, dead or alive.

Hania gives us both a big caring hug. "You know where I am if you need me, but you should go and get some rest before this evening. The shadow people will have drained your energy and you need to recuperate before your blessing. It will be a long night, believe me. Go and get some sleep."

As we walk away, I see Hania meditating on the treehouse veranda. As the sun goes down, I can see her shadow replicating her. For a second, I feel a moment of her inner calmness, and hope that I will also one day be able to achieve this, hopefully after the Day of the Dead.

CHAPTER FOURTEEN

At midnight we approach double iron gates to enter the ruins. A gentleman that can only be described as looking like a wizard greets us. He wears a long brown linen sheet tied around his body like us. He has long white hair, a matching long white beard and a wrinkled face. Some people have a face that looks lived in, his looks like it's had squatters. He looks sinister and evil looking.

"Password?" he demands in a stern voice.

"Earth, death, promise." Miguel answers.

He looks at me, scrutinizing me closely, "And your password?"

"It's the same." I reply nervously.

"Say it then," he orders in a deep frightening tone.

"Earth, death, promise."

He slowly opens the gates for us to enter and he nods to a young man who approaches us. He has the gentle features of a boy and smiles at us hesitantly.

"Please follow me," he requests.

The air is warm and there is a smell of smoke in the air that is combined with a smell of stagnant water. I can only presume that the stagnant smell is coming from the nearby cenotes and wells. It is pitch dark and bats fly above our heads and amongst the hundreds of surrounding trees. We tread carefully, watching our steps in the dark to avoid tripping or hurting ourselves on underfoot debris. In the far distance I can see a fire ablaze and I can now hear chanting that sounds like music.

I stop in my steps and Miguel stops by my side.

"You both ok?" the young man enquires.

I shake my head. "I am frightened. What happens?" I can feel my body tremble.

The young man looks down and doesn't answer.

"Please tell her, she is worrying," Miguel requests. "We won't say that you said anything."

The young man looks up, but I notice that his hands are shaking as he starts to speak.

"You have been reborn and found your past, or your past has found you. Most people don't know that they have lived before, or remember anything about having had a past life, but the souls from your past life have remained on earth at death, rather than having gone to heaven and have found you. It's believed that they want something from you."

"Do you know what is wanted?" I ask.

He tries to explain but doesn't really answer my question. "Destiny has brought you here today so that a spiritual guru and Ixmen can help you to work out what is wanted. They will aid you in finding your path in life without your past tainting your future. The guru will let you know the mysteries that are hidden, even from those who search the meaning of life. This will be shared with you if you seek answers and can only be shared on the evening of a full moon, which is why you have been invited tonight."

"Why are people chanting and what is the fire for?" I direct my question to the young man as I run my hand along my forehead to wipe away sweat. It's really hot.

"The chanting is a prayer and request to the Mayan gods. The fire is used for divination."

"What do you mean by divination?" Miguel asks.

I am having difficulty catching my breath and experience tightness of my chest. I can only presume that this is down to the heat and the smoke from the fire.

The young man ponders, "The fire is used to help foresee, and to be inspired by god. It helps the guru gain insight into a question about your situation by way of a ritual. This will then help the Ixmen prepare your collative spiritual awakening under the full moon."

I don't understand and looking at Miguel, I don't think he does either. I know that this young boy is trying to help but I wish that he would not speak in riddles. I find the information confusing and I do not like not being able to perceive what he is trying to tell me.

"What does that mean?" I quiz him.

He shakes his head, "I can't say anymore. We need to go because time is of the essence."

He starts to pace ahead, and Miguel and I follow holding up our linen sheets to prevent tripping over.

I feel the heat of the fire upon arrival at the ritual. It warms my body through to my bones and I feel my face aglow. There are approximately twenty people all standing around the fire holding hands and in chorus answering, "Amen," to a woman who circles the fire making statements. She wears a long pure-white gown that has a hood, long flared sleeves and she has a large diamond filled cross on a chain around her neck. She is obviously the Ixmen, the female priest. Her hair is straight, silky smooth and raven red. She looks over and holds her cross up to us. Miguel and I look at each other unsure what we should do.

We are surprised to see Hania in the circle. She appears to be assisting the Ixmen. She looks over and smiles at our arrival.

"I didn't know she was going to be here," I comment to Miguel.

"I had an idea that she may be," he replies distractedly, observing and trying to take in everything that he is seeing.

A lady approaches us dressed similar to the Ixmen. "Hello," she greets us warmly as she touches me gently on my arm. "You feel hot. Let me take you away from this fire. You aren't ready for it yet. You will see the Ixmen in a little while, but firstly I need to take you to a spiritual guru who is waiting for your arrival."

We follow her through intricate semi-sunken caves dripping with water, through many passages and eventually arrive in a small cave where candlelight flickers. This cave has many ancient carvings etched in the walls and precious stone formations resembling animals revered as sacred to the Mayans. I have never seen anything like this and I run my fingers along the etchings interested in their meanings.

Miguel whispers, "These magical creations are some of the most unique and supernatural features of the environment of Mexico."

We are both intrigued with the unusual drawings.

There is a large oval stone, similar in shape and size to a small coffee table, where the spiritual guru sits cross-legged. She points to the opposite side of the stone for us to sit and join her in discussion. In the middle of the stone I observe a crystal skull, it looks real and I wonder if it actually is a human skull from some sacrifice, that has been decorated with special gems. It is placed next to a large piece of quartz that looks really pretty as it glistens in the candlelight.

When we are comfortable, or as comfortable as we can be sat on a cold wet cave floor with our legs crossed, the spiritual guru introduces herself.

"Spiritual Guru," she announces and bows her head. I knew that and wonder if she has a name.

"Saskia and Miguel," we introduce ourselves, and bow back to show respect.

"I know," she confirms in a soft tone and clasps her hands together as though she is praying. "I have referred to my Sastun and communicated with the spirit world. I know all about you both and I can help you."

"What's a Sastun?" I have to ask if I am going to follow this.

"Stop asking so many questions," Miguel interrupts and elbows me in my side. "Whatever it is, it will hopefully help to provide detailed information regarding our lives, either in the past or the present, and will provide some kind of closure on our past life so we can move forward with our future."

Spiritual Guru smiles at us. "If you need to ask any questions then that is ok. I am here to help."

We both nod in agreement and she carries on, "In answer to your question, a Sastun is a tool of the Maya healer. My Sastun is this large piece of quartz." She points to the quartz on the rock table. "I use it to communicate with the spirit world. I use it alongside my crystal skull, in case you wondered what that was for." She points at the skull and takes a deep contented breath. "They work in unity together and are helping me to understand your situation. The spiritual guardians who communicate through these have shown me your window to the afterworld and a key to the afterlife."

Miguel nods, "So they work like a crystal ball, where you can see the future and the past."

Guru smiles, "I suppose they work in a similar way."

I look at Miguel and he seems to be absorbing everything that he is being told, but I suppose that I should resign myself to the fact that I am not going to understand this spiritual guru, Ixmen stuff. I suppose it doesn't really matter as long as they can help us resolve our situation and move on. We will be here all night if I keep asking questions, so I have decided to just keep quiet and accept what I am told.

Spiritual Guru carries on speaking and I observe my surroundings and the carvings on the walls. I can't help but wonder how I have happened to be in this situation and how many other people have sat in this particular cave, spoke to this guru, prayed with the Ixmen and come out of the situation normal, having found their life and lost their shadow people.

As I am thinking this through, I see shadows dance around the room, but I don't feel scared. The shadows feel friendly and calmer.

I look at Miguel who has also seen them, "What is happening?" I ask nervously.

He holds my hand, "It is ok. Everything will be ok, baby."

The spiritual guru is waving her hands over the Sastun and the crystal skull. The quartz starts to change a multitude of rainbow colors, which somehow creates positive energy. Whatever she is doing is keeping the shadows peaceful. I don't feel cold like I have in the past. I actually feel warm and don't feel in danger.

She looks up for a moment, "I am bringing together information regarding your life and your past. With the help of the spirits I may guide you through your present life providing some closure on your past life."

Guru instructs us, "Breathe slowly now, deeply now, you must learn to control your breathing, in and out. It's important you do this in rhythm."

We act as told and as I breathe, I feel a warm presence pass through my body. A sense of wonder melts my cares away and fills me with peace.

"Your lost soul has been feeling anxious, leaving you troubled. This breathing technique will help you connect. You shall feel a moment of calm and then you can work together to resolve your issues, as your past soul passes through your body and life."

We carry on breathing and I close my eyes.

Scenes from my life flash through my mind. Scenes from my childhood, memories of my wonderful caring grandparents, I remember planting daffodils with Grandma, I recall flying my kite high in the sky on the beach with my grandfather, building sandcastles as a family, I feel the distress of my grandparents' funerals, which appear in my vision like they were yesterday. I miss them so much and I feel a pang of loneliness pass through every vein and bone in my body.

Nothing else comes to me after the feeling of loneliness. It's as though this is where my life has ended for now. I open my eyes and see the shadows dancing round the room.

Spiritual Guru instructs me, "Close your eyes, Saskia, and carry on breathing just like before, just like Miguel."

I do as I am told and I experience a vision from my past life. Suddenly I feel like my body is no longer my own. A gentle warm breeze passes through me and takes over my mind and body. Scenes flash through my mind that I seem to recall, seem to remember, but do not know. I instinctively know they are visions from my past life.

I see siblings from my past life, and I feel a close bond between us all. I see a man who I recognize as my father. He is shouting but I am unsure why he is annoyed, it appears that he is annoyed with me. I see my past life mother and she is crying because I have upset her. What have I done? My mind recalls a caring and gentle father, but I have done something to upset him. I have upset all of them, and I feel the need to get away from them. I see myself run out of a house, it's the house where I lived with them, our home.

Everything that my mind recalls feels like it is actually happening here and now. I feel like my current life has been taken somewhere else, and I am in somebody else's body living their life.

My past life vision now takes me to a place where I go dancing and I love dancing. The rhythm takes away all of my worries, tension and concerns. Miguel is there, and we dance together perfectly. I instinctively know that we aren't supposed to be together, but we are, and it feels right because we are in love and it is forever.

I then see us enter a car laughing and we drive away together. We are happy, really happy, we are running away to be together. This feeling is short lived, as I next experience our car skidding. The car leaves the road and descends off the cliff. I look over at Miguel and now feel a sense of misery, a sense that this life has reached an end. Our moment of happiness has ended and there is nowhere to go, just a sense of loneliness as we say to each other, 'Goodbye'.

I now feel the upset of my past life soul, my ghost, a shadow stands looking down at the cliff. I feel her sense of loneliness and a wish to be found. Now was not her moment to go and her soul hasn't gone to heaven but has remained on earth with the man she loved. Miguel's shadow reaches out for her and holds her in his arms. If only they could have a second chance to live again, they would do things differently. They are now lost souls in a world they need to rediscover in a different way. They are here as spirits until the time comes for them to put matters to rest, put right their mistakes. Only then will they go to heaven.

I am left with the vision of my past life mother crying and mourning me. For some reason she blames herself for my death.

The vision finishes, and I am brought back to the present. Miguel looks over at me knowing we have just shared a similar past life experience, as we are brought back to current reality. The shadow people are no longer within the cave.

Spiritual Guru speaks first, "Sometimes major events seem to unfold around us that challenge our thinking and direction in life."

Miguel relaxes his shoulders, "I have found some comfort connecting with my spirit, thank you."

I agree, "I have found some comfort too, but I also know that we still have a long way to go. There was something that happened in our last life that prevented our past life souls from going to heaven and I still don't feel that everything has been revealed."

I hesitate as a drop of water drips from above, "After what has just happened, I think that our old ways are no longer valid, or of value. We need to move on and make a whole new start, a new life, but we need to rectify something from our past before we can do this. I just wish I knew what it was and wish that we were not in this situation."

Miguel interrupts my thoughts, "We are being given another chance to be together, Saskia."

Guru nods, "You have been given another chance, but you both need to broaden your horizons and make sweeping changes. Your future could move ahead in many and varied ways, but only if you let it. You need to let go of your past, but this will only be done if you can help your past souls be put to rest."

"What shall we do next?" Miguel enquires.

"You have learnt the lesson that life can end at any moment and that goes for all of us. It's how wisely we spend our time here that matters. You both need to turn a new leaf, sow new seeds, leave time for fun and spontaneity, get out there and dance if you like dancing, live your life together how you should, and how you want. What you need to do to help your past life be put to rest will be revealed to you in due course. Just get on with your life and you will know what you have to do when the time comes."

Miguel grasps my hand and looks me in the eyes, "We will, won't we? Let's make the most of our life together and do everything we can to be happy."

I smile and nod.

The Sastun and the skull have now stopped connecting and no longer glow. Spiritual Guru stands up, bows to them, closes her eyes and says, "Amen."

We both follow her actions as a sign of respect for the help and advice offered. We follow her down the dark corridors of the cave until we see light at the end of a tunnel. The fire is still in full blaze, but it does not feel as hot as on our previous encounter.

"I now feel that you are prepared for the female priest," Guru informs us. "It is time for you to step completely into a new version of you. Let go of everything in your life that does not matter and only keep what is important. Resolution comes with letting go. Follow this instruction and everything will fall into place."

Miguel and I look at each other with a look of confusion, wondering what is going to happen next.

Guru advises us, "This is a very sacred place in which rituals and dances that honor different gods of the Mayan mythology take place. A blessing shall be performed by our female priest in the beautiful moonlight. Pure fresh water from the cenote is an important part in this ritual and a purification bath is prepared for you. Mayans believe the cenotes to be an entrance to their underworld, where their gods live and sometimes spirits reside after death. You need to pass through the underworld in order to move on with life. Your shadows will hopefully soon return to heaven, where they belong."

I don't like the idea of passing through the underworld, but I know that it has to be followed through. Guru kisses us both on each of our cheeks and wishes us all the best with our life and future. As she turns her back and walks back into the cave, we are greeted by the Ixmen.

CHAPTER FIFTEEN

Standing around the fire, the Ixmen holds her cross up at us and then draws a cross in the air. As she finishes she says, "Amen," and falls to her knees on the floor. Miguel bends to help her up, but she shakes her head refusing his help and slowly rises of her own accord.

"Welcome to spiritual history," she greets us. "These cenotes are more than a natural phenomenon. They are considered sanctified occurrences, proving the existence and caring nature of the gods."

The cenotes seem somewhat mysterious and I am intrigued by what she is saying. She has a husky voice that somehow draws you in and gains your attention.

"I need you both to relax," she says. "I need to address the force of nature in you in order to provoke a certain mood."

She starts spinning around in circles. I worry that she will become dizzy and fall in the fire. I step forward to pull her back, but I feel Hania's arm in front of me blocking my movement.

"Just relax," Hania advises. "Until you relax, the Ixmen can't relax, and won't be able to help you."

I nod in agreement and step back, relaxing my shoulders and body.

Hania informs us, "The Ixmen is going to speak and at the end of each statement, you need to say Hallelujah."

I glance at the Ixmen who appears wild and crazy. She is more insane than the people I met at rehabilitation. She dances around the fire in bare feet, twirling around in circles with her long red raven hair flying behind her. She has the appearance of an innocent child, without any cares in the world, but at the same time she has a glow that draws you close.

Hania places a bucket of water in front of us and the Ixmen circles toward us. She places her hands and long white sleeves in the water, then splashes us and runs her hands down our hair and faces.

She talks to us and I listen carefully, "Salt water mixes with fresh. You must surrender to the flow of water. It isn't a time to resist for everything is out of your control. Your world may feel like it's been turned upside down. Take it as an opportunity to see your life from a different perspective."

Hania nods in our direction and Miguel and I say together, "Hallelujah."

Hallelujah is a word known worldwide, but I don't really understand it. I believe the exclamation 'hallelujah' to translate to 'God be praised'. I also believe it to be an expression of worship or rejoicing. If I am going to use this word, it would be good to use it correctly. Ixmen clicks her fingers in front of my eyes and gains my attention again.

"About the fire we do dance, round and round in a trance," Ixmen spins in a circle in front of us whilst chanting.

Miguel elbows me gently to remind me to speak. "Hallelujah," we repeat.

The Ixmen falls to the ground and then gently rises again, "This is life, this is power, now is the time and now is the hour, remember this day forever."

"Hallelujah," we say again.

"Skulls, bones and breath, are everywhere we go in life and death."

"Hallelujah."

The Ixmen looks at the bucket of water and waves her hands through the steam that has started to rise from it. She nods at Hania who removes the bucket from in front of us and throws it on the fire. The fire calms and the behavior of the Ixmen also calms at the same point. She slowly takes a deep breath in and out and runs her hands down the side of her body as though she is massaging herself.

She advises us, "A purification bath has been prepared for you in the cenote and it will welcome you into a world of silence and rest. The cenotes are pathways to the afterlife and will help provide you with the truth of your being. The water visibility is infinite and will give you the feeling that you are flying into another planet, just go with the flow of the water."

"Are you saying that we have to swim in the cenotes?" Miguel asks, looking worried.

She spins around. "Just go with the flow, the flow of the water, the flow of life. Look upon it as a holy encounter with life, death, gods and goddesses."

Hania approaches, "If you want closure and peace, it is something that has to be done. No harm will come to you both."

We descend to the cenote by a rock staircase. The Ixmen and Hania walk ahead of us with a candle for light. We eventually reach a small cavern with a lake inside. I hold Miguel tight, wondering what is in the water beneath us.

The Ixmen tells us, "Do not touch or remove anything from the cenotes. Everything here belongs to the underworld and needs to stay here. Even if there is something that grasps your attention, remember that it belongs to the underworld. Take only the memories and leave nothing behind."

"What happens after?" I ask.

"Time will tell and your soul from your past life will decide when that time is. Enjoy your experience."

They exit, leaving us in darkness.

"This isn't an experience I am enjoying," I confide in Miguel. "I can't believe she said enjoy it."

He shakes his head and stares at the water, "I know, but we are in this together. Shall we just jump in and get it over with?"

I nervously reply, "Shall we just exit and run." I mean what I say.

Miguel shakes his head, "We would have to live with the shadows forever, never knowing. Our souls from our past life deserve rest. We need to live our life how we want without being tormented. This is something that we have to do."

Shadows suddenly appear darting through the cenote and make our decision easy. Miguel grasps my hand and together we take a deep breath and descend into the deep cold water.

Below the surface is a world of turquoise blue, a world of formations, hidden tunnels and also a blackness of the unknown. The path is wide enough for us to swim side by side and we keep tight hold of each other's hands, as we flow with the movement of the water. I almost forget that we are underground and underwater, with only a layer of rock between us and air. One dazzling passage follows another, and we kick our feet calmly behind us, observing everything in our path.

Surface lights occasionally penetrate the water and I soon become aware that we are surrounded by life and death, past and present. Tropical fish approach on all sides and swim amongst the items below and around us. We pass beads, bracelets loaded with glass, silver beads, charms and vintage brass. These are obviously things that belong to the underworld spirits. The items are similar to what I saw the boy at the ruins selling.

I see a heart locket glistening on the bottom and let go of Miguel's hand to approach it. It reminds me of a shiny penny and I want to touch its magical beauty. As I get deeper and closer, I am suddenly presented with skulls, skeletons, and praying hands of skeletons entwined. The shock makes me start to cough and splutter and prevents me from holding my breath under the water. Miguel grasps my hand and we move to the top of the water, leaving only bubbles behind us.

We rise in a spring hole that leads to a giant cave where vines hang down. As we pull ourselves out of the water, I carry on coughing and Miguel gently rubs my back.

"Are you ok?" he sounds concerned.

I shake my head in shock. "We are surrounded by life and death, past and present. We are alive, and some fish and the bats are alive," I say looking around, "but then there is evidence of death, with the skulls and skeletons and past belongings." I start to cough again and find myself being sick.

Miguel puts his arm around me, "I know. The ancient Maya believed that cenotes were pathways to the afterlife and would sacrifice humans and items of value. There must be hundreds of cenotes in Mexico like this. It's disturbing to witness."

I nod, gaining my breath again after coughing, "I saw the items of value, the silver beads, bracelets and vintage brass. They reminded me of what a young boy was selling at the ruins when I first experienced the shadows. He showed me a bracelet and said that it was a shrine to remember the dead. Perhaps all these items are shrines to the dead."

"It's possible, but you haven't got to touch anything. Remember what the Ixmen told us. Everything belongs to the underworld and we are only to look."

I know, "But I saw a heart locket on a chain and it was shiny and there was something that attracted me to it, and I was only going to…" I stop and recall what I was going to do, "I was going to touch it and I shouldn't." I shake my head disappointed with myself.

Miguel looks at me concerned and I think before carrying on, "I passed lots of other items but didn't want to touch them, so why that?"

Miguel shrugs his shoulders, "The Ixmen said only to take memories. You must not touch anything, and she said it for a reason, Saskia. Perhaps the locket you saw brought back a memory from your past life."

He's right and I am truly sorry, but I know that we need to move on. I want to put the past to rest, keep special memories, but leave the cenote and live for the future.

Baroque limestone swirls and crystalline icicles glitter like jewels under the rays of gold and blue light which now pokes through the holes in the cave's roof.

Miguel looks up, "Daylight is here and is peeping through. Perhaps it is time for us to find a way out of here and leave."

Time seems to have passed us by.

We take a deep breath and penetrate deep into the water. Some memories from my past life appear subconsciously in my mind as I swim over shrines from the past. I don't recall everything about my past life, I don't know everywhere that I have been, but having said that, I also don't know where my current life will take me. I just hope that time will help work things out.

The water has been crystal clear but now appears like an incredible fantastic cloud. We find ourselves rising in an inlet surrounded by lagoons, to take breath.

"What has happened to the water?" I ask.

"It's where the salt water mixes with the fresh. I think that we are near the end of our journey. A little further on and we should see more daylight."

We take a final deep breath and our bodies flow with the movement of the water as it washes over us, offering some kind of purity to our bodies and minds.

I don't recall the end of our journey. It's almost like I blacked out. I vaguely remember surface lights penetrating the water before finding ourselves on an empty beach near Miguel's wellbeing resort.

The Ixmen told us before our journey through the cenotes, before our purification bath, that we would find the truth of our being. I have found my reality of absolute consciousness, a pervasive sense of 'me' as a separate self.

Miguel hasn't discussed his feelings, but I would like him to. I feel that there is something that he doesn't want me to know. I want him to be open with me and share his thoughts and feelings. I've shared everything with him and if we are to move on, there can be no secrets between us.

I can't help but wonder what the 'Day of the Dead' will bring and hope that there is some conclusion, like Hania and the Ixmen have insinuated. I hope that time will tell, but for now we are exhausted and need some sleep.

CHAPTER SIXTEEN

e awaken just after lunch, holding each other close. We are still fully dressed in our linen gowns and I can't help but wonder what possessed us to go to bed in the gowns, they would have been wet when we returned. They have obviously dried whilst we have slept but the sheets feel a little damp.

I feel safe and comfortable in Miguel's arms. I can hear the sounds of the tropical jungle, the whisper from the sea and the music of a humming bird in the far distance. I find it tranquil and relaxing.

Miguel looks up at the ceiling fan spinning around and around above our heads keeping us cool, "I wonder when all of this spinning will end, and we can proceed with our lives without the worry of the shadow people."

I was enjoying my relaxing moment but in the light of the day I am again faced with reality, the fact of our death in a previous life.

"We only have two more days until the 'Day of the dead," I remind him, "and I presume everything will then be revealed, one way or another."

Miguel's eyes widen, "That's what worries me."

I sit up in bed and position a cushion behind me for support whilst I look down on him. "What happens at the 'Day of the Dead'? I know that I have never been to a Day of the Dead event in this life and can't recall going in my previous life. I would just like to know what it is like."

He shrugs his shoulders, "It is more special than what I ever realized. It is a ritual to try and give meaning to human existence. Death is considered to be the passage to a new life."

"Well they are certainly right with that," I confirm.

Miguel makes himself comfortable, folding his arms above his head on the pillow. "Communities enthusiastically prepare for this festivity. Houses and cemeteries are decorated with flowers, elaborate wreaths and fruits from the region."

"It sounds beautiful."

He nods, "Commemorative altars are created in family homes and offerings are arranged for dead relatives. Tables are covered with fine cloths and decorated with sugar skulls, flowers and paper skeletons along with plates of food that the dead relatives used to enjoy. For each deceased relative a candle is lit. The light is thought to guide them on their way back. Incense is also burnt so that the aroma will help guide the returning souls."

I absorb what I am being told, "Our families from our past life are therefore preparing for our past life souls to return. I wonder if they know about the possibility of being born again after death."

"Possibly," Miguel answers.

I stare in a trance at the fan swirling around and a worrying thought suddenly occurs, "What will happen if we end up meeting family from our past life? It could happen, couldn't it?"

"They won't know us," he concludes.

"Somehow, we knew each other when we met, so it's possible."

Miguel looks worried, "I don't want to talk about this situation. I was telling you about the 'Day of the Dead' and what happens, so I will therefore carry on."

I want to talk about what happens if we should meet past life relatives and how we should deal with it if it happens. I don't understand why Miguel would not wish to discuss it. He appears frustrated though, so I will leave it for now.

Miguel carries on telling me about the Day of the Dead. "The bells of churches start to ring early in the morning, calling the deceased souls and the living relatives to attend a ceremony. Later, families go to the graveyard to clean tombs and decorate them with offerings. Here they pray and chant for the eternal rest of the souls."

"Do you think our past life families are going to pray and chant for our souls and help us be in peace? Do you think this will be the end of our ordeal?"

He doesn't answer but scowls, raises his brows and sits up pulling the flowered duvet above our bodies.

"There is something that is really bothering me."

"What's that?" I ask.

"It is meant to be a ritual to happily remember the dead relatives, their life and give meaning and continuity to human life. Our life has continued, but what has happened to our personal possessions?"

I can't help but wonder what a strange question that is. "Well, mine are back in England in my friend Catherine's flat and yours are here around you," I reply, confused.

"Saskia, you don't understand. Death is considered to be the passage to a new life. In Mexico the deceased are buried with many of their personal possessions because it is believed that they will need them in the hereafter. What do we have as proof that we are from a past life? We don't have any personal possessions from our past life. We have nothing that could have been buried with us when deceased. We have nothing that has come with us to our new life."

I think about what would be buried with you, such as jewelry and I see that Miguel has a valid point. I suddenly remember the locket that I saw when swimming in the underworld. I reached out for it thinking that it was mine.

"Could those possessions be the shrines that we saw in the cenote?" I question. "Perhaps our possessions are with the shadow people, our past life souls, and haven't been passed on as they are still on earth, rather than in heaven."

I look at his serious expression and know he is thinking about it, "The possessions are supposed to be in the hereafter and we have nothing from our past lives."

"We are fortunate enough to have each other. Whatever else could we possibly want?"

He doesn't answer my question but carries on talking about the 'Day of the Dead', as though he is trying to avoid something.

He rambles, "At nightfall the most impressive celebrations begin. Parties are held in streets and people dress up in Halloween masks and clothing. Picnics are held in graveyards under candle light. Folkloric dance is performed as part of the celebration and fireworks are displayed in the evening sky."

I interrupt as I want my question answering. I feel that he is distancing himself from me, and I don't know why. I feel closer to him than I ever did, so I'm concerned if he feels different.

"We have each other, what else do you want?" I ask again.

He doesn't answer, and I feel myself burning up. I'm not sure if it's the heat of the covers being pulled over my body or anger at him avoiding my question.

Am I not enough for him, does he not want me anymore? Has something happened in the cenote? Has the purification bath cleared his feelings for me? Am I just being paranoid or has something changed?

I climb out of bed and disappear to the bathroom where I splash cold water on my face and look in the mirror at my reflection, my image of life. Every line and wrinkle on my face tells a story just like a photograph tells a story. This is an important story to me as it's the story of my life in this life, not the story of any past life. Yes, Miguel was in my past life in some form and I know from somewhere in the depths of my mind that I loved him, but now I am thinking about if I am supposed to love him in this life. He's in my memory, he's in my past but should he be in this life and the future? Is he supposed to be in the makeup of this life, or am I just living in the past due to the shadow people? Are we only together because our past life souls have brought us together, because they want us to have another chance?

I have spoken to Miguel about my visions from my past life and told him everything, but thinking about it, he hasn't told me anything about what he knows about his past life. He has just pacified me, telling me that he loved me. The purification bath has made me come to my senses and realize that there are gaps of information from our past life that need to be filled, and there is only one person that can help with what I need to know, and he is in the next room. I can't help but wonder why it has also taken so many years for me to meet him again in this life. Over thirty years is a very long time.

Miguel is sat on the edge of the bed with his head in his hands when I return to the bedroom.

"We need to talk," I insist. "I want to know what you saw in your vision at the ritual and anything else that you know. There are gaps of information missing that I need to establish.

He looks up and I can see that he has been crying, "I know, but I am scared you won't understand."

"We are both scared, but unless you open up to me, this problem may go on forever. The purification bath was for everything to be revealed."

"You aren't going to like what I am going to tell you."

I can tell from his expression that I probably won't, but I don't honestly believe that anything else can shock me after what we have been through. I can only hope that what he has to say is part of the purification process and will allow us to move on with life, either individually or together.

He seems angry, pent up, and suddenly shocks me when he thumps the bed putting me at unease.

"I was responsible for killing you. I killed you." He thumps the wall agitated and sits rocking on a chair in the corner.

I am in shock and pace the room thinking about his announcement and erratic actions. I recall the nightmare and remember that he was driving the car when we skidded off the road, but it was definitely an accident. He did not do it on purpose. We had plans for a future together, so why would he have wanted to kill us?

I play the scene through my mind again and confirm that it was certainly an unfortunate accident. I clearly remember the panic between us in the car when we skidded off the road and went over the cliff. He was as fretful and upset as me and he wouldn't have been frightened if he had planned it. I have had to live with the nightmare for as long as I can remember. I would know if Miguel had done it on purpose. I would know…wouldn't I?

I believe that we were together in our past life but there are enormous gaps missing that I can't recall. I have experienced visions of my past life family, recalled places that I have visited before, but I am unable to remember everything about our relationship which makes me question things. What is the true story behind our past life relationship? Why is he angry and behaving so strangely? He is frightening me, and I feel worried.

I need air and I feel that the room is coming in on me as I struggle to breathe. I run out of the bedroom, through the lounge, along the deck and down the steps onto the beach. The salty sea air grasps my breath making me cough. A small group of Palm Resort residents are participating in yoga on the beach and I am relieved by their presence, even if they appear to be cut off from what's going on around them in a world of their own relaxation. I feel safer with them there.

I take a deep breath absorbing the fresh air to clear my mind and then carry on running, holding up my robe. I am now not only running from the shadow people, but am also running from Miguel, the man that I thought I loved.

I hear him shout my name, "Saskia, Saskia, please don't go."

I don't look back, I can't stop running. I run and run until I reach the main road. I wave my hand at a chicken bus approaching. I don't know where it is going but it will help me get away from here. I just want to get back to the safety and comfort of my hotel. I just want to escape my past in every way possible.

It is quite a journey back to the hotel, stopping and starting along route, but it gives me plenty of time to consider what has just happened. If Miguel wanted to hurt me, or kill me, like he claims he did in our past life, then he would have done it by now. All that he has ever done is cared for me and loved me. I can't understand why he has just told me that he killed me in our past life.

I feel like arranging a flight back to England and running away from my past in Mexico. Reality prevents me from doing this though, because even if I leave Mexico and Miguel, the shadow people won't leave me, and my nightmares will prevail. My soul from my past life is in some sort of purgatory and I feel like I am in a place of temporal punishment. The Day of the Dead is approaching and whatever it is that I have to do to help my soul from my past life rest, I will do. My soul should be in heaven, not in purgatory, and Miguel and I need to be freed from torment.

The reception of my hotel is quiet when I enter but Miguel is there, pacing around with his eye continuously on the door, awaiting my arrival. He is dressed in a grey suit and wears a white shirt with the top buttons open. Despite all of my worries and concerns, I can't help but adore him. How can I really adore a man who told me that he was my killer in my past life? He looks pasty white and drained of energy. He walks towards me and hands me a beautiful bunch of daffodils. He smells more beautiful than the flowers and as I inhale his scent, it somehow calms my senses. Perhaps there is an explanation.

"I'm sorry," he apologizes and looks at me with his amazing ocean blue eyes that look tired and weary.

"I am confused," I confess, "You killed me? You told me that you killed me in my last life and I don't understand."

He looks down at the floor in shame. "Since the Ixmen and the purification, I have been worrying about what is going to happen at the

Day of the Dead. I am scared by what events might unfold or occur and what you could find out. Neither of us know what's going to happen there."

He moves forward and touches my hand sending butterflies through my stomach. "I won't hurt you, Saskia, I love you."

He feels a connection between us, and pauses for a moment before continuing, "You have told me everything that you know, but I haven't shared everything with you. I think that the time has come for me to be honest with you and to fill you in with the missing story. I don't want to lose you, but feel that I may, if I try to hide the truth. It may present itself on the Day of the Dead and compromise our relationship."

Tea and coffee are readily available in reception and I feel that my nerves deserve a cup of tea. I shake as I pour two cups. I can't help but remember what my grandma used to say, "There's nothing like a good old cup of tea to make everything feel better." As I take my first sip I feel my tension ease.

It is unusual what your memory recalls. My grandma remains forever in my thoughts and feelings. The daffodils Miguel has just given to me remind me of her and her garden. The dead always stay with you in some way or other. I can say that with confidence.

Miguel and I sit in a quiet corner where we can talk without being disturbed. I see a few guests look over at us, probably wondering what a freaky disturbed woman dressed in dirty sheets is doing talking to a handsome gentleman dressed in a suit. He's changed before coming to see me. They probably think that we look worlds apart. If only they knew the real truth about different worlds.

We sit comfortably next to each other and talk quietly so as not to draw any more attention to ourselves. I relax back in the sofa and listen to why and how Miguel killed me.

He shakes his head in disbelief and disgust with himself. "Your parents were amazing and very special people, but I was disrespectful to them." I see disappointment and upset in his eyes.

"What happened?" I am desperate to know.

"I didn't have a loving family in my last life like you Saskia. A loving family was all that I ever wanted, but I was an orphan. I was passed from one home to another, but I was never for keeps, I was always moved on. I don't know why."

I sit up protective of him and lean forward stroking his arm, "That must have been terrible for you."

He nods, "When I eventually reached an age that I could look after myself, I found a job on a farm. I was really pleased for myself. I was given a little cottage and the owners of the farm welcomed me into their family. They treated me like one of their own children. They had a large family who were also very good with me. They had a daughter a good number of years younger than me and as she got older I become very fond of her. It was obvious that she also had strong feeling for me. Sometimes you just know, don't you?"

I know. I am now recalling some of the gaps in my knowledge and remember living on a farm. Miguel worked on the farm for my father and I was attracted to him when I first saw him. I used to go and flirt with him, whilst he was working, and I knew that he liked it.

Miguel carries on, "As our fondness grew, our relationship became passionate. You used to tease me at work and we would make love in the haystacks. You would sometimes sneak out of your parents' house late at night to spend the night with me at the cottage. I was loved up more than anybody could imagine and hoped that you would one day become my wife and we could live the happy ever after story."

I smile with contentment at his feelings for me, but I wonder what could have possibly gone wrong.

He closes his eyes as though recalling something. "One day your parents went into town and we were making the most passionate love in the haystacks. We were both naked and you were screaming with enjoyment. Unknown to us, your parents had returned early from their trip and they caught us. They did not know of our relationship, and thought I was taking advantage."

I gasp, "That's why my mother was crying and my father shouting." I remember, "I saw the scene in my vision when we were with the spiritual guru in the cave. My past life passed through me and I saw my father shouting and I didn't know why. I had two visions of my mother crying and this must have been the reason for one of them, the reason for the other was my death."

Miguel closes his eyes again for a moment, containing his sadness, "Your father was disappointed with me. He was disgusted with me. He didn't know that we had been seeing each other and claimed that I had abused my position. Even though you were eighteen, you were still his little girl in his eyes. He did not want you in a relationship with anybody, especially me, as I would not have been good enough for you."

I recall, "He was very protective of me, wasn't he? That's why we hadn't told them."

Miguel nods. "Your father told me to leave the farm and never come back. I explained that I loved you and wanted to marry you, but he spat in my face and said that he would kill me if I ever went near you or his farm again. I could leave the farm, but I wasn't willing to leave you." He looks up at me, "As far as I was concerned you were my soulmate."

I am recalling more and more information and remembering everything about my past life. I was happy on the farm, but only because of Miguel. He was my food, my water, my moon and the sun in my life. He made every day special. I loved my parents and siblings, but it was Miguel that made my heart beat. He was my universe.

I recall that my family were annoyed with me and said that I had brought shame and disrespect on them. They were exceptionally strict, but I knew deep down that it was only because they cared. My father called me a slut that day.

My father shouted, "You are a dirty little slut, bringing disgrace on our family. I will never forgive you."

I don't think that he meant it. He was just upset with my actions.

He shouted, "You will never see that boy again, never. It is over between you forever."

There was no convincing them to change their mind, but I was not going to let them stop me living my life how I wanted. I wanted to be with Miguel as I loved him.

I was sent to my room and told to stay there, but I climbed out of the window. I was going to run away to the Mariachi. They believed in the rite of courtship, and dancing made everything feel better.

Miguel continues, "I was packing my things together and I saw you running through the fields. I had heard your family shouting and knew that you were running away. There was only one place that you could be going…."

We say together, "The Mariachi."

Miguel and I loved to dance. We used to dance the official dance, the Jarabe Tapatio, otherwise known as the hat song. I remember now. It was the song that we danced to when we first met in this life, at the Destruction Tequila beach party. I now know why I could dance and knew all of the moves. Traditionally, the dance tells of love and courtship between two people and if you dance with the right person, it is an easy way to get close, have fun and check chemistry.

Young members of opposite sexes were once kept apart in society, but the Mariachi participated in the rite of courtship. They would sing and play the Jarabe Tapatio in secret locations and bring young lovers together. We attended together regularly and knew that there was a dance that evening.

I remember that night clearly, our secret was out, and if my father and family would not accept that we loved each other, then we would just have to run away. Nobody or anything was going to keep us apart. We were soulmates.

I recall to Miguel, "We had a wonderful evening with the Mariachi and danced continuously to the Jarabe Tapatio. Everybody there knew how strong our love for each other was and supported our decision. We had been secretly meeting at the Mariachi for over a year and had made friends with other members, who were also kept apart from the rite of courtship. That night I was convinced that I was doing the right thing. We danced like never before, we danced with closeness and chemistry. I knew you were the only man that I could ever want and need in my life. Nobody else mattered."

Miguel recalls, "Our spirits were high as we left. We didn't know where we were going or where we would end up, but we would be together, and that is all that mattered. For those that could not or would not accept us in unity, they were history in my mind."

Miguel knows that I am remembering what happened and moves closer. "Do you remember our plans?"

"We were going to run away after the Mariachi, so that we could be together."

Miguel's eyes fill with tears again, "I am so sorry."

"Why?" I question. "I was happy."

"I should have left quietly and let you live your life with your family. The trouble would have eventually been forgotten and you would have had a happy life. You could have met somebody else who made you happy and who your father and family approved of. Instead I killed you."

"How did you kill me? I don't understand?"

He takes a moment, "I was keen to steal you from your family. I hated them for the trouble they caused, and I resented them for trying to split us up. I loved you and knew that we needed to escape fast, so that they would not come after us and take you away from me."

He pauses, "You didn't know but your father had bought you an old car. He had been working on it secretly. He was planning to give it to you for your 19th birthday, when it had been fully renovated."

"Was that the car we died in?" I swallow hard and feel dryness in the back of my throat. I feel a pain and sickness in the bottom of my gut.

"It was only two weeks off your birthday and I presumed that the work had been completed. It was going to be your car, so I took it for us to get away in. I was disrespectful of your father and I took the car with no thought, consideration or care for the feelings of your family. I selfishly wanted you to myself."

There is a long silence between us.

"When we were driving down the cliff, I realized that the brakes had stopped working. He must not have finished the work properly and everything is therefore my fault. I blame myself for killing you." He starts to cry, "I killed you."

I take a deep breath then let out a loud sigh. "It was an accident and accidents happen."

"It was more than an accident. I should not have taken your car and I should not have taken you from your family. I blame myself for everything. I blame myself for your death."

I have always wondered what it would be like to be part of a large family. Even though I was brought up with my grandparents and I really loved them, I always felt that there was something missing, people missing in my life. Now I realize what those feelings were. The missing feelings were the family that I left behind when I died in my past life, the family that I deleted from my mind the night I decided to run away, the family that I once loved and who in return loved me, but the family that I will never see again. I will never be able to apologize for my actions or explain my feelings, and there will always be a hole in their heart for me and a feeling of disappointment for what I did to them.

Miguel didn't kill me, it was a fatal accident. I don't blame him, and I certainly don't want him to blame himself. I just need some space and time away from him to think everything through. I look at the worry on his face, but I can also see an element of relief at his confession. Everything is now out in the open and tomorrow is the Day of the Dead. I wonder what else is in store for us and, more importantly, if we can get through it.

I watch him leave the hotel, almost dragging his feet with exhaustion and his head held low. He fully understands that I need time to mourn my own death and feel the grief and sorrow of losing a loving family. I know that I have been here in a previous life and have been recalling past life experiences, but now that I have all of the facts, I feel a pain beyond words.

I smell the underworld cling to me. The stagnant smell of the cenotes, the anguish of death and the feeling of sadness clings to my body making me feel emotional and dirty. Back in my room, I pull off the robes and climb into a rose petal bath. I cry until no more tears can be found. I don't cry for myself. Instead I cry for the family that I left behind. I mourn my past.

I stare in agony at the beautiful pink petals floating around me. The life of a flower ends the moment it is picked, similar to the way life ends at death, yet these beautiful remaining petals bring me some contentment. The sweet smell reminds me of how beautiful life sometimes can be, but also helps me pay homage to my past life.

The scattering of flower petals on the grave of the deceased is not only a ritual for honoring the dead, but a reminder of the shortness of life and a means of honoring their memory. The custom of funerary flowers is an ancient tradition and as tomorrow is the Day of the Dead, I intend finding my gravestone from my past life and taking some flowers.

As I climb out of the bath and wrap my body in a fluffy dressing gown, I notice some of the rose petals are turning black in the steamy hot water. Perhaps black roses do not always mean death, they could really mean rebirth. Thinking about flowers, daffodils return every year as though they are reborn. I can't help but wonder about the circle of life and where my situation exactly fits in this crazy world.

I lie on the bed and close my eyes. I am really tired and emotionally drained. Time is a healer, and hopefully things will feel better and seem clearer tomorrow.

CHAPTER SEVENTEEN

I awaken to loud knocking on my door and hear Catherine's voice, "She isn't in Joshua. She must still be out with Miguel."

I hear a moan from Joshua, "But I want to show her my sore knees."

It's lovely to hear them and despite feeling down, I really want to see them. They are the next thing to family in my life, they are the only family I have, and after what I have just been through, family means everything to me.

As I open the door I see Joshua with each knee wrapped in bandage. Blood has leaked through one of the bandages and I feel his pain. Protective of him, I pick him up in my arms, walk back into my room and give him the biggest cuddle in the world. Catherine follows behind me sighing.

"What have you done to your knees, Josh?" I ask as I kiss each better.

Joshua half smiles loving the attention, but puts on a sad voice, "It was horrible, Aunty Saskia, I only wanted to be a butterfly."

Catherine sighs again, "Don't give him any sympathy because he doesn't deserve it. We were by the pool and he decided to climb up on a bar stool and suddenly jump off without giving any warning, trying to fly. He was lucky that he has only cut his knees and not broke his legs."

Joshua stamps his feet, "I only wanted to fly like the butterflies, but I couldn't."

He looks up at me with a cute look, "Can you teach me to fly Aunty Saskia? I want to fly away from Mummy, because she is angry with me."

I sit on a chair and he climbs on my knee and cuddles into me.

"I wish I could teach you to fly, Josh, but I can't fly. We don't have beautiful wings like a butterfly, because we aren't meant to fly."

I think about the butterfly dome, "Not in this life, anyway."

He looks up at me again, "But I want to fly."

Catherine snaps, "Well you will just have to be a pilot when you grow up and fly a plane. Won't you?" She rolls her eyes.

Joshua looks down and cuddles tighter into me.

"I'm pleased that you can't fly," I say. "I don't want you to fly away from me like a butterfly would. I want you and your mummy in my life forever. Where would we all be without each other?"

Joshua nods, "I wouldn't fly away from you. I love you too much and will be with you forever."

I agree, "I hope so. I really do."

I hold him tightly in my arms and cuddle him. I feel lucky to have people in my life that are so special to me and enjoy the warmth and meaning of his cuddle.

Catherine pours herself a large glass of white wine from the minibar and places herself down on the small sofa near the patio doors. I can't help but think to myself that she has a special glow about her this evening, and it isn't her suntan. She is wearing a beautiful low-cut red dress that suits her, but it is more than just the dress that makes her look different.

I look at her and smile, "You look lovely this evening. Have you done something different with yourself?"

I am trying to ascertain how she looks different, but I can't work it out.

Catherine smiles at my pleasing comment, "I went to the hotel hairdressers and they blow dried my hair. I thought that I would treat myself. Do you like it?" she asks, gently running her fingers through her long hair.

I nod, "It looks great. You should treat yourself more often. You look lovely tonight."

She nods, "I thought I would make a special effort. There is a party at the hotel tonight and you never know who you might meet. I saw a few good-looking men around the pool today."

She raises her eyebrows and smiles with mischief. "Do you want to come with us, or are you seeing Miguel again later?"

"I will be seeing him tomorrow, but not tonight. Anyway, looks like I am coming out with you tonight if you plan to pull. Who will have Joshua otherwise? I will play gooseberry and nanny."

She throws her head back and laughs, "I never pull anybody'.

With the help of Catherine and Joshua, I pick an outfit to wear. It is a simple knee length chiffon white dress. Catherine nips into the bathroom and as I look in the bedroom mirror, Joshua looks me up and down.

"You make a good ghost, Aunty Saskia."

I feel myself go pale, wondering if Joshua can see something that I can't.

"What do you mean?" I ask nervously wondering if he can see my shadow.

"For the Dead Party, you look like a ghost in that white dress."

I am still absorbing what Josh has just said and I hear Catherine exit from the bathroom in her high heels.

She overhears Joshua and informs him, "Joshua, I have told you, and have already explained, it's not a dead party. It's a party to celebrate the Day of the Dead which is something they do in Mexico. It's a Mexican tradition. Aunty Saskia isn't dressed as a ghost. It is just a beautiful white dress."

She looks at me, "Ignore him, Sas, I've tried to explain this to him earlier, but he doesn't really understand."

He scowls at his mum and I can't help but laugh at his cute face.

I smile at him. "I will be a ghost if you want me to be a ghost, Joshua."

No wonder he doesn't understand the Day of the Dead. He is only a child. I'm still trying to come to terms with its meaning.

He smiles at me showing his cute teeth, "And I will be a butterfly, but one that doesn't fly, because I don't want to leave you."

We decide to dine formally before the party. We haven't spent a lot of time together since they arrived. We have typically opted for room service on the nights we have spent together, usually due to Joshua being tired, however tonight he is full of energy, full of beans.

"You are full of Mexican jumping beans," Catherine jokes with him, and he jumps up and down on the spot.

The restaurant is lit with beautiful candle light and soft music is playing upon our arrival. We sit ourselves near the window looking out over the beach, the ocean and soft lighting in the far distance. Joshua is distracted by the beautiful view and the pirate ship in the distance as we talk.

"Aunty Saskia," Josh interrupts us.

I look up and listen to him.

He points through the window at the pirate ship, "If I can't fly like a butterfly, I could be a pirate and have a patch."

I laugh as he closes one eye and covers it with his hand. I am sure that he will change his mind about that too, especially if he ever meets the glass-eyed American.

Catherine and I chat casually about anything and everything over dinner, and it is great to catch up. We discuss Joshua, work, worries, love and life in general. We talk about Daniel, which is a short conversation. We both believe that you meet everyone for a reason and the reason behind us both meeting Daniel was to bring us together. We laugh and nearly cry at points, but that is life, and I am proud and pleased to share my life with two people that are so special to me.

I may not have my family from my past anymore, I don't know where I am going with Miguel, but I have Catherine and Joshua who bring love and meaning into my life, and I would be lost without them.

CHAPTER EIGHTEEN

Time sometimes just passes you by and it is certainly the case this evening. We haven't spent much quality time together in such a long period and we have a lot to catch up on.

By the time we arrive at the Day of the Dead hotel party, it is in full swing. It isn't how I expected it to be. It isn't how Miguel described it, but having had said that, I don't think it is supposed to be. Let's say it is more like a Halloween party with no precise meaning other than to entertain holiday guests and let them have fun. Tradition and meaning does not come into this scenario.

Lots of guests are in Halloween-type outfits, such as ghosts, witches, zombies, spiders and anything else that goes with Halloween. Joshua's mouth is wide with excitement looking at all of the colorful costumes and makeup. He looks at everybody, absorbing what is around him.

"I want to be a spider," he quietly announces, eyeing a gentleman in a spider-type black costume with lots of legs.

Catherine nods, "So, do you want eight legs instead of two wings and a patch."

"Is that the most legs a spider can have?" he quizzes, still thinking about what she has said.

"You can be whoever and whatever you want to be tonight," I advise him. "I just want us all to have some fun and quality time together.

Catherine shrugs her shoulders, "Well at least if he's a spider, he won't be jumping off stools and hurting his legs." Laughing she carries on, "Even if he does, at least he will have another six to get him about."

I laugh, "That was a terrible joke."

A teenager dressed as a skeleton with RIP written on his back runs past me screaming and I feel a slight sense of nausea. I recall the skulls at the cenote and wonder if they are in purgatory, and if they will ever rest in peace. I wonder if I will ever have peace, or if I will be haunted by my past for the rest of my life.

I try to put the thought to the back of my mind. Tonight, is about the three of us. Following recent events, I now realise that you need to enjoy and appreciate your time with the people that you love. I don't want my past to spoil this evening. I want to live life to the full, with the people that matter to me.

There are local and international acts to entertain the guests and one of these is 'Thriller'. Michael Jackson music plays loudly, undead actors begin to rise out of their graves and zombies dance on stage. The crowds cheer and dance enjoying the show, but I feel a moment of sadness. If only these people really knew what I know.

"Do you not like this?" Catherine shouts over the music in my ear. "You look really pissed off with it. It's written all over your face."

I shake my head, "I just find the situation a little distasteful and the music a little loud."

She shrugs her shoulders, "It's a great atmosphere, but you are a hard lady to please."

"Why am I hard to please?" I ask, alarmed.

She smiles and places her hand on my shoulder to comfort me. "You just need to let yourself go, Saskia, and have some fun. Stop being so highly strung and letting things bother you. Be a free spirit and you might actually start enjoying life."

I know that Catherine didn't mean what she said to be offensive. She cares about me and doesn't have a nasty bone in her body. She must be able to tell that I am a little stressed, and it is her attempt to help my situation. She doesn't know that I am worrying about tomorrow and I would never discuss my situation with her. She would probably think I was going insane and rush me back to mental rehabilitation. I suppose that life can be crazy, but my life just appears more nonsensical than most.

Catherine waves her hand in front of her face to fan herself, "Let's go and get a drink, it's hot in here. I think the bar is open near the swimming pool. I would appreciate some sea breeze to cool me down."

I can't agree enough.

The pool area is beautifully lit and little stalls have set up selling momentums for the Day of the Dead celebration. The products are similar to what I saw at the ruins, when I first saw the shadow people. There's jewelry, incense, religious icons, masks, candles, shrines and crosses. The list of things you can buy is endless.

There is a small stand selling sweets and desserts associated with the theme. A lady offers onlookers the opportunity to taste one of the foods.

"It's a dessert called Calabaza en Tacha and is made of pumpkin, cinnamon and piloncillo," she informs me as she directs a spoon towards my mouth.

It's delicious and but for having already eaten, I would easily enjoy a full bowl. All of the edible goodies on offer look amazing. There are skulls and coffins made of sugar, chocolate skeletons, amaranth seeds and special baked goods, including sugary sweet bread topped with bits of dough in bone shapes, which are meant to represent bones of the deceased. The lady points to some unadorned dark breads molded into humanoid figures which she calls souls.

"Would you like to try?" she asks.

"I am tempted," I answer, "but I have just finished dinner, so I am full." I rub my belly to express myself.

"Would the little boy like to try?"

Joshua shakes his head and looks up at me, "Please can we get some of the sugar skulls, Aunty Saskia. They look really good and I have never seen them before."

I wonder who came up with the idea of making candy skulls. I mean, who on earth would want to eat a skull? In England, I have always bought nice sweets like chocolate mice, Percy Pigs, jelly teddy bears, bananas and shrimps but never skulls. Having said that, I have bought jelly babies and I used to get great enjoyment biting their heads off. I suppose that people here may find that a little weird.

The lady hands Joshua his sweets and he seems more than content sucking them quietly. Catherine is pre-occupied looking at all the different jewelry. She is like a magpie at times, attracted to anything and everything that glistens. She picks up a locket and waves at me to come over and look.

"Isn't it beautiful?" she asks, holding it up to her neck. "It is sterling silver and look at all of the small stones placed on the actual locket." She holds it up for me to look at closely, "It is hand-finished and the attention to detail is exquisite."

I agree that it is beautiful. It reminds me of the locket that I saw at the base of the cenote, the locket that I was allowed to look at but not touch. I saw lots of things in the water but that is the one item that really stood out and seemed to mean something.

The lady on the stall has been chattering away to Catherine. I'm not sure what she has been saying, I haven't really been listening. I have just been looking at the unusual dolls, the prototypical Catrina dancing skeletons in their beautiful dancing gowns.

The lady fastens the locket around Catherine's neck and she stares proudly at it in the mirror.

"I will take it." Catherine turns to me, "I've got to have it, Sas. It will be a memory of our holiday. I shall put a picture of all of us in it and treasure it forever."

I smile at her beautiful thought, then instantly wonder what possibly could have been in the locket at the cenote. Whatever was in it wasn't revealed to me.

Further along there is a stall where you can practice carving pumpkins. Some have been completed and candles have been lit inside them. They line up almost smiling at me as the candle light shines through their carved features. I think about candles being lit to guide souls from the past to the Day of the Dead and wonder if any of these candles have a meaning. I wonder if any of the candles have been lit by people wanting to guide their dead relatives. Spooky shadows surround the stall where the flickering of candlelight catches the fancy dress outfits of the guests who are carefully carving and scraping. Joshua sits on a chair watching intensely but doesn't say anything. He is still happy sucking his sweets and taking in his surroundings.

Further along the line there is an apple bobbing competition stall. People are dunking their heads in water barrels to try and catch an apple with their teeth.

"I'd have a go if I hadn't had my hair done today," Catherine says.

"I bet you wouldn't," I tease.

We laugh at the apple bobbing competition stall where guests are getting soaked, and I don't know how it's happened, but I even come away soaked.

"You would have been less wet if you had dunked yourself," Catherine notes.

The last stall that we come to sells paintings. An elderly gentleman sits and paints without being distracted by our presence. He paints skeletons who are riding bikes, dancing, working and playing.

Catherine studies the paintings in detail, "What an unusual thing to paint," she observes. "Skeletons doing chores of the living."

She screws up her face disturbed with the images.

I smile, "I felt exactly the same when I first came across similar paintings and drawings at the ruins, but I now understand the paintings, and feel that the artist fully understands the meaning of life after death."

I place some money in the hat he has put on the counter for tips, and as I walk away he winks and smiles knowing that I appreciated his work and efforts.

A DJ is now present in the main ballroom, so we decide to go for a dance. We both hold Joshua's hands and swing him to the beats. He laughs his little head off with enjoyment.

"More and more," he shouts.

We hop, bop, groove and move.

"You have moves I didn't even know existed," Catherine says as she watches me dance and tries to copy with Joshua.

"I have moves that I didn't know I could do before I came here."

She looks me up and down and laughs as though I am joking. She should know that I am not joking because I have never had co-ordination, I have never been able to dance, and she has been out with me enough to know this.

Spooks surround us in Halloween attire on the dance floor and despite my first reservations about this party, I am actually having a good time. I expect that tomorrow won't be light-hearted and fun, but I am not going to let the thought spoil our evening tonight. I am going to put it to the back of my mind and live for now. I'll worry about it tomorrow, when the moment is actually upon me.

As the evening draws to a close, a Mariachi band plays music on the terrace, whilst magnesium fireworks are displayed in the sky. We cuddle together watching the spectacular, awesome, thrilling and breathtaking vision. The fireworks choreographed with the music create impact and lasting memories for the three of us. This is a moment to be cherished and never forgotten.

Making our way through reception back to our hotel rooms, I see Scott talking to the receptionist.

"Scott," I shout out, pleased to see him. I have wanted to introduce him to Catherine all holiday and this seems a perfect opportunity. He turns around and smiles his Colgate smile, pleased to see me.

He pecks me on each cheek and tickles Joshua under his chin. Joshua lifts up his shoulders and grins. I think it's fair to presume these two have taken a liking to each other.

"Did you like the butterflies?" he asks Joshua.

"Yes, I chased the flying flowers, but didn't touch them."

Scott smiles, "You have a good memory little friend."

Scott turns to me, "Have you had a good evening? I hope you have been drinking lots of Destruction Tequila, as it was us who organized this event."

I laugh, "Yes, we have had a good evening. I should have known that it had something to do with the company you work for. You are everywhere."

"I know," he admits proudly. "Anyway, are you on your own with Joshua again?

"I'm with the friend I told you about. She's here to be introduced to you."

I turn and realize that Catherine is no longer at my side.

"She was there a minute ago," I claim, feeling confused as to where she has gone.

Scott looks puzzled, "I never saw anybody with you, apart from this little guy."

"She is definitely with me," I tell him.

He looks around, "Well unless she is invisible, I am struggling to see her."

After a moment, he jokingly holds out his hand and pretends to shake hands with somebody, "It's nice to meet you Saskia's invisible friend."

He starts to laugh knowing that his behavior is winding me up.

I give him a sarcastic glare, "You are such a big head and think you are so funny, but I am not amused."

Joshua starts chuckling then immediately covers his mouth as though trying to stop. Scott and I look at each other unsure of the source of his amusement.

"Perhaps she has gone to the ladies or left something in the ballroom." I am looking for excuses as to why she should disappear, "Maybe I should go and look for her."

Joshua chuckles again, "Mummy's playing hide and seek."

"What do you mean, Joshua?" I ask baffled.

"Mummy's hiding and she doesn't want you to know where." He chuckles again looking in the direction of some sofas in the corner of the reception area.

Scott raises his eyebrows. "Your friend sounds like loads of fun and I would love to play hide and seek with you, but it's a bit difficult when I don't know what she looks like."

I provide a description, "She has long red hair and she is stunning. You can't miss her."

We all head in the direction of the sofas and I witness Catherine shuffling around a large three-seat sofa on her hands and knees.

"Catherine, what on earth are you doing?" I ask, puzzled with her behavior.

She places her finger up at her mouth, trying to hush me.

Scott walks towards us, "Take it you have found her?"

I nod, "Scott, please let me introduce you to my absolutely crazy best friend, who is currently on her hands and knees. It's taken a while to get here, but I am sure that it will have been worth the wait to meet her." I roll my eyes.

Catherine shuffles up from behind the sofa looking embarrassed with a red face.

I know we are at a Halloween-type party, but Scott stares at her as though he has seen a ghost, "Catherine," he says with astonishment in his voice.

"Hi Scott, I thought it was you from a distance and yes, it's me."

She brushes herself down and tries to look dignified, despite dust and bits having clung to her knees and dress.

She lifts up her hands in the air to express herself, "My hair's a lot longer and my boobs a bit bigger."

Scott smiles and looks her up and down. "You've changed."

She relaxes her arms by her sides, "I had a boob job, but yes, it's still me."

She shrugs her shoulders and they stare at each other.

"You two know each other?" I ask, confused with their reactions.

"Meet my ex," they both say together.

Things are now starting to make sense. Scott had previously spoken about his ex-girlfriend who was originally from Ireland. He'd explained that she had a child with somebody else, but he had never mentioned her name to me. Catherine has spoken to me about the ex that she claimed to still be in love with and she had also mentioned things that described Scott. Why had I not put two and two together? The thought had never once crossed my mind.

"I was looking forward to introducing you to each other and you already knew each other." I ramble, "What a surprise – for me."

Scott speaks whilst still looking at Catherine, "It's a surprise for all of us."

Catherine smiles at him and tries to break the ice, "It's a pleasant one."

"It is for me too," Scott says looking pleased.

Despite there being an unusual atmosphere between them, I am fully aware that they need some time together, they need to talk. I know that they are still both in love and should build whatever bridges are needed in order to be together. Catherine has told me that she still loves her ex, and Scott has also told me the same. It's about time that they just told each other.

"Perhaps you guys have things to catch up on," I suggest.

Catherine nods, "Please could you take Joshua to bed, Saskia, it's getting late for him."

"I'll take him to my room. I get the feeling that you both have a lot to talk about and I could do with getting myself to bed. I'm seeing Miguel tomorrow and don't want to be tired"

"Thanks, Sas, it would be a great help. I will come to your room in the morning to collect him."

I head towards the lift with Joshua, but I notice that Scott and Catherine are still standing opposite each other in silence.

I walk back towards them to offer some advice. I feel that they need a little help and encouragement.

They both look up to listen to what I have to say, "Sometimes you might only get one chance to say what you need to say and express your feelings. I think that you are both being given another chance, so take it whilst the opportunity is here. It may not ever come around again."

Scott smiles at me. We have had many heartfelt conversations and he knows where I am coming from.

"Thanks, Saskia, and thanks for the cherub you gave to me. It has worked its magic powers and I know what is needed."

With everything that has been going on in my life, or should I say double life, I had forgotten about the cherub and how it is supposed to help you find your soulmate. Catherine and Scott are made to be together, and despite them dating and separating, the cherub has helped them find each other again, because they are meant to be. Some things in life are just inevitable. I suppose that love and soulmates go together, even in the most complicated situations.

If the cherub has done this for them and I can see this clearly now, then I should start to appreciate that it has also brought Miguel and me together too, but this time from a past life rather than a present life.

I have been wondering if we are actually meant to be, if we do make a good couple, looking for reasons why perhaps we shouldn't be together, but the truth is that I love him, and I do want to spend the rest of my life with him. I would want to spend the rest of every life with him because he is my soulmate.

I remember my grandma saying, "You will know when you have found the one."

The truth is that I have always known that Miguel is the one.

Cherubs obviously have magical powers. I am undecided as to whether they are supernatural beings, spirits or maybe angels that serve God, but they are responsible for making humans fall in love and perhaps this is an instruction from heaven.

I hope that the gods and angels above are still looking out for us, despite our past souls being in some form of purgatory. The fact that Miguel and I have been brought together makes me believe that they are taking care of us, and this makes me feel more confident about what may happen at the Day of the Dead tomorrow.

Some couples are said to go through thick and thin together. Miguel and I have gone through life and death together. I just hope that we come out of the other end, wherever that may be, still together.

I help Joshua get in bed and kiss him gently on his head. "Goodnight sweetheart."

"Night, Aunty Saskia."

He is certainly very tired because he closes his eyes straight away. It must be wonderful to not have a worry in the world and to sleep so peacefully.

I can't remember having had a proper night's sleep in my whole life. If I haven't had nightmares about my past life death, there has always been something at the back of my mind bothering me, disturbing me, telling me to get up and pace the room, making me toss and turn a hundred times in a one-hour period. It's strange but you seem to clock watch throughout the night when this is happening, taking note of every hour, minute and second, almost wanting to fast forward the hours until daylight and another day.

I now stand on the balcony looking out at the dark ocean, looking out at the unknown and wish that I could rewind those years, days, hours, minutes and seconds. I wish that I could rewind my current life and be taken right back to my past life, even if it is only to say goodbye properly to the people I loved.

Following recent supernatural revelations, when my shadow person passed through me in the caves at the ruins, I should consider myself lucky to have shared a vision of my last life and seen the people I loved. I know the shadow was crying out to me, trying to explain why it was still on earth and asking for my help, but I begrudge being shown the trouble I caused before I died. I am now left with a vision of my past life family being upset with me, and I think this thought shall disturb me forever. I wish that I had been shown a happy memory rather than a sad one.

I know that I shared many happy moments with my family from the past and I can now recall these, but the vision of unhappiness has disturbed me more than you will ever know. I wish that I could put everything right, somehow and someway.

I return to my suite locking the patio doors behind me. There is a sense of eeriness in the air tonight, almost mysterious and uncanny, weird as in ghostly. Candles are being lit and incense burnt to guide souls from the past for the Day of the Dead, and I wonder if this is what I am sensing. The thought disturbs me and frightens me, inspiring a feeling of fear, dread and uneasiness to travel through my body.

My mobile phone beeps indicating a text message and makes me nervously jump. It's from Miguel and simply says, 'I love you, I miss you'.

I sit on the edge of the bed and absorb the words into my mind, before replying, 'I've always loved you and I have always missed you. I wish things were different, but I still want to be with you'.

I honestly believe that I have always been in love with Miguel. There had always been a missing feeling in my mind, body and soul all of my life. I searched high and low for where those feeling were coming from, even ending up in a mental rehabilitation unit. When I come face to face with Miguel, I just knew he was what I had been looking for. We just knew that we had been missing in each other's life.

I wish that he was here with me tonight to hold me tightly in his arms. I would feel safer with him by my side.

I receive another text, 'I need you tonight and I am here if you want me?'

I feel his presence and open my hotel room door where we fall into each other's arms, where we rightly belong.

As Joshua is sleeping in the bed, we take the bed settee, which isn't particularly comfortable, however, I would rather be here safe in the arms of the man that I love, than be anywhere else in the world.

CHAPTER NINETEEN

I awaken to shadows dancing around the room almost enticing me to get out of bed and join them. I remember that it is the Day of the Dead and I quickly pull the duvet covers over my head. It is dark under the covers, but it is somewhere I can hide from today, somewhere that I don't need to join in with the Day of the Dead events.

Miguel pulls the covers from over my head revealing the light of day. He puts his arm around me and pulls me towards his body.

"Everything is going to be ok, Saskia," he reassures me. "Whatever today may bring, we have each other and we will face this together."

I frown, "I have been thinking and if the Shadow People really wanted to hurt us then they would have done it by now, wouldn't they?"

Miguel nods. "I hope that they just want our help. I am sure that everything will be revealed today. Let's just go with the flow because it's no good worrying about the inevitable. If something is going to happen then it will happen, and it is out of our control."

I sigh, "Life and death are out of control. We know our past, but our future cannot be destined."

Miguel climbs out of bed and starts to get dressed.

"I have to go back to my hotel, but I shall pick you up at lunchtime. Is that ok?"

I sit up and panic, "Why do you have to leave? You said that we could face today together?"

He sits on the end of the bed and holds my hand, "You can spend some time with Catherine and Joshua this morning and I shall collect you by car at lunchtime. We then have to go and collect my grandma to take her to the daytime 'Day of the Dead' events. She needs to go to the local graveyard to visit my grandfather, and I said we would take her."

I had forgotten about meeting his grandma. Miguel had mentioned it on our first date, before we knew about our predicament.

"Does she know about our situation?" I ask.

He shakes his head, "Of course she doesn't."

I am worried, "Well, what happens if something occurs with the shadows whilst we are with her?"

"If the shadows from the past appear we will just have to deal with it," he answers sternly. "I always take Grandma to the 'Day of the Dead'. I love her, and I am not going to let her down, or my grandfather who passed away. Grandma will want to visit his grave and spend some time there. The shadows will just have to respect our time, and if they want our help, they shall have to wait until we are available. We shall only stay with her for a couple of hours, because she will be tired and need to get home after that."

"You don't appear scared of the shadow people anymore," I observe.

"They need our help and we will do everything we can to help, but we also have to live for now and for us in this life. I know that we need to be freed from the shadows in order to carry on with our life, but there need to be boundaries."

He kisses me on the head and walks out of the door leaving me in thought.

Thinking about it, Miguel is right. The shadows have made their situation known to us, but they can't overtake our life. They are the past and we are living in the present. I want to help them escape purgatory so that Miguel and I can move on and they don't haunt us, but that doesn't mean that they can frighten us, and leave us looking over our shoulder all of the time, so to speak. We are here to help them, and they probably need our help as much as we need theirs.

I get out of bed and boil the kettle to make myself a cup of tea. A cup of tea makes everything better. Joshua wakes up and bounces over to me full of energy.

"Can we go swimming, Aunty Sas."

"We need to get breakfast first. We also need to find out what your mummy is doing."

It feels really hot in the main dining room, so Joshua and I opt to sit outside on the balcony overlooking the beach. I don't feel particularly hungry, probably due to being churned up worrying, so I don't eat, but I have a strong cup of coffee. I enjoy watching Joshua tucking into his breakfast.

"Jam on toast is my favorite," he informs me with red-seeded teeth and his mouth full.

Catherine approaches and stands directly behind me with Scott, beaming his Colgate smile. I bet his teeth have never seen sticky jam.

"Joshua, you have terrible manners. You should never talk with food in your mouth."

Scott pulls his tongue out behind Catherine, and Joshua laughs spitting his chewed toast over Catherine.

She rolls her eyes, "You shouldn't laugh when you are eating either. Honestly, Joshua, I don't know why I bother trying to teach you manners sometimes."

Scott leans over the table, "Suppose I had best rescue you from this jam on toast." He quickly takes a bite from a slice and starts to talk.

Catherine elbows him, "I've got two of them to contend with now. Look what I have got to put up with, Saskia."

Scott and Joshua both pull their tongues out behind her back and I smile.

"I am sure that you would have it no other way, Catherine, having your two favorite men in your life."

She frowns in disapproval at my comment.

Scott goes to order some coffee and takes Joshua for some orange juice. Catherine and I watch them walk away from the table laughing and joking between themselves.

"They seem to be getting on really well," I notice.

Catherine smiles, "Good job really. Scott and I have had a really good chat and we have decided to give it another go."

"That's wonderful!" I remark. "What about after the holidays though? I mean, you live in the UK and Scott lives here in Mexico. It's a long way to commute to see each other."

"Yes, I know, we still need to discuss the finer details, but the good news is that we are back together. Scott's work contract with Destruction Tequila lasts for another twelve months, so we have talked about me coming over with Joshua for that time, and then perhaps going back to England after that, just in time for Joshua starting school."

"That's good, but have you spoken with Daniel about this. I mean, he is Joshua's dad."

She sighs, "Gosh, the man cheated on you, and here you are worrying about him. I don't get you at times, Saskia."

I don't get myself at times, but she can be so abrupt at times.

I take a deep breath. "I am not worrying about him at all. What you and Daniel do is no business of mine, but I am just worrying about that little chap missing out on time with his dad. For all of Daniel's faults he does love Joshua. Surely you know that?"

"It's fine," she reassures me. "I have talked to Daniel this morning."

"Ok."

"He is fine about it all, honest." She softens, "Apparently he was telling me that he has been thinking about renting his house out and doing some travelling in order to find himself. I told him that he didn't need to travel far. He just had to look up his asshole and he would find himself."

"You didn't?" I ask, shocked.

She laughs loudly, "No, not really, but I felt like doing. He is so wrapped up in his own importance. Even if I stayed in England, he wasn't planning on staying around and spending time with Joshua. He is going travelling."

I think about it for a moment, "He doesn't like to travel. He hates flying."

"Well, he reckons that whilst on his journey to find himself, he will visit Mexico and see Joshua. Perhaps he will come by boat and with a bit of luck it will sink."

"You can be so nasty, Catherine," I remark.

She laughs, "I am only joking. I don't wish him any harm really. He is the father to my son after all. I do hope that he finds himself on his travels though. I am sure there is a nice guy in there somewhere."

She has such a weird sense of humor at times.

"So, are you and Scott good?" I ask.

"God Saskia, I have missed him, in fact I didn't realize how much until last night. He is so good in bed and…"

I cringe, and interrupt, "Please spare me the details, Catherine. I really don't want to know about your sex life."

She holds her head back laughing and then ties her hair back in a ponytail.

"Sorry, I am just so happy. I haven't felt so good in ages and everything just feels right between us, like it is meant to be."

Scott and Joshua appear back at the table listening to the back end of our conversation.

"It's you we need to thank Saskia," Scott states. "If you hadn't come to Mexico, then Catherine wouldn't have followed you, and we wouldn't have met again."

He strokes Catherine's hand and she stares into his eyes all loved up.

I am pleased that they are happy.

"There's no need to thank me," I tell them. "I think that it was just destiny that you were meant to meet again, and to be together."

Joshua interrupts, "Please can we go swimming?"

"Ok," I reply. "We will leave these two love doves to have some time together. I can't swim for long though as Miguel is picking me up at lunch and I need to get ready."

Catherine suggests, "Perhaps we could all do something together later?"

I hesitate, "I am meeting Miguel's grandma this afternoon and then just the two of us have plans later, but maybe another day."

Scott raises his eyebrows and grins his pearly cheeky smile, "I think she wants him all to herself, Catherine."

Little do they know, I wish that I could have him all to myself without the shadows and any tainted past.

Catherine jokes, "Oh yes, what have you got planned?"

I laugh along, "Sorry guys, but I don't kiss and tell."

Joshua pulls at my costume, "Come on Aunty Sas, or we won't have time to swim."

It's my perfect time to escape and face no more questioning.

After placing Joshua's armbands on, we hold hands tightly, count to five and jump in the pool making the biggest splash ever. We rise to the top, both laughing.

"Again, again" Joshua laughs.

I look at his beautiful little face which expresses excitement and happiness. I can't help but think that there really should be more laughter and joy in people's lives.

"Let's do it one more time, but then I need to get ready to meet Miguel," I inform him.

Joshua nods, "I wish that you could stay and play this game with me instead."

I feel the same. At least I am in control of what's happening here, I haven't a clue what's going to occur later.

I have been deliberating over what to wear today. As it is the Day of the Dead, I opt for a black outfit as it is the customary color to wear at funerals. I obviously never went to my past life funeral, but as I intend finding my grave to share my respects, it feels right. As it's hot, I wear a short dress, which is loose fitting. I also wear flat sandals for comfort.

I take a good long look at myself in the mirror and wonder if I will look at myself the same again after whatever happens today. I then wonder about the last time my past life looked in the mirror, before the accident and death, and wonder what she saw.

Perhaps she saw a reflection of a young beautiful girl with a happy future ahead of her and dreams of her family coming to their senses. I think this is what she would have seen, or at least wanted to see. Who could possibly predict that her end was close, and that after her death she would be reborn, but her soul would not go to heaven, but would end up lost on Earth in some form of purgatory.

I feel the need to take a deep breath and then breathe deeply in and out like I did at the ruins. There is a presence in the room and I see shadows circling me, but I know they don't want to harm me. I feel a warm sensation pass through my body as my past life spirit enters me, making my body jitter and taking over my mind and train of thought.

I don't know where time has gone, but I was not my own person for some time. When my past life shadow vacated my body, I knew what was needed from me, and it is the same thing that I want. We need to say goodbye to our past family and ask for forgiveness. When forgiveness is given, my past life soul can go to heaven.

I know now what is needed, but I haven't a clue where to start, and if I can't carry out this task, then my past life soul shall remain on Earth in purgatory, and I will carry the guilt of what happened forever.

CHAPTER TWENTY

Miguel arrives punctually at 12.30pm to collect me. He is driving a black Mercedes E-Class that Palms Wellbeing Resort use to collect guests from the airport.

He climbs out of the car dressed smartly in black linen trousers and a black open-necked shirt. He must have had the same idea as me in regard to dress and commemorating our past. I smile at him as he opens the vehicle door for me, but he pulls me back from entering.

"I have been worrying about driving this evening," he hesitates, "after what happened in the past, but we need to live our life for now."

"I know, I trust you," I reassure him.

He looks relieved, "I shall drive carefully."

"The past was an accident. I know you will take care." My lips quiver.

We drive through many villages and towns on the way to Miguel's grandmother. I can see that everywhere that we pass is dressing up with beauty and mysticism. Although this celebration is associated with the dead, it is not actually a morbid or depressing time, but rather a period full of life, happiness and meaning, and there is excitement in the air. Today, the celebration of the Day of the Dead is cherished, and death is seen as life.

We go through villages where people have created and adorned altars to honor their dead loved ones. They have taken great care in creating altars that are lovingly arranged and perfectly decorated, laid out with gifts and offerings which include candles, incense, flowers, a variety of foods and sweets, drinks, photos of the deceased and items that once belonged to them.

Through each town we hear chants and prayers to encourage visits by the souls, and there is a strong smell of incense, a distinctive smell of marigolds and candles being burned to direct the souls.

Scenes of skeletons hugging, dancing and laughing are seen in window displays on the streets. Towns and villages are filled with color as people in costumes dance with skull shaped masks and Mariachi music fills the air. The whole occasion is festive, and everyone I hear talks of the dead as if they were still alive, remembering, re-living and enjoying. All of this is to honor and celebrate the lives of the dead. All of this is to welcome the souls of the dead to enjoy the pleasures that they once had in life.

Miguel pulls up at the side of the road where we see people climbing on winged boats.

I observe the boats with interest, "Why do the boats have wings?"

He looks on, "They are called butterfly boats."

I remember what I saw and read at the butterfly dome.

I ask, "Where are all of those people going on the butterfly boats?"

"They are travelling to an island in the middle of a lake where there is a cemetery to honor and celebrate the lives of the dead. Apparently, the island is famous for having lots of butterflies, hence the butterfly boats. Some people say the butterflies are the souls of some of the dead, and will show themselves to their relatives as beautiful, fluttering colors."

"Yes, I read about that at the butterfly dome."

There is a lady attending a small stall selling an array of colorful flowers and people queue patiently.

"I am collecting some flowers for my grandfather's grave," Miguel says. "We always come here as they are fresh and last a long time. My grandma insists on marigolds."

"Why marigolds?" I enquire.

"These yellow flowers are a symbol of death, referred to as the 'flower of death'. It's believed that the distinctive scent of the marigolds attracts the dead."

I'd already noted that marigolds were popular, "We also passed lots of villages and towns where paths of marigold petals had been scattered by families. I don't know where the paths went, do you?"

Miguel knows, "The petals are scattered by families from the door of their house to the cemetery. The ghosts, spirits, souls, shadows or whatever you want to call them can find their way home by following this golden path. The souls are not usually seen but their presence is felt."

It suddenly dawns on me that there are hundreds of cemeteries throughout Mexico and our grave from our past life could be anywhere. We could search for years and never find it.

I panic, "How will we find our graves from our past life."

He answers immediately. He has already given it some thought. "We shall just have to hope that there is a yellow path of marigold petals for our shadows to follow and we are directed, otherwise we shall have to face the reality and future of our past life souls being on earth with us, but in purgatory."

I feel a shiver run down my spine. It's the last thing that is wanted by all concerned.

Whilst Miguel buys marigolds for his grandmother, I purchase daffodils for our graves ready for if and when we find them.

"Why are you buying daffodils?" Miguel asks.

"My grandma loved daffodils because they brought happiness and enthusiasm into her life. Enthusiasm is what is needed at a time like this and I hope happiness shall be the result, so they feel appropriate."

Miguel's grandmother is awaiting our arrival, standing on the doorstep of her house. She lives in a large town where all of the houses are painted in different bright colors. Some are red, some blue, numerous ones are green and lots are yellow but they all have a different tone.

Miguel gets out of the car, "Please wait and I won't be a moment."

His grandmother rushes over to the car throwing her arms around Miguel and holding him close. She is a small, slim lady with long silver hair and a class of elegance about her. They appear to chat for quite a while, before he opens the passenger door for me to join them.

She stands on the doorstep and looks me up and down smiling, before throwing her arms around me and welcoming me to her home.

"Thank you for coming, Saskia, I am Marcia, Miguel's grandmother. I have heard all about you and I am happy that you can join us today."

"It's a pleasure and thank you for having me."

"I know you are very special to Miguel, so you are also special to me. Please come into my home and meet Miguel's grandfather, Alejandro."

She waves her arm directing us in and Miguel smiles, happy that his grandmother has taken a liking to me and accepted me.

It is dark inside due to all of the curtains being closed and there is a very strong smell of copal and incense being burned. We walk through a large lounge with a cold marble floor and sparse furniture.

Miguel pulls at my arm holding me back, "Don't be disturbed by what you will see, because it is normal for this day."

"What am I going to see?" I ask, slightly disturbed.

"It is an offering to the dead. It's an offering especially for my grandfather, Alejandro, and others that have moved on. My grandmother has built a shrine in her home for him and others. I just want you to be prepared for whatever you may see."

"I will be fine." I am sure.

We walk through to a dining area that is completely lit with scores of candles. Some have been freshly lit and some look like they have been burning for hours. The dining table is draped with a rose tapestry tablecloth and has numerous things covering it. There is a large cross, statues of the Blessed Virgin Mary, pictures of Miguel's grandfather at different stages of his life along with photographs of other people, who to use Miguel's words have 'moved on'.

The table is also decorated with plates of food, sugar skulls, sweet bread, liquor, cigarettes, flowers and there is a plastic skeleton.

Miguel picks it up and shares a memory, "My grandpa helped me make this for the 'Day of the Dead' when I was just a little boy. We had lots of fun together and I hope that he enjoys the offerings that are here for him today."

His grandma smiles, "I welcome his soul. He returns every year to enjoy the pleasures that he once had in life. I have given him the most elaborate food and drink that can be afforded. The candle light, along with the marigolds and the smell of copal incense, will help his soul find his way home."

We sit around the shrine and Miguel offers a prayer. I close my eyes and hold my hands together offering my respect.

Later I listen to Miguel and his grandma telling anecdotes about the deceased in the photographs. By the time we have finished smiling, laughing and even crying at some of the stories, I feel that I know everybody whose photograph is on the table, and I am happy to be invited to celebrate the life of each and every one of them.

In the corner of my eye I see a shadow pass over the shrine, but then I see a candle flicker and presume that is what I have really seen.

Marcia bows her head and crosses her chest, "I feel Alejandro's presence and I think we should now visit his other home." She walks off into the kitchen.

Miguel whispers in my ear, "She is referring to his grave when she says his other home."

Marcia walks out of the kitchen with a basket filled with further offerings including the marigold flowers that we brought.

I hold Miguel's arm, "I just saw a shadow pass over the shrine. I thought it was a candle."

He smiles, "You saw my grandfather's shadow. He is here for the 'Day of the Dead'.

Marching out of the house, we follow her almost in a rush, as she pulls the petals off the marigolds and spreads a trail behind her. We follow her without speech, passing numerous houses, streets and celebrations until we reach a steep cobbled lane. I can hear church bells ringing and Mariachi music playing in the distance. We stop for a moment to catch our breath and then carry on until a large cemetery and church emerge in front of us.

Marcia looks ahead and addresses Alejandro's grave as she walks calmly ahead, "I am here my darling. I am here for you on this special day."

I realize that today, the Day of the Dead, is a cherished holiday celebration where death is seen as life. It is a holiday when both the living and the dead come together in the celebrations of the 'continuum of life'. Despite understanding this, it still all feels weird.

Miguel watches his grandma rush to her lover's grave but doesn't follow. He grabs my hand holding me back.

"We shall let them spend some time together before we join them. It will give us some time to look around and see if we are given any clues that our graves from the past may be here."

CHAPTER TWENTY-ONE

It is the most beautiful cemetery that I have ever seen and it provides a sense of tranquility. Its scenic charm, elegance and history are captivating, and the lawns and foliage are meticulously maintained.

Composed of graceful crypts and stately mausoleums, not once do I see what I would describe as a normal gravestone. The graves are built up with white washed cement, covered with patterned tiles or painted in bright colors. Inside each grave, or on each grave, there is something brought and left by the living from when they have visited. The graves have places in the headstone, like shelves, where candles, incense, statues or photographs are displayed and left for the departed.

"I know why Marcia referred to Alejandro's grave as his other home," I say to Miguel. "The cemetery doesn't look like a place for the dead. The graves look more like little houses lined up within a beautiful garden of memories."

He agrees, "Some of these houses look newly decorated with bright colors, furnished with flowers, candles and ornaments to comfort their home. They are the perfect place to celebrate and remember the life of someone special."

In one part of the cemetery, some of the little houses are faded or grey. Some have broken glass and rusty furnishings. Candles have burnt out or melted, statues and photographs have faded beyond beauty and the once loved flowers are dead and rotting away.

"Perhaps there is nobody left to care anymore," Miguel comments.

I nod, "Perhaps those that once did care have also moved on to another place where they can join their departed, so it doesn't matter anymore."

"The dead are everywhere. Everywhere you look there are homes for the dead," I comment.

"Yes," Miguel agrees. "They range from classically beautiful and over the top displays to faded headstones.

I agree, "They are little houses built by the living for the dead. The houses are kept as a place to visit, a place for memories."

We stop at a cenotaph, an empty tomb, a monument erected in honor of a person whose remains are elsewhere. It is dedicated to the memory of an individual. Red rose petals cover it and there is a marigold cross placed on top.

Miguel and I both look on in despair as it dawns on us that we may not even have a grave.

I worry, "What if we don't have a grave? What if our remains were never found after the car crash?"

Miguel frowns, "Perhaps that is why our soul is in purgatory, because our bodies were never found to be put to rest."

I absorb the fact, "Well, even so, we should still have a cenotaph somewhere, surely?"

"Possibly," Miguel says, "but nothing would surprise me. We should just prepare ourselves for anything and let destiny take its course."

I look around the cemetery and it is slowly filling up with visitors. Families busily maintain the graves and bring gifts for their loved ones. They bring chairs, mats, food, drink and blankets so that they can remain throughout the evening and stay warm when the sun has passed. They sit around the little houses, telling and listening to stories of those gone before.

Prayers waft through the air mingling with the scent of flowers, candles and incense and I reflect on the number of dead souls that will be called for by their relatives on this popular day. I find the thought peaceful and beautiful, but not scary. Everybody is relaxed and happy as they cherish, honor and reminisce about the past. Miguel is right, it is the perfect place to celebrate and remember the life of someone special. It's a place where on the Day of the Dead, life and death reunite. Today, communication really does exist between the living and the dead.

We go to Alejandro's crypt. It's a stone chamber beneath the floor of a burial vault where his coffin is displayed.

"Grandma has been busy cleaning and decorating his grave and it looks pristine," Miguel notices.

I observe, "It does look lovely, furnished with flowers, crosses, statues of the Blessed Virgin Mary and lots of candles. She has made a lot of effort."

We open a polished metal gate and walk down some narrow steps to the vault where the coffin is protected behind a glass screen. Marcia jumps as we enter the small room, disturbing her quiet time with her husband.

Miguel offers his apologies, "Sorry to frighten you, Grandma."

"I am sorry," I apologize for both her loss and shocking her.

The vault has a smell of earth and mustiness, yet it has been freshened with the flowers and incense that is burning. It is dark but lit with the flickers of candles. I feel claustrophobic and nauseous as I stare at the thought of death, with the coffin directly in front of me. I look at the silver framed photograph of Alejandro displayed on his coffin and feel Marcia's loss. It has been a couple of years ago since he moved on, but I can feel his presence in the small partly lit room.

She stands and starts folding some pillows and blankets that she has brought with her, "I brought these so that Alejandro can rest after his long journey from heaven to see us. His remains and past may be in this vault, but his past life soul has travelled from heaven to be with us today."

Miguel puts his arm around her, "Grandfather will appreciate your consideration, but now let's sit down. I think you need a rest."

We sit on some little stools and face the coffin where all conversation is addressed. Marcia sits between us and holds each of our hands for comfort. To be honest, I am happy to hold her hand as I feel nervousness run through my body and I can feel myself tremble. I have never been in a situation like this before. The last time that I was with a coffin was at my grandma's funeral. The disturbing thought has never left me. Here, it is like an open grave that can be visited regularly, yet it appears to bring comfort.

"Things will never be the same without you here," Marcia says, addressing Alejandro's photograph, "You always told me that I should find somebody else to love, when you moved on, but I couldn't do that because nobody could ever take your place. You are my soulmate and I wish my time would come, so that I could join you."

"My grandma felt exactly the same when my grandfather moved on," I comfort her. "She was never the same after he left her. She wanted her time to come so she could join him wherever he may be. She believed he would be waiting for her."

She looks at me, "When you really love someone…" Her eyes fill with tears, "When you love 'that one', nothing else really matters."

I nod, "My grandma felt the same, but you must not let yourself go, we want you here with us for as long as possible. I know that I have only just met you, but Miguel has told me a lot about you and I would like to get to know you well."

Marcia sheds a tear, "I would like that too. It would be nice."

Miguel interrupts, "It's normal for you to cry and hurt but you need to hold on. Grandfather would want you to be strong and not let yourself go. He always encouraged you to be strong and when your time comes to leave us, it will happen, but now you need to enjoy your life with us. Grandfather will be waiting for you when your time comes. There's no need to wish your life away in order to be with him in another world, wherever that may be."

He reaches over and touches my hand.

"Yes," she agrees, "Alejandro visits me once a year for the 'Day of the Dead' and I know that he will be waiting for me, when my time comes."

She addresses the coffin, "We are soulmates, aren't we darling?"

The candles flicker despite there not being any wind and I am reassured that he is here with her.

She starts to talk about her dying again, so Miguel walks out of the vault, containing his upset and his anger at the way his grandma is speaking. He strokes my shoulder as he leaves the vault.

I stand, "Perhaps we should go and get some air and find Miguel." I feel claustrophobic.

"You go. I will follow you in a moment," she instructs me.

As I leave, I hear her talk to Alejandro, "It's getting harder for me to stay..."

A tear comes to my eye.

Outside Miguel crouches next to the grave, and cries under the hot Yucatan sun.

I kneel down at the side of him, put my arm around him and kiss his cheek.

He looks up, his eyes red with crying. "I am sorry," he apologizes. "This is all wrong."

"What do you mean?" I ask. "You are just overcome with emotion, and it is acceptable."

"Life and death, it stirs up a complicated mixture of awe and despair and I am finding it hard to deal with. Our situation isn't normal."

At that moment we are distracted by a Mariachi band playing live music around an open grave. A few mourners are attending, and many others are arriving and being dropped off by vehicles. Beside the grave, I see a number of angels and cherubs that seem unique to Mexico and as I put my hand in my bag to reach a tissue for Miguel, I find the cherub that I gave to Scott.

It grabs Miguel's attention, "Where did you find that?" he asks puzzled, taking it off me.

"I am surprised to find it in my bag," I say shocked. "I gave it to Scott to help him find love. I really wish that he would look after things."

I am quite annoyed with Scott. He promised that he would look after the cherub, yet this is the second time that he has lost it. Luckily, it seems to keep finding its way back to me.

"Look," Miguel says enthusiastically, placing the cherub on his grandfather's grave, "It is the perfect fit."

I stare at the grave which is decorated with a number of angels and cherubs and it fills an empty area where a cherub has broken off. It fits perfectly. I know that it has now found where it belongs. It has found its home.

Miguel explains pointing at the grave, "There has been a cherub missing for years and this is the right cherub because it fits." He grabs hold of me and kisses my lips, "Thank you so much, where did you find it?"

"My friend Julia gave it to me," I answer astonished and shocked, wondering how this has happened.

"Julia?" He quizzes.

"Yes, my friend from rehabilitation. I am sure that I have told you about her. She told me that she had travelled. She must have been here at some point."

Miguel doesn't take much notice of what I am saying, but busily fixes the crystal cherub to the grave and I watch it glisten in the sunlight. I know this is its rightful home and I remember what Julia told me before I left rehab, "Everything that happens in life, be it good or bad, happens for a reason. Sometimes people come into our lives and we know that they will affect us in some profound way, almost to serve some sort of purpose. The people that we meet along the path of life help to create who we are."

Like she promised, the cherub shot its arrow to help guide me to my true love, but the cherub has also then found Alejandro's grave where it rightfully belongs, obviously after helping Miguel and I come together. Julia really did help me in a positive way and will remain in my thoughts forever for giving me such a wonderful, thoughtful gift. It was also my destiny to bring it here for Marcia and Alejandro.

Marcia descends from Alejandro's crypt, "Is that what I think it is?" she asks, looking at the cherub in amazement.

Miguel finishes fixing it, "Yes, Saskia found it."

She grabs hold of me and cuddles me, "Thank you so much, Saskia."

"I am pleased to help," I say.

"I wonder where it has been all of this time."

I answer, "I am sure that your cherub has been helping other people."

She looks at me, puzzled, and I can understand why. I don't want to explain everything, so I just carry on talking, "I am just happy the cherub has returned for this special day, the Day of the Dead."

"I agree," she smiles with gratitude.

"I think that we need to go soon, Grandma," Miguel advises. "Saskia and I have things to do."

I suddenly notice that it has started to go dark and the graveyard is lit with just candlelight.

She nods, "Please may I just have five more minutes with Alejandro. The cherub has helped to bring us back together, and my husband wants me to stay a little longer."

Miguel is anxious. I shrug my shoulders, "Surely five more minutes won't harm?"

"Ok," Miguel answers. "We shall wait near the entrance, but only five minutes."

As we turn to walk away, we hear the music of a band around Alejandro's grave, but there is no band in sight, just the noise of a band. We both turn and see Marcia dance on her husband's grave. She dances and moves to the official Jarabe Tapiatio dance, the Mexican dance that tells of love and courtship between two people.

"Why is she dancing?" I ask.

Miguel stares, "She is dancing on his grave to celebrate his life. It is a Mexican tradition."

I don't want to upset him by telling him of the version that I know, that you dance on somebody's grave because you are happy they have died. I have never heard of the tradition that you dance on a grave to celebrate somebody's life, but things are different here.

"Why the Jarabe Tapiato dance?' I question.

Miguel smiles and holds me tightly in his arms, "It tells of love and courtship between two people. The Mariachi participated in the rite of courtship and if you listen carefully the Mariachi band are playing for them now, bringing them together again."

"But, there is no band."

"Perhaps it's a Mariachi band from the past."

I look on with admiration and I see an outline of a man dancing with Marcia, I see the shadow of Alejandro, who is visiting on this special day to dance with the woman that he loves. I also see shadows stood around them playing instruments.

It is a mystical moment and I am a believer.

As the music stops, Marcia stops dancing and looks up in the dark sky blowing a kiss with her hand. "Goodbye, until next year darling. I love you and will never stop loving you, but you already know that."

Miguel and I look up and see a glow of red streak through the air. It looks like it has come from one of the candles, but I believe that it is Alejandro's soul returning to heaven following his visit.

Marcia is quiet as we walk back to her home following the petals that she scattered earlier.

As we approach her house, Miguel hands me his car keys, "Please wait in the car and I will settle her in. I am conscious about time. We really do need to go."

I cuddle Marcia at the door. "We shall see each other again soon," she promises.

"I hope so." I really mean it.

Miguel isn't long with his grandma.

"Is she ok?" I enquire as he gets in the car. I am concerned about her.

"Yes, she did what she normally does after returning from her visit on the Day of the Dead, each year."

"What's that?" I'm curious.

"She pours herself a large brandy and listens to Vera Lynn sing 'We'll Meet Again'."

"I love that song. I haven't heard it for ages," I comment. "My grandma used to like it too."

"I'll put it on for you." He goes through his collection and it starts to play.

"My grandma will be fine. She is a tough old bird."

I smile.

"What now?" I ask. "Where do we go from here?"

His blue eyes stare through me and I recall the nightmare of our past. He starts up the engine, "We drive, just drive until something tells us to stop."

I nervously recall a flashback, "That's similar to what you said the night we ran away in our last life. You said we should just drive, until destiny took us to where we should go." I feel uneasy, "Things did stop when our car went over a cliff and death was our destiny."

He frowns, "That was then, this is now. We are here to face our ghosts and put things to rest, and that is what we are going to do, no matter what the conclusion may be."

He seems edgy and I feel wary of him. Why do I have an uncomfortable tension in my stomach as though I am about to relive the past? My body feels frozen as though I can't move, and I can do nothing other than go with him, and be his passenger, like in my past life.

I close my eyes and wish that this journey can have a happier ending.

CHAPTER TWENTY-TWO

As we drive, we are distracted by a large carnival being set up alongside the road. Colorful native Aztec dancers and Mexican music intermix with performing artists to celebrate the day.

It is hot in the car, "Please may we pull up and have some air?" I ask. "I am feeling a little nauseous with the heat."

Miguel parks, "Perhaps this is a sign and we should spend some time here."

Cars are lined up alongside the road for miles. A gentleman approaches us, "It is five pesos to park here."

Miguel roots in his pocket to find his money and I take a look at our surroundings. I can see a graveyard in the distance that appears to be lit with fires that are lighting up the dark moonless sky.

Miguel looks in the same direction, "Should we head that way?" He nods towards the graveyard and our feet spontaneously move us in that direction.

The evening celebrations are in full swing. Fireworks are lighting up the sky and there are hundreds of people dressed up in Halloween attire. Some people carry candles that flicker in the gentle breeze casting spooky shadows of the people in ghostly attire, others carry dolls of the dead, Catrina dolls. The chill of the breeze sends a shiver up my spine along with a feeling of déjà vu.

"I feel like I have been here before." I comment.

"I know we have been here before," Miguel replies. "I can feel it in my bones."

We pass skeleton celebrants on stilts and skeletons riding bikes. Stalls are everywhere you look selling food and souvenirs for the Day of the Dead.

"Are you hungry?" Miguel asks as we pass a stall selling beautiful smelling fresh bread.

"I am starving," I declare. "All of this food smells absolutely wonderful."

"Yes, I know what you mean. I could eat all of it."

There is a lady at the stall who smiles as we approach, "Would you like some pan de muerto, or bread of the dead?" she asks. "It has been freshly baked today."

The bread is baked in many shapes including skulls, human figures, skeletons, crosses and teardrops. They have all been sprinkled with sugar. The heat of the night makes them smell like they have just come out of the oven.

"It's such a difficult choice," I tell the lady. "They all look fantastic and smell beautiful."

She smiles with gratitude at my kind comment. "The festival for the departed souls begins with the food. Please let me choose something for you both."

She hands Miguel a cross-shaped bread. "The dead will rest in peace," she comments.

She hands me bread in the shape of a tear, "Tears are a natural and normal part of saying goodbye."

Miguel bites into his bread first, "If the festival for departed souls begins with the food, then this is special."

I start to eat my bread, I know exactly what he means.

Children in costumes roam the streets, asking people for a 'calaverita', a small gift of money or candies.

Two young boys approach us, "Calaverita? A small gift of money or candies please?"

Miguel laughs, "I remember doing the same when I was your age. I would walk the streets asking for money and candies, and everybody was really kind to me."

The two boys look at each other, probably never believing that he was once the same age as them. I suppose that time just seems to pass you by.

I smile at their expressions, "Miguel, I think that the boys are asking for a gift, not a walk down memory lane."

"Yes, they are," he acknowledges.

He pleasantly smiles at them, "Follow me, and I will get you some candy from a stall."

I follow Miguel along little cobbled streets and the boys skip merrily behind us, without a care in the world.

We walk through the crowds until we reach a stall selling elaborately decorated candies and sweets. "Choose something each," he tells the boys. He then informs the gentleman stall holder, "I will be paying."

The boys seem to instinctively know what they are having. Despite all of the choices, they choose a sugar skull each, thank Miguel and skip off into the distance cheerfully.

He watches them disappear, "It's nice to see people happy."

I am curious, "How did you know that this candy stall was here?"

"I could smell it. I could smell the sweetness."

Come to think about it, so could I.

Miguel hands over payment for the sugar skulls and also purchases a small bag of candies.

Miguel speaks to the stall holder, "Your candies are beautiful. They are elaborately decorated. It must have taken a long time for you to make them."

The gentleman nods, "Everything has to be ready for when the souls of the dead arrive. The smell of the food shall attract them. Their favorite foods need to be ready for the offering. My elaborately decorated candles emphasize that death isn't the end of life or something to be mourned." He pauses, "It is an extension of life."

I am touched, "That is a lovely way to look at it."

The gentleman nods and starts to serve waiting customers, unaware of our situation.

The large cemetery is a ten-minute walk from the main road. Outside the gates, the carnival is in full swing, but at the other side, a candlelight vigil takes place by the graves. In the graveyard we see people sleeping on mats, fires built beside the graves with cook pots that provide food during the long visiting hours. The cemetery is magnificent. There are thousands of candles lighting up the faces of people huddled in blankets enjoying being with their deceased loved ones.

This cemetery also has graves that are like little houses. They are lined up side by side, decorated with flowers, candles, photographs and gifts.

This garden of memories is a lot busier than Alejandro's, but having said that, it is much larger. It is almost a town in itself.

Miguel holds my hand, "I have a strange feeling."

"I have just had a shiver run up my spine." I grind my teeth. "Do you think our shadows are here?"

He shakes his head, "I don't know. I can't feel their presence and maybe I am just being paranoid. I just want to draw a line under all of this. I want us to be able to get on with our life."

I look down, "I worry that if we are in the wrong place, our lost souls will remain in purgatory."

He shrugs his shoulders, "Let's walk around here and see if there are any signs."

We are respectful to the picture-perfect families who sit around the graves reminiscing about the past. I see families smile, laugh and cry, and children listening to stories of those gone by. As we walk around the graveyard I hear people recount favorite memories, places and activities shared. I wonder if I ever cross the mind of my family, the family that I left behind in my last life.

My teeth chatter, "I wish we could find whatever it is that we are looking for."

"You look cold," Miguel observes. "You feel ice cold. Are you ok?"

"I feel fine, but the air is cold this evening."

A Purepecha man waves at us and shouts, "Chijpiri jimbani."

We walk towards him, "Pardon? I don't understand," Miguel states.

He waves his hands to join him, "A new fire. I am lighting a new fire and it will keep you warm."

I am grateful for his invitation and sit down on the floor next to the fire, where I can warm myself up. He places a blanket around our shoulders and hands me a bottle of Tequila.

"Please have a drink. It will keep you warm."

For the first time in a while, I am actually happy to be drinking Tequila. I thought that I would never drink it again after the way Scott pushes it, but tonight it actually tastes great.

The man stares at the grave, a beautifully decorated home, covered in flowers and food, and there is a photograph of a beautiful woman with long black hair.

He points to the photograph, "That is my beautiful daughter. I have come a long, long way to visit her, but this is where she wanted to be when she moved on, and I respected her wishes."

"Where have you come from?" Miguel asks out of curiosity.

"I live in the Northwestern region of the Mexican state of Michoacán, principally in the city of Cheran. I am known as a Purepecha man and this is my beautiful wife." He points to a lady walking over with a basket of food and drinks.

His wife doesn't say much but kindly hands us refreshments from her basket. I take a sip of water and listen to the hospitable couple.

The man speaks, "My daughter is a very clever girl. She got a job here and loved her life. She lived life to the full." He laughs remembering her lovely life, but then his face saddens. "Unfortunately, she became very poorly, and we knew that she was going to leave us. She wanted to stay here when she moved on and we respected her decision. We never stood in her way."

I look at the photograph, "She is a very beautiful woman."

He pulls his wife close and smiles, "She takes after my gorgeous wife - she has her beautiful looks and personality."

His wife crosses her chest, "We got to say 'goodbye' in our own special way before she moved on. She is a special person, in a special place, and we will see each other soon."

Miguel wipes my face with a napkin. I hadn't even noticed that I had tears streaming down my face.

The man hands Miguel a tissue and frowns with compassion at my upset. "Please don't get upset. I told my daughter and I am telling you; Death is nothing to fear. It is just another stage of life. I can still feel my daughter living, dreaming, loving and smiling."

I look up, "Can you really?"

"Yes, the Day of the Dead is just another part of life. It is our way of conquering death, by bringing back our dead loved ones each year."

His wife adds, looking around, "This takes weeks of preparation. After the food is cooked, the candles are lit, the graves are cleaned and decorated, the fires lit and then we prepare for the arrival of the spirits. Our daughter is on her way."

I feel the love they share for their daughter, which leaves a warm sensation in my heart.

Miguel looks at his watch, "Thank you for everything, but we need to go now."

"Who are you here to see?" the man enquires.

Miguel and I look at each other and answer together, "The past."

He smiles, "Yes, everybody has a past." He takes a swig of his Tequila and looks away. I know that now is his time with their daughter.

We carry on walking through the cemetery and something catches my eye. It is the number eighteen, which I have always believed to be my lucky number, a number that I have always thought to be special to me.

Miguel stops, "Why have you stopped? What are you doing?"

I look at a beautifully dressed cenotaph on plot number eighteen. There are two photographs placed on top. I recognize one as being a photograph of Miguel and the other as being of me. We look different to how we look now, but I know that it is us. I suppose your memory remembers. The photograph is of that girl who looked in the mirror for the last time, wondering how to fix her life, and a photograph of a boy who loved her and wanted to be with her forever.

I observe, "The cenotaph states we both died on the 18th, the same date we were both born, or should I say reborn as the people we are today."

Our cenotaph is an empty tomb, a monument erected in honor of us both. The wording simply reads our names and the date we died along with the following:

Deep in our hearts your special memory is kept, to cherish, to love and to never forget. Until we meet again.

Miguel bends down at the side of me and puts his head in his hands, "I don't know if we should be here. Your family may recognize us if they come."

I shrug my shoulders, "We look different. I don't think that they would know us."

He kisses me on my cheek, "I am sorry, but I need to go, I can't stay here." He reaches his hand out, "Please come with me."

"Where will we go?"

"I don't know, just somewhere away from our cenotaph." He looks around frightened.

I shake my head. "I have found my past and something is telling me to stay here. I can see that you are uncomfortable with this situation, but it's ok for you to go. I will meet up with you soon."

As I stand there alone, I see a shadow darken over my cenotaph and I know that my past life is present and about to join me. Whatever is going to happen is going to happen now, and I need to go along with it. I feel my body go cold, ice cold and then I feel the shadow enter my body taking over me again. My body, mind and soul are redundant, and my past is now controlling my thoughts and actions.

In the haze and the darkness, I see a path of bright marigold flowers and I know that I have to follow them. They are leading me to where I need to go. They are known to direct the dead and I have to follow them as my past life soul is now in control.

I follow them and slowly disappear away from the crowds and the carnival. As I take each step the smell of sea salt in the air gets stronger, and the crashing of waves against rocks becomes louder. I find us walking down a winding cliff road. There are no cars present and we pass only a few people. The flickering candles that these people carry cast spooky shadows and make me feel that demons have come to haunt me. The chill of the sea breeze sends a shiver up my spine, along with a feeling of déjà vu.

The marigold flowers carry on lighting my path until they come to an end, where I find myself stood on the edge of a high cliff, looking down into the dark deep ocean. The waves crash louder and ricochet off the cliffs. I look down at my past destiny. This is the place in my nightmares. This is the place that I died. This is the cliff where Miguel and I left behind everything and everyone that we knew.

I kneel down observing where I died, and I hear footsteps behind me. I turn and see an old lady walking towards me. She looks familiar and as she gets closer, I realize that I do know her. Holding my arm, she encourages me back from the edge of the cliff and we sit on a memorial bench in my memory, that is positioned in the vicinity.

She looks at the cliff edge in despair, "You shouldn't get close to the cliff. It's a dangerous place and the sea has been known to take people."

"I know," I acknowledge. "I know how dangerous a place it is."

I put my head in my hands and she gently rubs my back with her left hand, as though she cares for me. She holds something in the palm of her right hand and with her fingers she strokes whatever it is that she is holding.

"You look similar to my daughter," she tells me. "She was planning to be a professional dancer and she loved to dance." She speaks proudly about her.

I sit up and face her. "She was going to be a professional dancer?" I query, "Does she not dance anymore."

She shakes her head. "She was a good girl, a very good girl, but we had a disagreement and I don't see her anymore."

"That's a shame."

She nods and looks sorrowful, "She was in love with a young gentleman, but both her father and I disagreed about their relationship. We tried to put an end to it." She wipes tears from her eyes with her handkerchief. "She had a beautiful future ahead of her and we were worried that she was making a big mistake. We shouldn't have interfered. We tried to put an end to their relationship and instead put an end to their lives altogether."

"What happened?" I ask. I fear that I already know the answer as this is my mother from my past life.

"She ran away from home with her lover and she never returned. I believe that they were in a car accident. Both me and her father blame ourselves for that." She looks sad.

"Why do you blame yourselves?" I ask sympathetically.

"We had bought her a car, which was supposed to be for her birthday. My husband had been renovating it for her in one of the outbuildings, but he hadn't finished working on the brakes. It was supposed to be a nice surprise for her, not bring her to an unfortunate fate." Tears fall from her eyes. "My daughter and her lover took the car so that they could get away from us and be together. I should have accepted her decision about being in love and being with him. In hindsight he loved her and would have looked after her. I wish that things had been different to how they have turned out."

I look down with embarrassment at the upset I caused, "I am sure that your daughter does too. I think she regrets what she did and would be sorry for causing you so much upset."

"Yes, I know she would," she agrees. "If I could turn back the clock, I would have had a different approach. Sometimes major events that happen in our life challenge our thinking and our direction in life. Sometimes, something unpleasant happening leads us to a new path to follow."

I nod in agreement, "Sometimes we have to put the past behind us. You can understand life backwards but can only live it going forward."

She reveals what she is holding in her right hand. It is an oval-shaped gold locket on a long gold linked chain. Engraved on the locket is the wording 'Always'. She swings it in front of me and I note that it is the same as the locket I saw and wanted to touch at the cenote.

"My daughter died here. Witnesses saw the car drive off the cliff and said that there were two people in the car that matched the descriptions of my daughter and her lover." She sobs again. "Their bodies were never found. It's been hard to deal with."

I agree, "It must be terrible for you."

She hands me the locket and I open it discreetly. Inside the locket are two photographs of Miguel and me in our past lives.

She looks and smiles, "They really did love each other. We didn't know, but their friends knew. They came forward and told us stories after the news broke. Apparently, they used to go to Mariachi dances to be together. They had a special bond and I hope that they are together now, wherever that may be. They were soulmates and meant to be together.

"They are beautiful photographs." I keep looking at them and remembering the past.

She coughs and distracts me from my thoughts, "It is believed that you should bury the possessions of the dead along with their bodies. That way they can take them with them to their next life. Death is considered to be the passage to a new life and so the deceased should be buried with their personal possessions, which they would need in their hereafter. As their bodies were never found, I was unable to do this and have therefore kept hold of the locket. It is all that I had left of them as a memory."

She sighs deeply looking at the photographs in the locket. "I don't think that their bodies will ever be found, so the locket can then be buried with them, but I am now ready to come to terms with that. I feel that I should throw the locket into the sea, over the cliff, where they moved on together. I hope it will find its way to them. I am now ready to let the locket go and release their souls."

"Release their souls?" I question.

"Despite knowing that they had moved on, I couldn't let them go, but now the time has come to say goodbye."

I think about Miguel, "He will look after your daughter, you know."

She nods, "He was a good man and really loved her. We should have realized that. I hope that wherever they may be, that they forgive us."

I confirm, "They do."

She stands and throws the locket in the air, out to the ocean and speaks aloud, "I have been unable to let go of you, but the time has come to say 'goodbye'. You will always be with me in my memory and heart though. There was a lot of misunderstanding and I am sorry, I am really sorry for everything, but I love you more than you will ever know."

A man appears from nowhere. He vaguely looks at me as though he recognizes me from somewhere, and then puts his arm around his wife to comfort her. I know that it is my past life father.

"Has the time come?" he asks her.

She answers, "It's time to let go and move on."

I feel a tingling warmness inside of me and feel my past life shadow leave my body. It brushes softly past me touching my soul, leaving a message of thanks. I hear a whisper, "Enjoy your life for both of us."

My past life mother and father are still looking out to sea, but suddenly smile and their hearts rejoice. I see my past life shadow putting her arms around them. I don't know what is said, but I presume matters are being put to rest and a final goodbye is being said on this special night of the Day of the Dead. I stand back, not interrupting their special time together.

Sky lanterns are appearing in the sky floating higher than I knew possible, but there is one bright flash that stands out amongst them and I witness my shadow person leave earth. It travels as a bright light to heaven, blending in amongst the small fires in the sky. I wave goodbye and am pleased that I could help. For some reason, I now feel something missing in my life, but feel contentment that I can move on with my life - this life.

I stay seated on the bench watching my past life shadow disappear to eventually reach the peace it deserved. My past life parents join me and stare in astonishment at the sky. I don't think that my past life shadow has told them about me. She has allowed me to get on with my current life, without any of the past. They are happy and relieved to have seen their daughter on the Day of the Dead and bring matters of the past to a final conclusion.

My past life father breaks the silence, "I suppose that life can end at any moment for any of us. We should spend our time here wisely. Our daughter told us that she had lived life to the full and done everything that she ever wanted."

My past life mother speaks, "You need to be serious about some aspects of your life, but you need to leave room for fun, spontaneity and love. I loved her sincerely and I still love her, more than she will ever know. Whilst we are alive, we should show people how much we love them. You may not always get the chance when they are gone." She holds her husband's hand, "At least we did get the opportunity to say 'Sorry' and to express our love for her."

He agrees, "I was unable to let go, but now that I have been able to say goodbye, it achieves closure on everything and saying bye is my final gift of love."

My time here is finished so I stand to walk away. I need to find Miguel and check that he is ok.

"Goodbye," I say with a tear in my eye as I depart from my past life parents.

"We never caught your name, sweetheart," says the old lady.

I blush, "Its' Saskia."

They look at each other surprised and he speaks, "Our daughter was called Saskia."

I nod knowing, "My name is Saskia, too."

My past life father looks me up and down. "Please may I offer you some advice? I should have offered it to my daughter, but I didn't get chance."

I nod, "Yes, I would appreciate that."

"When people are close to death, they sometimes wish that they had done things differently. Some wish that they had kicked up their heels more often, been more carefree, danced longer and shown others how much they loved them. Live your life to the full and enjoy it. Do everything that you want and can."

I realize that I am still carrying the flowers that I bought earlier in the day. I hand them over, "I came to say goodbye to somebody really close, but I could not find their grave. Perhaps you could put these on your daughter's cenotaph for me?"

He looks down and speaks quietly, "The cenotaph is for both her and her lover. We appreciated that they should be together, when it was too late. He was called Miguel and he was her soulmate. He was a good man and I am comforted knowing that he will look after her now"

I smile, "I am sure that he will. Please leave these flowers for both of them."

My past life mother smells the flowers, "To the Aztecs, death was part of a cycle of life that was completed by returning to this life with the aid of flowers, offered by the living life."

They both give me a hug full of emotion and I know that it is now my time to leave them.

I make my excuses, "I'm sorry, I need to find somebody special."

Energy burns within me and I run for miles through the windy streets of the carnival and celebrations. People are everywhere I look, but I am unable to find Miguel and wonder where he may be.

I hear church bells ring and hope that it is a sign. I head in the direction of the sound and eventually reach a small crooked church on top of the cliff edge, with magnificent views out to sea.

Miguel is sat on a bench and turns as I slowly approach him.

"Are you ok?" I ask concerned.

"Yes, it is all over. We have our life back, Saskia. It just feels strange with our past not being here anymore."

"Yes, I know," I agree.

Miguel informs me, "Our past has been put to rest. I said goodbye to my shadow as it left this world and I saw it join your shadow on the way to heaven."

"It is all behind us now, Miguel. Purgatory is something of the past. I saw my past life parents and forgiveness and love was given. All we can do now is live for the future. We should live the life that our past wanted to live."

"Our shadows had something special."

I agree, "And so do we. We have been reborn and given another chance to be together in this world. Our past wants us to be happy together.

He smiles admiringly at me, "Shall we go home? And be blissfully happy together forever?

I beam back, "It's all that I ever wanted."

He pulls something out of his pocket, "I have something for you."

"Is it a present?" I smile.

It's the locket that I saw my past life mother throw over the cliff.

He advises, "It's the locket that we saw at the cenote."

"Where did you get it from?" I ask, confused.

"My past life shadow gave it to me. It's ours for the hereafter."

He fastens it around my neck and kisses me gently.

As we walk back to the car we pass through the graveyard. Sat around our cenotaph are six people. All of their faces are unforgettable. We see my past life father, mother, my brothers and sisters. When you really love someone or have loved someone, you remember them. Your memory never forgets the people or things that are special to you.

They sit around our cenotaph eating, drinking, talking, laughing and expressing continuity to human life. I love them all, despite the fact that they have aged, and changed since I left them.

I look over at them and I feel a little upset, "I am a memory already fading. I am a memory that will die."

Miguel shakes his head, "You are a memory of the dead, but you have been reborn. We need to put the past behind us and move on with our life in this life."

"I will always have room in my heart to love my past life family."

"They will all look after each other and will always have a space in their hearts to love you too, but they loved your past life and don't know your present."

His words ring true. The dreams had brought back memories of things I'd felt that I'd been through, but the dreams and memories belonged to another soul.

As we walk away, we see that the Day of the Dead celebrations are highlighted by the construction and flying of giant kites. Children run around in the wind laughing at their various designs floating high in the sky. I stop and smile.

"What is it?" Miguel asks amused at my interest.

"Remember, I told you that I used to fly kites with my grandparents. Well, seeing this just reminds me of them."

"Why, because of the memory of your past with them?"

"I never really understood the meaning of what my grandma had said before she passed away, but it is clear now."

"What did she say?" he is curious.

"I can't remember exactly, but it went something along the lines of, 'The beat of my heart will disappear from Earth but will still ring loudly. I will feel the mourning of the ones left behind, but I will come back to Earth to celebrate my life.'"

"How do you interpret those words?"

I shrug my shoulders and smile. "She is here somewhere for the Day of the Dead celebration. I can feel her presence."

I stare up at the flying kites and cuddle into Miguel.

CHAPTER TWENTY-THREE

I wake up bright and early, but Miguel still appears to be asleep. As I lie by his side, I study his face with its dynamic expression lines, all of which are part of his life and story.

I watch his nose twitch, but then a little smile appears on his face. "I can feel you watching me, Saskia."

I laugh, "You must be psychic. I wondered if you were dreaming."

He opens his eyes and turns to put his arms around me, "I was having happy new dreams."

I smile, "We have now found our happy."

I am excited about spending my life with Miguel. Although we still have to discuss our plans for the future, I want the rest of our life to start as soon as possible. I want to spend forever making memories of us, which will tell a story, that may be shared after our lifetime. Only now do I appreciate the true value of a moment becoming a memory, after having experienced what we have.

I appreciate that being happy won't mean that everything in our life will be perfect, but it will be about finding what lights us up and warms our souls. It will be about being thankful for everything and everyone that we have in our life.

We make fresh coffee and drink it on the veranda, looking out at the calm ocean. It has been raining during the night, but this morning the sun is trying to shine through. I admire the rainbow that has formed as the light from the sun meets the raindrops, and the colors light up my spirit. It serves as an obvious symbol of peace and serenity to me.

It is said that at the end of every rainbow is a pot of gold. We don't find any gold, but we have found a treasure more precious than anything. We have found our life and we intend to live it to the full.

As the Day of the Dead is over and I stare out to sea, I think about the ones that we've lost on the way, those that are gone from our touch, but never our hearts and minds.

Memories are special and bring everybody together, those on Earth and those in heaven.

Until we meet again for Dia de los Muertos. Amen.

ACKNOWLEDGEMENTS

I gratefully acknowledge the invaluable help of so many people throughout this process, most particularly Russell Holden, Joe Ward, Damaris Broadhurst, Ruth Moulden, Sharon Keeley-Holden and the team at Jam Butty Photography and Video.

Thank you to my family for your love, support, advice and laughter. You all mean the world to me.

Others who have contributed know who they are, and how thankful I am.

Thank you to everyone who has welcomed my book into their life. You've made me smile.

Finally, thank you, Saskia and Miguel, for choosing me to tell your story.

AUTHOR BIO

Maria Broadhurst lives in Lancashire, a ceremonial county in North West England.

A country girl at heart, you will often find Maria hiking to the top of chilly Pendle Hill, world renowned for the tale of Pendle witches, or following in the steps of J.R.R Tolkien, walking the landscapes around the historic village of Hurst Green, situated in the Ribble Valley.

Married to Jason, they have two grown up children, George and Damaris. As a family, they love to travel to experience things and places that are completely unknown or different to them. Maria likes meeting new people, visiting new places and experiencing different cultures, all of which give her inspiration to write.

MariaBroadhurstAuthor

@MBroadhurst_

mbroadhurst_